STARCRASH

STEALING THE SUN
BOOK 6

RON COLLINS

STARCRASH

STEALING THE SUN: BOOK 6

Cover Image
© Philcold | Dreamstime.com- Facing the Unknown

Skyfox Publishing

ISBN-10: 1-946176-16-8
ISBN-13: 978-1-946176-16-5

For Lisa.

As are they all in the end

That's one small step for man, one giant leap for mankind

Neil Armstrong

INTRODUCTION

Have you ever had one of those days where you had everything planned out, and you were getting things checked off the to-do list right and left? One of those days when the moon and planets were lined up and everything was flowing like clockwork (to mix a couple metaphors), when life is just humming along in perfect lock-step...and then something happened that changed everything?

You know what I mean, right?

A day when you think it's all coming together, and then next thing you know, you get a fender bender and everything stops.

That's kind of what happened on this series and with this book.

I mean, when I originally envisioned *Stealing the Sun*, it was supposed to end at six books, and book six was due to be published in mid-2017. I was writing along, doing wonderfully, and then I had this fender bender. Or maybe I should say the water heater burst and I suddenly got a pool in my basement. Whatever. The main thing here is that after I "finished" this book the first time, I knew it wasn't right.

I didn't like it.

So I went back and worked on it for another month, just trying to wedge things in to make the whole thing work like I knew it could.

Silly me.

The problem, it turned out, was that I was trying to tell at least two stories in one book. I can say this is true because immediately upon thinking about it this way, I lopped off the last third of the work, and realized that the story that remained was a stand-alone story. This means I've got seven books in the series, not six.

Aside number one: When I told her this revelation, my lovely daughter Brigid, who is a better writer than I am and who clearly knows me too well, just sighed, looked at me kindly, and said, "This seems to happen to you a lot."

Aside number two: I think Brigid said what she said because the same dynamic happened with my fantasy series *Saga of the God-Touched Mage*, which was supposed to be seven episodes, and wound up being eight.

Anyway.

You get the idea.

Perhaps as a result of all this, *Starcrash*, it turns out, may be my favorite single volume I've written in any series. I loved returning to Eden. I loved thinking about the social structures of the place, and I enjoyed getting back into the characters, which I did in a much stronger way during this last rewrite than I had in the first effort. This book is about them, after all. It's about the effort it takes to survive and about exactly what it means to survive. It's about love, and relationships, and what it means to be close to someone. It's about what societies do to exist, what we expect from leaders, and how things happen for reasons that can make sense and not make sense at all.

Or, at least that's what I think it's about.

If, however, there's one thing I've learned from listening to other people talk about my stories, it's that you guys are going to take something away from it that will be unique to you.

That's totally cool with me, of course.

At the end of the day, I'm proud of this book. I'm happy to have taken the extra time, though I admit it was painful at moments.

Now I'm on to book seven, which I expect to be the last.

Unless something changes along the way.
I've heard that happens to me a lot.

Ron Collins
    September 2017

PROLOGUE

"'m going to miss Lelo," Ezi said.

Brada Waganat, son of Baraq, stood at the window and pressed one six-fingered fist into his opposite palm. The sweltering pressure coated him like a blanket. His robes stuck to his skin, and his exposed back plates glistened with perspiration. Eldoro, the greater heat, was near the horizon. Tiny Katon was still blazing brightly though, and still high in the sky, still chasing her brother as she had even in the time before the clouds began to disappear. The skies were clear most heats now. In a way, Brada felt kinship with Katon. She was a match to his own work: small and easy to ignore until her cover was thrown off, but then glaring and bright, impossible to dismiss.

Outside the window, quadars gathered, accompanied by the usual ring of observers the Families always sent when he announced a public conversation. This was good. The Families needed to be aware of what was happening here for his plan to come to fruition. They needed to know the scope of *hedgie* resistance so they could make the right decisions.

Still, anxiety made Baraq wring his hands.

This speech would be the culmination of everything they had worked for.

Ezi put her hand on his arm. The crest over her primaries widened and her central dilated. "Are you all right?"

"I'm sorry," he said, starting. "You don't deserve to be ignored like that." He knit his fingers together and gave an unconscious grimace.

"It's all right," she replied. "The time before a talk is always the worst."

"Yes, it is."

"Don't worry. You'll be brilliant, as always."

He returned his gaze to the crowd, giving a neutral click from the back of his throat that he immediately regretted as being too dismissive. "I hope you're right," he said.

"Of course I'm right."

He raised the ridge over his central, but said nothing.

"You'll be brilliant because they believe in what you are saying," Ezi added. "They won't let you be anything else."

"They believe in what *we* are saying," Brada replied.

Ezi gave a pleased click. "Inclusion will get you everywhere," she said.

A grin played across Brada's lips. "I think I've heard that somewhere before," he said.

Breeze stirred the gauze covering the window.

Esgarat City was busy.

Electrified motor carts rolled along pathways that had been cut haphazardly around buildings below, and the sounds of "progress" echoed across the distance. Even here, far up in the preparation room, the air smelled of baked rock and the sharp residue from builders across the pavilion. A heaviness draped the city now, a heaviness that hadn't been there when he was a whelpling.

Brada gave a series of nostalgic clicks from deep in his throat.

"Thank you," he finally said to Ezi. "I hope we don't let them down."

"You've said it yourself, Brada. They see the world changing around them. They see burning rain and the melting mountains. Feel the heat that makes it hard to breathe. The diseases that eat their skin.

True quadarti see the world is killing us, and they watch as the Families and council pretend this is normal so they can stay focused on their currencies. They know something must be done."

He clicked again, this time warmer.

The quadars gathered below were energetic and vibrant, mostly young.

They wore colors the Families would consider garish or distasteful. Given the time, most of these quadars were risking an array of punishments to be here. As a Waganat, Brada understood the concept of Family well. There were businesses to run. Idle hands led to empty stomachs.

Ezi put her hand on his shoulder.

They had been pair-mated for nearly two full years.

Brada was who the public thought of when the topic of the Orange Ring came about. He was young and he had a certain charisma to him. He could think quickly and turn a phrase when debating. Arguments came to him in ways that they didn't for Ezi, and the people following him spoke of his energy and his passion. But they had built this group together, grown it from nothing into one of the most controversial clubs in the Esgarat. Ezi was a master tactician, and a brilliant organizer. Many of his best phrases were actually created inside Ezi's mind and refined over time by the two of them. She was part philosopher, part politician. Together they were far stronger than either one was apart.

It didn't hurt that she was also intensely attractive to him. He liked the vivid nature of her central and the slope of her neck as it disappeared into the collar of the robes he most certainly planned to remove from her later this evening. Standing beside him, she smelled good.

Outside, the quadars were stirring.

"Look at them, Brada," Ezi said, motioning toward the audience and getting on to business in the way only Ezi could. "All these quadars. Here for you. Quadars from the Families, *as well* as the *hedgies*. They understand that the whole of Esgarat is bigger than them."

Brada took them in.

Ezi was good at this, he thought—pointing out certain facts of a situation that had relevance. He hadn't really planned for this kind of response, hadn't even considered the endgame at all. When they first started, these *hedgies* were their only audience, the poorest of quadars born to independent and lesser families. None of them were aligned to claims, and no *hedgie* family had lease-right to any product or service, hence they had no bargaining power except as a supplier of labor. When they first started, all Brada was really trying to do was to get quadars to think.

Now, though, Ezi was right.

The concept of quadars being stronger if they threw off the Family Rubrics of Commerce, which said only those in the ranking Families could carry decisions and own properties, spoke to the younger generation. The new ideas of fairness that Brada and Ezi had planted in their midst had taken root.

Now it was time for it to bear fruit.

He put his arm around her waist. "Do they understand what's coming?" he said.

She set her face in a fatalistic expression. "We've told them."

He chuffed from the back of his throat.

She was right about this, but it was easier for her. She didn't come from the strongest of the Families. She didn't truly understand the depths to which the lead Families, like his own Waganats, would go in order to maintain the order.

"Fair enough, I suppose." He reached to the stand where his mask lay.

Lelo's mask, anyway.

It was a *Shensi*, the traditional covering of the philosopher, intended to separate pure thought from the person thinking it. Brada had made it himself when he first took the name, back when he was a school whelp. Formed of clay and fired in a mountain kiln, its surface was smooth and clean, painted the color of desert rock.

Metaphorically, the mask set him apart from his worldly being.

He wore it in school pavilions and alley corners, then slowly over the cycle he found himself at small gatherings held in homes and at informal sessions of committee. He met Ezi at one of these sessions. She was beautiful and passionate. She understood his message, often understood it more deeply than even he did. She helped him see what he felt, and helped him put what he felt into words others could understand.

The real Lelo had been an underling of Shensi, who was the namesake of the mask, and Brada admitted he felt a certain connection to the past when he wore it. Pragmatically, it hid his identity, and let him speak freely and without the burden of Family, council, or churches. It protected him from direct retaliation from established power. *Hedgies* had always made the bulk of the quadarti. As such, they always had the capability of making their interests heard, but no one had ever brought them together before, no one had given them the tools to make their voices clear.

Until Brada-as-Lelo, that is.

He turned the mask over in his hands.

Wearing it, Brada Waganat, a member of one of the most powerful Families across the whole of the Esgarat, had found the glue to bind masses of the quadarti together, regardless of Family lineage.

He had changed everything.

With this speech, he would change them again—or further, anyway.

The plan called for him to lay out steps to the future.

To list how these quadars would take control over their lives.

It called for broader control of production, and doing *something* to find the cause of the rotting disease that suddenly had quadars wasting away to die in the streets. It called for forcing the Families to examine how the quadarti might use mountain caves for emergency safety zones and driving them to use their technology for greater good rather than commerce.

"Together," he would say, "we can free ourselves of the powers being lorded over us."

With this speech he would lay out the process of what he hoped would be a peaceful transition of power from relatively few Families to the large numbers of quadarti, each with a role.

But, despite the numbers at his disposal, it would not be so simple.

This is why, when this speech ended, he would pull the *Shensi* away, and reveal exactly who "Lelo" was.

It was this revelation that he hoped would turn the tide—showing by his own example that the Families could work on the side of common good.

Ezi ran her hand up his arm.

"I'm proud of you," she said. "I know I argued at first, but you were right. The new quadarti order needs to be based on truth. They need to know their leader was once a Waganat."

"The voice of the people is not a face," Brada quoted Shensi.

"But sometimes the face matters."

He clicked in warm agreement. Showing a Waganat was ready to give up control would cement the quadars around him. It would give him leadership of the revolution.

"I will miss Lelo, too," he said. "Is the motor cart ready?"

"Yes," Ezi replied. "We will ensure you can exit when the talk is finished."

He pulled back the gauzy drape one more time.

The gathering was complete. In the distance Family security was waiting, too, which made him happy. Bad judgment leads to rash decisions, he thought as he took them in. If violence was to be avoided, the Families needed to know what was happening.

He pressed the *Shensi* to his face.

It felt odd there, the edges riding over his cheek and along his jawline. A familiar sense of claustrophobia came over him. He drew one more cleansing breath and shook out his arms. The moment picked up an essence of precision.

"All right," he said. "Let's get to work."

ADRIFT

Alpha Centauri A System:
U3 Star Drive Ship *Icarus* Shuttlecraft *Aurora*

CHAPTER 1

Torrance Black gave a violent shiver as he came awake.

The profound coldness of the shuttle compartment was like a blanket of ice over his entire body. His face felt stiff and brittle.

The pilot seat pressed hard against his shoulders. The small of his back burned and his entire body ached. Moving anything was like being stabbed from all directions at once.

He lay still and let the world around him come into focus.

The smell was stale and metallic. The sound of an engine firing from far away rumbled through the shuttle's framework, but otherwise the cockpit was silent. The control panels flickered with a steady stream of green and blue. Stars gleamed from outside the viewing screen.

Torrance raised himself up, and his leg burned with electric pain.

He cursed and fell back to the headrest, panting hard.

His ankle—Holy Mother of God, moving like that had his ankle burning like a goddamned sonofabitch.

And his thigh.

Crap.

His memory snapped into place.

Universe Three, a terrorist organization headed by Deidra Francis, had been using *Icarus*, the Star Drive Ship they originally hijacked from the United Government, to place a wormhole gate into the heart of Alpha Centauri A. That wormhole was to be connected to a black hole.

If *Icarus* had been successful, that black hole would drain the star.

He wasn't a good enough physicist to know if the pull would be able to slow this shuttle down or not, but he knew that if it was actually set, the black hole would destroy every Star Drive spaceship Interstellar Command had attached to the star. That was the U3 plan, after all. Block the United Government's ability to travel the galaxy by cutting off the flow of Star Drive fuel.

He had tried to stop them.

Yes. That's what had happened.

Alpha Centauri A was behind him now, Eden ahead.

Had he succeeded?

Had he managed to keep them from planting the wormhole?

All he could remember with certainty was that a guard had shot his foot as he ran through the docking bay, and that he had crawled all the way to the shuttle he was piloting now.

His gut twisted up with the memory of wormhole pods launching just before an explosion ripped *Icarus* to shreds. It didn't matter that the crew inside were Universe Three. After *Everguard*, the idea of any spacecraft tearing itself up would always leave him with visceral memories of being trapped on a dead carcass. Fear filled him, and for a moment he thought he smelled smoke and heard warning sirens blaring.

He shivered again, the specifics of his situation becoming clearer.

Torrance was alone, adrift in one of *Icarus*'s shuttles, headed toward a planet that most scientists said was lifeless. If he had kept the U3 pods from creating the black hole, he still stood a chance, but if the wormhole was set and Interstellar Command was confined to the Solar System, only Universe Three would have the resources it would take to rescue to him. The third possibility, that he had disrupted things enough to simply break the wormhole gate, didn't seem much better, but at least it would mean Interstellar Command could jump to get him.

Assuming they knew he was here, anyway.

And assuming he lived through whatever was going to happen next.

At best it would be almost two weeks before he would arrive at Eden, which meant he needed to ration his resources. Then, even if he somehow survived entry into the planet's atmosphere, and even if that atmosphere could somehow support him, no one would know he was here until they received his radio message—which, given the speed of light, would be something more than four years from now. The chances of surviving on a wild planet were small to begin with, and that was before taking into account that most scientists he knew said that Eden was desolate and most likely poisonous.

It all added up to say Torrance Black was a dead man.

Christ.

Just north of seventy standards and this was how he was going to go.

Poetic justice, he supposed. He pursed his lips.

"All right," he said out loud. "One problem at a time."

As he sat there, small bits of his ancient survival school training leaked into his mind. It was silly to worry about anything he couldn't control. That's what they said anyway, though nothing seemed particularly silly to Torrance right now.

"Let's get to Eden before we get to worrying about anything else," he said to himself.

He looked at the command panel.

"Abke," he said. "Any chance we can turn up the heat?"

"Of course, sir," the computer assistant replied. "The current thermal rating has been set to reduce power draw."

"I need it warmer."

"Setting?"

"Let's start at eighteen Celsius. We'll see how we're doing then."

"Aye, sir."

A scan of his instruments showed he was off-course. Nothing he couldn't correct. He took a preliminary assessment of the burns along his leg. His thigh was reddish and raw, with clear liquid seeping at the edges.

Clear was good, right?

Fibers from his pants were embedded in the wound, though.

He couldn't remember if he was supposed to leave them there or pick them out to avoid infection. Probably best to get them out, but the thought of picking around in his wound made him nauseous.

Regardless, he needed to do some disinfecting. No walk in the air lock, either way.

The ankle was better news. A laser blast had cauterized a hole between the Achilles tendon and the bone.

He was damned lucky. Both of these wounds would hurt like hell, and he may not walk right later on if he didn't get the ankle done properly, but he thought he would heal if he kept everything clean.

The first…umm…pressing matter…however, was that he now realized he needed to pee. The rest could come along on its own time, but you gotta go when you gotta go.

The lavatory was across the cabin.

Torrance unclipped his belt and let microgravity lift him from the chair.

Thank God for zero-g, he thought for the first time in a while.

When he was a kid, he enjoyed flying through the middle of rooms and corridors, but time had made him far too serious for anything like that now. Zero-g—or, really, the mix and match between artificial gravity and zero-g—was a pain in the butt that seemed to exist mostly just to make it hard to get around. Telomere extensions be damned, life was too short to mess with these kinds of things.

Now, however, the lack of gravitational force meant he could move through the cockpit without putting extra pressure on his leg.

Even so, the motion of pushing off from the seat brought him pain, and the momentum of catching himself at the end of his "flight" brought him a sharp suck of pain.

He hung there, shivering in the cold and muttering *sonofabitch, sonofabitch, sonofabitch* until the pain faded, then he proceeded.

The lavatory consisted of a vacuum stool and a urine containment device.

Torrance did his business, then still shivering, found blankets in the passenger compartment and returned to the pilot seat.

He strapped himself down, put the blanket over his good leg, and examined his burns again.

The emergency kit behind the second seat had scissors, gauze, and antiseptic spray. A canister of PlastiSkin would be useful after he healed a bit.

He prepped the scissors with alcohol, then stared at his open wound. The fibers sat there, glistening in his flesh as if silently taunting him.

"Enough kicking the can down the road," he said.

Then he gritted his teeth and began to dig the debris out.

It was like holding a hot branding iron against his own leg.

He screamed as he pulled fibers away, first calling himself every name in the book and a few more he made up on the spot, then talking himself back down. As time passed, his vision wavered and his jaws ached from clenching. When he finished, Torrance rinsed the wound with a tube of water, a process no less painful than the extraction, but considerably shorter. Finally, he hit his entire leg with antiseptic.

Panting and sweating, he lay back to rest.

He was exhausted.

His throat was raw and ragged. Even in zero-g, his arms weighed a ton.

He should be hungry, he thought, but the pain was still too much to leave any desire to eat. The only good news was that the compartment was warmer now.

He closed his eyes and soon found himself drifting on gray waves of unconsciousness.

CHAPTER 2

When he woke the next time, Torrance was hungry.

The shuttle had been designed to serve as a quick transfer vehicle, which meant it had no kitchen service beyond a freeze-dry bin the crew could use to throw a few energy cakes or fruit sticks into. He got lucky and found a small stash of sandwiches in the bin. Not many, but Academy survival school had drilled into him the idea that a person can survive on minimal food. What was there should last until he made the planet if he was cautious.

More pressing was his need for water.

The juice and water dispensers were operational, though both would run dry earlier than he wanted. He would have to be stingy.

Torrance pulled out a sandwich and tore the package open. It was dry, some kind of composite protein, but he was happy for it.

He went back to the pilot seat and tweaked the navigation parameters, then checked fuel and power levels. He should make the planet with room to spare on the energy envelop he had left, so he bumped the heating system again. Assuming the automated routines for atmospheric entry were any good, he now needed to prepare to survive on the planet's surface for as long as he could. At least it made sense that he should plan to survive since planning for the alternative scenario was essentially finished.

He laughed at himself for that thought.

"All these years and you finally become a comedian," he said aloud. "Or maybe you're just insane, eh?"

Who said a man who talked to himself was sane as long as no one answered? He didn't know, but then, what the hell did it matter? You deal with what you have. He was going to have to get used to being alone.

The air-lock bay contained a locker with three EVA suits folded and stored one atop the other. A boxful of water tubes sat in a cubby, count of twenty-four. Better than nothing.

The suits were all orange, and all tight-fitting.

Just the idea of pulling one over his damaged leg made him want to barf.

"Heal faster," he said to his leg.

The leg didn't respond.

"Score one for sanity," he said.

Clear helmets lined a shelf above the suits, each held in place by connectors that fed data to active nano-displays that coated their insides. Two of their air systems were full, the third was down a quarter. Combined they should last something beyond a standard day outside the vessel. It wasn't much, but at least he might see what was around if it came to that.

It hit him then that these air systems may well hold his last day of life.

If he survived the trip and the entry into Eden's atmosphere, and if he managed to land the shuttle, there was a reasonable chance that he would die on its surface when the air in those systems gave out.

He didn't know how to feel about that. Oddly lucky in a way. Maybe.

Some people lived their entire lives without learning the truths they sought, but assuming he landed safely, at least he might get a day on the surface of Eden, which meant he might learn for certain what was there. On the other hand, knowing he was on borrowed time sucked major balls. The conflict between fear and hope set his mind into contortions that would have made a circus act proud.

"Stop it," he said, feeling stupid. "Focus."

He picked his way further through the locker.

A utility box held a rebreather. That would make for another day or so. The exchanger was clean, so maybe longer.

He gathered blankets, a flashlight, and a tool set.

The emergency kit came off its hinges, and inside he found more water tubes and a set of hand tools.

Suddenly tired, he bundled everything into a single package, then practiced slinging it across one shoulder, making sure the loop was big enough to deal with the added bulk of an EVA suit. He practiced a few times, but in zero-g he wasn't able to get a feel for its real bulk. Still, he was happy.

It felt good to be doing something.

When he was finished, he stowed the bundle under the right-hand seat, checked his coordinates, then sat back in the pilot seat, scanning his leg and willing it to heal.

Whether he was really ready or not depended a lot on how well those wounds healed.

"Take a chance, right?" he heard himself say as he drifted off.

As far as he knew, he didn't respond.

CHAPTER 3

"Abke?" Torrance said to the shuttle's computer.

It felt strange talking to Abke now. Where was this creature he was interacting with? What was its foundation? He thought about its code, the processors it looped its logic through. He wondered how it actually thought, considered again its learning algorithms. Could it feel? Did it have emotions? The questions seemed to highlight his isolation. They made him feel exactly how alone he was.

"Sir?"

"Do you have the topographics of Eden available?"

"No records are tagged such."

Having studied every piece of data taken from Eden for more than a quarter century, Torrance knew the planet's topography like the back of his hand. He also knew roughly where the energy bursts that delayed that fateful first launch of wormhole pods had come from, and he knew the coordinates he had sent the wormhole pod to.

Those facts alone determined his entry target.

"All right. Please run radar scans of the planet over the next twenty-one standard hours to ensure we get reads across an entire day. We'll need those to plot a proper course to our final landing location."

"Commence now?"

"Please do. Once the scans are complete, please search the result for a ring of mountains in the northern hemisphere. There's a huge peak at the southernmost lip of the ring. Please devise a proper set of navigation instructions to arrive at a point just south of that position and let me know when I can review them."

That location should be relatively flat.

"Yes, sir."

He nodded. "Thank you, Abke."

"The scan is complete, sir," Abke said the next day. "The calculation for reentry is on holo."

The display was of poor resolution but it showed the massive ring of mountains, a recommended point of entry, and a calculation for the predicted location of final touchdown. Though Torrance was no navigation specialist, the plan seemed to land them, within fairly gross tolerances, right where the radio signals he discovered had originated from. Still, he examined it for longer than truly necessary.

It made him miss Marisa that much more. This would have been right up her alley. It made him think of Kitchell, too. Thomas would have given his right arm to see this.

"Would you like to alter the trajectory?" Abke asked.

"No," he said. "Please run this profile every day as we approach. Update the parameters to optimize appropriately."

"Aye, sir."

The days progressed.

As the planet grew larger in the displays, Torrance found himself with nothing much to do. Though he had gotten a lot of practice at it over his lifetime, he had never been very good at waiting.

It didn't help that the shuttle's cockpit was such a confined space.

He wanted a place to exercise his leg as it healed. A treadmill, perhaps, or given the zero-g environment it would have had to be a centrifugal station. Instead, he used stretches and isometrics to work the leg as best he could. Still, the healing process seemed glacially slow.

"You're getting too old," he complained to himself more than once. He found a nook behind the second seat that let him press his back up against a flat wall and his feet onto the seat. It still hurt like a bitch, but at least he could build a little muscle.

Other times he watched movies, and skimmed books.

He played games.

He checked his pack, and continually tried to scavenge the ship.

He wrote stream-of-conscious journal entries.

Torrance thought about assignments he had been given, about his girls, about the day he proposed to Adrienne, and the day he proposed to Marisa and was turned down in the best way possible. He thought about the thousands of other times he had been anxious or frustrated. None of them compared to this. He ate small bits of sandwiches and the remains of a chocolate bar he found in a storage bin. He drank stale water and staler juice. He wondered whether Universe Three's wormhole pods hit their target or not.

Each day he cleaned his ankle and his thigh, pleased that the seepage congealed and the burns had healed up to the point his skin was a crinkly crepe. It made him think of Marisa and her skin treatments after she had been burned on *Everguard*. His pain paled in comparison to what she had suffered.

And, finally, he thought about the big picture of his life.

He had been a good man, hadn't he?

He did his best, anyway. He helped raise two amazing kids, even if he was really just inept at it when the final tally registered. He worked hard. Tried to do the right things in situations where the right things were both unclear and hard. Those things had to account for something, didn't they?

Something was missing, though.

Torrance felt a hole inside him as certainly as if it had been carved from his chest.

He felt small.

At first he thought he was just tired, just worn down by events. But that wasn't it. Sitting here alone forced him to face himself, and the fact was that looking at who he was made Torrance feel inadequate. He had been a part of so many of the most important events that happened across the Solar System and beyond, but he had been a cog. Just a wheel. A guy, doing his job.

He worked under the surface to nudge things rather than standing tall for things he thought were particularly right.

The realization cut into his gut.

"Take a chance," young Thomas Kitchell would say. And Torrance would go along, using that phrase at times to give himself permission to do things he normally wouldn't. But the fact was that Torrance had never really taken a chance, had he? He used that phrase to help him slide up to the very edge of the cliff, and sometimes even to put a toe over the edge. But he had never truly jumped. Never truly made a decision that put himself on the line when faced with power.

He had never been all-in against a force big enough to crush him.

Torrance Black had commanded system teams and negotiated deals for the United Government. He had managed science, and jockeyed with corporate leaders, military brass, and elite scientists, but he had never set the agenda. He had never taken control of anything he hadn't already been given. And that left him feeling like he was nothing but a piece of some big machine, one of a hundred gears, meaningless really.

Ultimately replaceable. Eminently useless.

Maybe this was why the planet was so important to him.

Something about this planet, orbiting a dying star all alone in the darkness of space, ignored by the rest of the cosmos, spoke to his heart.

He didn't need anyone to tell him how psycho that sounded, but it was true that Eden had latched itself to him the moment he launched the first wormhole pods. He had risked and essentially lost his family, his military career, and his professional reputation trying to save this planet throughout various parts of his life.

Now, here he was.

He found himself checking the clock and calculating trajectories constantly.

The nav system was showing progress every day. The fuel gauges dropped.

He knew the cabin must stink of him, but his nose seemed oblivious now.

If he played with the radio just right, sometimes he could find thin threads of broadcasts from the Solar System that came through in several languages. Once he picked up Portuguese. He knew just enough of the language to get by at cocktail parties but without physical communication methods to aid interpretation, the show quickly eluded him. He listened to the voice until he lost the signal anyway.

Was this what Magellan felt as he traversed the Earth? Lewis and Clark? Vasco da Gama? Maybe the first humans that walked across the Bering Straits?

"No," he answered himself aloud. "You're no explorer."

Torrance was just a guy in a space shuttle. At best he was on a rescue mission, at best he would die bringing a life-form a message. But more likely—far more likely—he was just a poor sop in a doomed lifeboat riding a current to a desolate and uncharted island.

CHAPTER 4

"Nearing entry point, sir. Shall I prepare a flight plan?"

"Please do," Torrance replied.

While he could handle routine piloting, he didn't want to bring a shuttle through a foreign atmosphere by hand. Best let Abke handle it.

The automated navigation procedure put the craft into a controlled descent, dropping velocity in staggered decrements to let the shuttle fall through the band of ultralow-density hydrogen and helium that existed in Eden's outermost region. Technically, the shuttle had been in the planet's atmosphere for the past thirty minutes, but the air density here was only a molecule or two per cubic kilometer at best.

Things would get dicey soon enough, though. The denser edges of the planet's stratosphere loomed.

He rubbed the scraggly beard that had grown over his face. Hunger pangs grabbed at his gut, but his heart raced too fast for him to worry about eating right now.

Torrance selected an EVA suit.

If he survived the descent, the suit would keep him alive—for a while, anyway. Scans of the planet estimated its surface temps to run very high, over 40°C, maybe as high as 45°–50°C, too high for a human to function for very long without a steady source of water even if he could breathe the air. The suit's environmental controls would keep him cool, though. His air would probably run out before his battery, though it would be close.

The skin on his leg was still shiny and hairless, but it was healed enough to manage getting the suit on. Just to be safe, he hit it with a blast of PlastiSkin from the emergency kit, and a pad ripped from a blanket. He pulled the suit over it, gritting his teeth against pain that wasn't as bad as he expected. A minute later he sat on the pilot seat wearing a full suit and carrying a clear pressure helmet.

He ate a full sandwich from the freeze-dry. It was something similar to peanut butter. When he finished, he slipped the remaining three into emergency pockets along the suit's legs, then donned his helmet, engaged the EVA system, and gripped the pilot seat.

It was time.

"Engage the reentry routine, Abke."

Abke enabled the heat shields. They grated with a metallic groan as they crawled over the portholes and view screens to clunk into place. Vibrations came as the spacecraft rubbed the planet's atmosphere. The sensations were comforting, actually. He visualized the components working together and imagined deflectors adjusting while the retro trims tweaked their vectors in response to Abke's course corrections. He recalled the air handling system's circuit diagrams, felt pressure nozzles monitoring the shuttle's dwindling oxygen cache.

Power supplies, thermal systems, air scrubbers, navigation systems: A spaceship was a beautiful thing, especially when you understood how each of their systems fed off every other system, how every part of a spaceship depended on every other part. A craft like this couldn't live for long unless every part of it was healthy.

His scalp itched and he smelled the reek of peanut butter inside his helmet.

The sound of his breathing felt very close.

Trim boosters fired like rumbling thunder as the shuttle entered the thicker ranges of Eden's presence. Numbers changed on the nav panel. A hiss sounded like the summer rain did when he was a kid in Wisconsin, but grew and grew until it was more like the sizzling of hot oil.

The shuttle lurched left and right, up and down.

His muscles clenched, and pain seared his half-healed leg. His stomach got twisted up, and he may have screamed. Metal squealed under sudden pressure. The cockpit rumbled and bumped. Red lights flashed with reverse reflections in his faceplate. A coppery taste came to his mouth.

The shuttle's silhouette spun on the holo display.

"Abke?" he called.

Something was wrong.

He didn't know what it was, but this wasn't right.

His feet and legs bounced in their restraints as the entire ship shuddered and shook.

"What's happening, Abke?"

Still nothing.

He didn't have time to deal with the computer system now, though.

The damned thing was coming apart. He overrode Abke instinctively, grabbing the yoke to take control. Only his good foot found its pedal.

He twisted the yoke to bring yaw into bearing.

Pitch came up.

The shuttle dipped and rolled before he got his other leg into position.

The yoke twisted from his grip.

Something exploded at the back of the craft, and suddenly he was spinning in violent circles.

He yanked the yoke back and pulled up. The shuttle responded but the reaction ripped the controls from his hands. Breathing felt like an iron band had been wrapped around his chest. Then the craft bottomed out with a slam, and a pressure that threw him against the back of the seat as if he was at the bottom of the world's angriest roller coaster.

The ride smoothed out then. By some miracle, the craft rose on a glide path.

He was level. For just a moment he was level.

He grabbed the stick back, and became aware of a warning beacon's blare.

A pair of trim rockets fired, and the craft nosed sharply down.

He was losing altitude. Holy crap. His ears popped as the shuttle raced toward the surface.

The yoke twisted right and left. Abke was back in control now, which was probably better anyway because Torrance had no idea how to land blind, better yet get them out of vertical.

His eyes widened in claustrophobic fear. Every muscle tensed. His heart pounded in his throat, and Torrance flashed on the thought that he would give anything to be able to see something outside, anything to know what the hell was going on.

When impact came, it was savage and immediate.

Metal screeched like death in the dark. Then the right side of the ship was suddenly gone and he was upside down. Shrapnel flew. The taste of sweat coated his tongue. The sharp grip of his restraints bit into his shoulders. His head crashed against the back of his seat with a thunderclap, and the craft bounced, flipped, and turned as it tumbled over land. The restraints held, but his arms flailed, and his legs were tossed backward and forward.

His faceplate shattered.

It was only then, at the very moment when his body was being clawed at by the forces of nature and the thin layer of reinforced plasti-glass shattered, that Torrance came to the dreadful realization he was not prepared to die.

Then everything went dark.

AFOOT

Esgarat: South Castanda Desert
Local Date: Convergence, Year of First *Piela*, Cycle 57

CHAPTER 5

Karshi Fael had just decided to find shelter when a bright light appeared in the distant sky.

It was midheat and she was on a high ridge of the foothills, a place she enjoyed because the rising currents of wind carried the scent of desert and because the view of the flat basin below stretched out beyond the great forever in a way that made her feel immense. This place was as much a part of her as her third heart. Like most free-rangers, Karshi was at her most comfortable while on the rock and in the wind.

She had been gathering root since Eldoro's arrival had turned the sky orange. Now the greater heat was nearing high point; the most dangerous portion of the heat and a time made even more treacherous by the fact that Katon was now racing nearly alongside, adding the fire of her heat to beat down upon the desert.

Quadars who were unprepared had always died in this kind of weather, but it was getting worse by the year. Even free-rangers like her could get themselves into trouble now.

The glare was bright enough that she had to close her central and hold her knobby hand up to protect her primaries. Even then she had to squint as she pulled her headgear's cowl away and stared up into the sky.

The sleeves of her robe dangled from her wrists.

Like her, the cloth was old and frazzled, but it cut the heat and kept her skin from burning.

Unlike Eldoro, or even Katon, this tiny new light in the sky left a blazing streak as it traced a path that reminded her of a *jah* hunting *piela*. But this was no *jah*. Dark smoke marked its pathway, and as it fell its brightness faded until only its tail was lit with blue. The front of the object, because Karshi could now see it was an object falling from the sky, gave a silvery brilliance as it reflected Eldoro's heat.

Instinctively, Karshi raised her arm to protect herself as the object hit the desert with a hard explosion, then bounced across the surface in a series of impacts, skipping, rolling, and disintegrating into bits as it broke into two and then three portions that each continued to tumble and roll until they all eventually came to rest or disappeared into crevasses. When it was done, the only thing remaining was a vicious rumble that echoed off the stone mountains before it, too, faded to nothing.

The area grew silent then.

It was one of those silences in which the entire desert seems to come to a halt, a silence like the ones that come when a pack of *neantha* go on the hunt—as if animals and plants across the whole of existence stop in place, and even the wind comes to a pause.

It was the wind that returned first.

Then the scent of blasted soil grew so faint in the wind that Karshi knew she was imagining it. The rustle of a single *pax* scampering into the protection of a crevasse filled her hearing. Dried bramble tumbled away below the ridge she stood on.

In only a few moments everything had returned to normal, everything, that is, except for the columns of black smoke that still rose from the places where the bright light had crashed to the ground.

CHAPTER 6

Torrance forced his eyes open.

He saw nothing, literally nothing but a dark cloud of gray pain. A smell like asphalt and rotting ocean nearly made him retch.

And it was hot. So hot.

Too hot to breathe.

It felt like he was baking, or like he was stewing in some gray cloud of nothing. Like he had stuck his head into a sauna filled with rotten eggs. A heavy layer of sweat coated his face. His stomach churned, and bile rose up. He swallowed it down and moaned for mercy.

His temples pounded and he tasted a rich mix of salt and blood.

Pain coursed from his shoulders and neck. His back pressed against a hard surface with intense pressure, his feet were flung…upward?

Though he couldn't see anything, he felt it all.

Was he sitting? Lying?

His joints burned like they had been ripped out of place.

Heat radiated from his whole body, which he realized now felt as bloated as it was hot. He was pretty sure he had broken a tooth. He drew a pain-laden breath and gave a groan that echoed so close it scared him. Yes, Torrance thought—his breathing was too close.

The act of expelling air hurt his chest.

He swallowed hard and closed his eyes. Everything felt upside down, a sensation not unlike sitting in a zero-g stress-test cockpit, feet up, tilted backwards, blood flooding into his head. In other words, it felt a lot like being an upturned turtle.

The good news was that even if he couldn't see shit, he could move his arms and legs, though it hurt and his wound didn't feel right. He ran his hand down his thigh. Yes, his leg was still there.

Where the hell am I?

Torrance reached to his head. His hand crashed into something with a resounding *thunk*. A shower of drops fell on his face, and sudden pain made him wince from every direction at once.

His helmet, he thought, the idea coming in a flash.

Of course.

His eyes focused on the mist in front of him, and Torrance finally realized he was looking at the safety glass of a faceplate that had shattered into a fine lattice. That's why he couldn't see a damned thing beyond the fog of dark yellow and gray.

Condensation covered the faceplate.

The condensation was his exhalation.

His sweat. That's why it was so hot. It was his body, seeping into the air inside his EVA suit.

Shit!

He was baking in his own goddamned suit!

His body came awake and he clicked the display control. Nothing happened. What the hell did he expect with a shattered faceplate? That meant everything was probably broken.

He tried to sit up, but was stuck to the seat.

It was the restraint system. Yes, the restraint system would be holding him tight. Pain in his shoulders said they were deeply bruised by the force of impact.

That made sense.

He started to release his restraints, but at the last moment his brain kicked in and he remembered his Academy commander screaming at him during his slim stint at survival training.

Look around before you cut yourself loose, goddamn it! Do you want to die?

That was a lot of years ago.

What was the guy's name? Torrance couldn't remember. Du? Yes, that was right. He thought it was, anyway.

"Focus, Torrance," he said to himself.

In order to see where he was he had to remove the helmet. Was the air was okay? It wasn't like there was any choice. Given those cracks in the faceplate, if it was bad he would probably be dead already.

He hit the helmet's latch.

It rolled away and dropped with a clank behind and below him.

For a beautiful instant the air was fresh and cool against his face, but then a rancid wall of sulfur stabbed the back of his throat. He gagged and blinked back tears. The air was horrible, and the act of coughing hurt. The O2 seemed breathable, though. At least he wasn't expiring on the spot.

He looked around.

Christ.

His pilot seat had been ripped free of the shuttle and was wedged into a crevasse, facing upward in the dark shade at the bottom of a gorge that was maybe thirty meters wide. Rocky cliffs rose fifteen or twenty meters up to the sky, veined with layered striations of dark minerals, but smoothed in places as if it had been worn by water flows.

Could there have been an ocean here once?

He shrugged at the question, the motion giving him a painful session of deep coughs.

All he could say for sure was that he was at the bottom of a big crevasse, and that Alpha Centauri A beat down from the slice of pale violet sky visible above the cliff walls. A thin swath of clouds was barely visible high up in that sky, literally disappearing as he watched. That, and the fact that the sweat on his face had almost evaporated spoke to how arid the planet was.

If he had his coordinates right, Alpha Cen B would be lower on the horizon.

Proxima would be too dim to see until darkness settled.

Part of the fuselage lay crumpled a distance away. One of the shuttle's landing assemblies had embedded itself into the rocky cliff down along the crevasse. The upper shell of the fuselage, complete with the passenger's bubble-shaped observation panel, teetered on a stubby mesa top some distance away from him.

Of his survival kit, he saw nothing.

And, yes, it was hot. Hot, hot, hot. Even here in the shade he guessed the temperature as high as 40°C, maybe higher. The lack of humidity made breathing workable, though. Barely. It was like inhaling fire, but he could do it. Torrance exhaled with another cough. His tongue was sticking to the roof of his mouth.

How long had it been since his last water?

He had two small water tubes in his side pockets, and the dried sandwich packs in his leg pockets, but without his emergency kit or without finding a natural source of water this place was going to crisp him.

Still, one problem at a time.

He had to get out of here.

Seeing it was safe, Torrance released the seat's restraint, then carefully guided his good foot to the ground and swung out of the seat. Putting pressure on his bad leg sent a spike of pain through his body, so he stood there like a stork sucking the caustic air while he let the sensation fade.

Memory of the rough landing came to him.

The new skin over his leg had probably torn again, and what little exercise he had given the ankle was pitifully inadequate. His muscles were weak from his lack of activity, which was a normal thing for a man of his age even if he hadn't spent a couple weeks in zero-g. They should come back if he worked them, but his brain was already growing fuzzy with the heat and all he had done was stand the hell up.

He needed to find water.

Soon.

He took a step and his bad leg collapsed. He twisted to avoid a rock as he fell, but he still hit the ground hard.

It took several moments for the pain to dissipate this time.

He was lucky he hadn't broken anything, but the leg was bad. He needed a crutch.

A titanium strut jutted out from wreckage ahead of him—originally it had been a channel designed to protect the optical fibers that ran through the craft, but it had been thrown clear somehow. It would make a better walking stick than a crutch, but beggars couldn't be choosers.

Torrance dragged himself toward it, sucking breath.

His leg throbbed and his vision blurred. His EVA suit was as broken as his helmet so it wouldn't help with the heat, but, again, he had to deal with one problem at a time.

He reached a hand out to claw his way forward.

Something dark and fishy flashed below his fingers.

"Ahhh!" Torrance recoiled and collapsed in a wave of pain once again.

It was a lizard of some kind, maybe a quarter meter long with black, peeling skin that was pink underneath. It was obviously as afraid of him as Torrance was of it. Its head swiveled twice before it raced away, a retreat made to the scratching sound of snakeskin against leather.

Torrance rolled onto his back, letting what had just happened flow through him.

A lizard.

Life on Eden—life beyond bacteria or viruses, anyway, life considerably more complex than paramecia or whatever primordial goo various scientists occasionally speculated about, something better than jellyfish swimming in stagnant pools.

Eden was not a dead planet.

He rolled onto his back, clenched both fists and raised them to the sky.

"Yes!" He yelled at the top of his lungs, his voice echoing in the cavern. "Yes!"

CHAPTER 7

Karshi Fael stopped her descent and let her central register subtle differences in the rock's temperature along the path the light had tumbled through. Her primaries took in the few thin trails of smoke that still rose into the sky. She extended her arm and spread her fingers, noting the span to the wreckage was the width of four of her six fingers.

Not too far. Most of the day, maybe. If she could stay in the shade, anyway.

She reached her water bladder from her belt and hefted its weight. There was enough.

She looked back over the route she had come from, then returned her gaze to the smoke. Whatever fires had created those trails were burning down but she had already marked their origin well enough that she could now find them in her sleep.

The difficult part of the descent lay before her, though. The cliff was quite sheer below.

So it was decision time.

On one side of the ledger, she had promised Gar'et that she would meet up with him in two heats, which meant she was due to return to Extico—the small free-ranger post where they had first met. He had been more than eager to make such arrangements when they parted, and though she considered his attentions to be of dubious merits, she mostly liked it. Being focused on like Gar'et focused on her was nice for a while, and after such a long time alone there was always value in physical pleasure. It would, however, be only natural for him to expect any attentions she accepted to be returned, and that step took effort she didn't always have patience for.

She looked at the expanse of the desert, and felt its call.

If she followed the path to the light, she would be late to Extico and Gar'et would be mad.

He would forgive her, of course. That was who he was. But it was a nasty thing to do to another free-ranger, and it made her feel bad to think it.

She considered her situation.

Be late to Extico, or let the light lie.

Her mind fell once again to the legend of Taranth, a story passed among wiry, desert-dried free-rangers like her—quadars who lived their lives in places like Extico, Harshish Point, and any other nooks and crannies that could be carved out of the vast and open expanse of the southern desert. Taranth had been one of them, an old tracker said to have led a pack of whelplings across the desert to search for a Light That Fell from the Sky. No one knew if Taranth's quadars had found what they sought, but no one had seen Taranth after he and the rest of his party had left Harshish Point the last time, either.

That meant the legend had different endings, depending on who told it.

Some said the light opened up and took the party to another world where they were today eating a never-ending supply of *katja* root, drinking, and having games whenever they wanted. Another said the light was the cause of the clouds leaving, and that it ate Taranth and the whelps for disturbing it. She glanced at the sky as she recalled that version. The lack of clouds promised that no burning rain would fall anytime soon and that sudden dustups of wind were unlikely until later in the heat. Its expanse seemed to taunt her, like it was goading her to enter, nudging her to pursue the light that way.

When she was young the skies were a gauzy mesh of pink and

orange that were often shot through with dark cords that swam through them like the fish that swam in deep cave ponds. When she was young, the burning winds came often. Now the winds were calmer, but the rains could tear gauges into the rock.

Personally, she assumed the desert had simply claimed Taranth and his party—that they had gotten caught by *rela* or *neantha,* or that a burning wind had eventually scattered their bones to the distance.

The desert played no favorites, after all.

Such loss happened, even to gnarled experts like Taranth.

She ran a thick-skinned hand over a rain-smoothed section of rock. Could this light she had just seen be part of Taranth's story? Given the orientation of the mountain and the light as it soared from above, it was possible she was the only quadar in existence to have seen it. If so, what would that mean? Would there be value? What would happen if she let it lie?

Why was she the one given this insight?

The final lines of smoke dissipated and the sky became clear. She extended her arm and raised her hand to block Eldoro and check her path once again.

The heat would be harsh, but she had her robes and she had water with her. If she worked the land properly, several segments of the path would be shaded. If things got too bad, she had the water trap, too.

It shouldn't be too dangerous to press on.

She scowled at that thought.

Only those who wanted to cease living should ever think of the desert as anything except dangerous.

If she was careful, she should be fine. And, yes, Gar'et would forgive her for being tardy, especially if she gave special attention to his needs when he eventually calmed down.

With that, Karshi slipped her pack over her shoulder and began the descent toward the vastness of the desert floor.

CHAPTER 8

Sweat beaded on Torrance's face, and he panted as he hauled himself over the lip of the mesa. *I'm working too hard,* he thought, *working too hard to just get to the top of this goddamned rock.* He needed to figure out where he was, though. If he was going to stay alive here, he needed to understand his situation, and sitting at the bottom of a crevasse wasn't going to get him anywhere.

It had taken several excruciating minutes of climbing to make it to the top of the mesa. Now Torrance lay on his back, groaning and baking in direct sunlight while he caught his breath.

He mopped his brow and covered his eyes.

The heat from Alpha Centauri A was so intense it felt like he was burning on the spot. It was a weird sensation, a feeling like bugs were crawling over the parts of his skin that were exposed. Sweat made the EVA suit feel rubbery. It made him feel slimy. Like he was swimming in oil. The whole thing had to go, but he wasn't dumping his only protection without another option.

At least the wind picked up here.

When it blew, its touch was almost cool. But then it would stop and the heat would commence to baking.

Torrance didn't know much about heat and the human body, but he understood that after a point the basic cellular structure of a person would break down unless they got water. Certain parts of the Earth had been almost uninhabitable late last century due to heat. He was pretty sure this place was above that point.

He had to get the hell out of here.

He rolled to a sitting position.

The view took his breath away.

The landscape was desolate. Broken and distant.

The sky seemed endlessly deep, touched by only a small band of gauzy clouds that looked like they were made of watercolor spilled over the sky.

The ground was nothing but orange and brown rock and sand that stretched to a dark line of mountains in the direction Torrance knew was north. The most prominent peak of what was most likely a volcano lay directly ahead, standing like a sentry with its chest out and chin exposed. The peak was tall and strong, unmovable, its crest shrouded in drab clouds of billowing smoke that gave testimony to why the planet smelled so strongly of sulfur. The mountain ridge continued both east and west, making a toothy profile that faded into the horizon. To the south, the desert was broken by only the occasional formation or rocky point.

On "his" mesa, scraggly brush clung fiercely to cracks in the baked rock.

He saw more in the distance, withered growths on other parts of the desolate surface that clawed desperately at the ground.

Plant life.

That meant water, somewhere. He wondered if he could eat any of it, and his stomach gave a twinge in response.

Water.

Soon.

The thought made him feel even more parched.

Torrance used his walking strut to stand up.

The ground was pitted and burned where the shuttle had bounced during its tumble. Bits and pieces of debris were scattered about, but no major component was obvious. Most of the wreckage was probably at the bottoms of crevasses like his section of the cockpit had been. Jesus, but he had been lucky.

On the other hand, he saw no sign of the survival kit, nor any obvious source of water.

His tongue stuck to the roof of his mouth. The pair of suns beat down on him. He had two tubes with him, but he had to wait if he could.

He limped a step, then cupped his hands to his mouth and yelled.

"Hey! Can anybody hear me?"

His voice faded into the wind.

As he turned to scan the whole view, he caught a gleaming flash of light.

It was one of the spare helmets, sitting like a lonely conch shell a short distance away. He hobbled to pick it up, then turned it in his hands as if it were a Ming vase.

"I'll be damned," he said, chuckling to himself. "Not a scratch."

He attached it to his utility belt.

"Never turn down a lucky piece," he said, happy for the tone of his own voice.

Shielding his eyes from the daylight, he considered his options.

He needed to find water.

Time to go exploring.

Less than ten minutes later, Torrance half-slipped and half-fell into a shaded crevasse large enough to huddle down into. He backed up against the wall, and let himself slide to a seated position.

His leg hurt and his brain felt addled.

It was just too goddamned hot to work. He could barely catch his breath. What was the O2 content of this place? No. He didn't want to know. Maybe when he was younger he could have handled the load here but, life extension or not, his seventy-one-year-old body couldn't take it.

His chest hurt, and he wondered if his heart was giving out.

Or if the air was poisonous.

He ran the arm of his suit over his forehead. He should take it off, but the idea of being naked against heat felt more dangerous than not. When he had first come to he was just a little queasy. Now he was feeling flat-out sick.

He pressed his hands over his temple and stretched his neck.

No option now but to drink what he had.

He broke the seal on a water tube and let the warm liquid flow down his gullet. It didn't help as much as he wanted it to, but he had only one more tube so he had to stretch it if he could.

Torrance retrieved the freeze-dried sandwich from its pouch, then ripped the package open. The "sandwich" inside was a melted mass of undecipherable goo. Scooping it with two fingers, he layered it into his mouth and laid his head against the rock while he finished chewing.

He wasn't going to make it.

The idea of stepping out into the baking heat again made him cringe, so he would stay here for now. Travel at night when only Alpha Centauri B's more distant light would leave the going cooler. But facts were the facts. He wasn't going to survive out here for much longer.

He closed his eyes.

A moment later he was asleep.

CHAPTER 9

Karshi pulled her hood down to better protect from the heat. There was no wind here now, which was a bad break.

She had scaled the sheer cliffs and made her way into the rugged foothills. She wanted to continue, but knew better than to press too far.

To her left, a line of broken rock jutted upward and caught the crosshatched light of Katon and Eldoro to create a patch of shade. If the lack of wind was bad luck, the vein of root growing from recessed cracks in the shelter was a boon. She pulled the root, and chewed it as she disrobed. Once naked, she stretched, then sat down and pressed the three plates along her back against the surface of the rock to let her blood cool to something closer to normal as it flowed through the plates. A wave of relief passed through her body, and her toes tingled. Always a good sign. Blood that got too hot turned to mud. Tingly toes meant no mud.

Using rock like this for rapid cooling was a trick free-rangers had used since the first days there were free-rangers, though in the past it was rarely needed unless the heats were in the harshest times of Convergence. Now, with both Eldoro and Katon in the sky, she used it almost daily.

The root was sharp on her tongue and made her nasal passages expand, which was good, too. Spreading the surface area helped everything cool.

It would save her several sips of water.

She ripped another bite of root and chewed it as she put her head against the rock.

The image of Gar'et sitting alone in Extico came to her.

It was wrong to leave him like that. He would worry, a reaction she understood but still annoyed her. Whether Gar'et meant it or not, his concern said he didn't think she could handle herself. At one point she had tried to explain that to him.

"You don't understand me," she had said.

"Tell me," he replied with his central wide and the skin around his ridge pulled back in that overdone expression of compassion he was so good at.

They had been together for two heats. Given that she had been attractive in the time before the desert had broken her skin and the mountains had hardened her manner, she was familiar with the sensation of being smitten over. Still, she had to admit to being surprised that a grizzled free-ranger like Gar'et could fall like he had.

"I was born inside the ring," she explained. "My da spent everything he had serving the Families, and he wanted me to pair-mate into one of them so I could have a comfortable life instead of scrounging in the gutters like he did. For the longest time that's what I thought my life would be."

"I'm glad you didn't agree with your da."

"It's not like that," she said, probably too harshly. "I would have accepted whatever my da wanted, but no upper-house quadar would take me for more than a side servant. I left, but only because bedding great Family quadars was never my strong suit."

The answer stymied him.

"But I stayed here because I love the wilds."

"So do I," Gar'et replied, obviously trying to move the topic away from the city.

"Do you?"

"Of course."

She scowled then. She had known Gar'et for only two heats, but already she could tell that he, like almost all the others, was lying to himself about why he was a free-ranger. It was in the words he used, and the hard edge to his voice when he told his stories. Gar'et respected the desert. He understood it. But he didn't love it. Instead, he lived in the desert because the Families chewed up quadars like him. He liked the soft conveniences of those who lived inside the Great Ring of Esgarat, but he was a quadar of little patience for the politics of people. He wasn't the kind to succeed in cities. Quadars like Gar'et went crazy inside the ring. They did bad things and found themselves punished and placed in workers' prisons or worse. So, instead, quadars like Gar'et took to the expanse of the desert and to the cool shelter of the caves, not because the life of a free-ranger was what they loved but because it was the cost of being able to live outside the reaches of the Families.

He tried to argue this point, but Karshi had learned long ago that opening that vein was a sure way to break a friendship, so she just left it alone.

But from that time on, she understood the difference between them.

While Gar'et was here to be free, Karshi truly loved the desert.

She was here because this is where she belonged.

"Sometimes," she told Gar'et that night, "when I sleep I put my ear on the ground and wait for the land to speak." His expression was uncertain then, almost confused, and she knew she was right. "If I'm just the right amount of tired, the world hums to me," she continued. "It wraps its arms around me and lets me know I'm important, that I'm part of something bigger than the quadarti, something bigger, even, than the desert that we walk over and the air we breathe," she said.

Gar'et nodded then. Yes, he said. He understood. But she didn't need much intuition to feel the truth. Gar'et didn't understand her because he couldn't understand her. And he couldn't understand because he, unlike her, was not actually of the desert and the rock.

Life for her was not about deals. Not dwellings or technologies. Not Families taking advantage of other Families. Instead, life was about listening to the world as it moved around her, about giving the land her body and her blood, and sometimes, when the desert was kindest, life was about letting it respond with a gift that was so simple and pure that it could rock you to your hearts.

That's what she was thinking about as she let the cooling breeze slide over her naked body.

A vibration, she thought, feeling the rock behind her.

A vibration was a gift from the mountain, a present from the desert.

Alone in the dim shade of the shelter, she finished chewing the root, then stood and stretched. The sound of *jah* calling came from the distance. It made her think of stealth, which gave her to flash on hunting patterns and the way that the smell of death from the *jah*'s kills eventually brought *rela* beasts to chase them away if they didn't eat fast enough.

She flexed her hand, sipped from her water bladder, then got back into her robe.

It was time to move.

CHAPTER 10

lpha Centauri A had already set when Torrance woke, Alpha Cen B nearly so.

It was growing dark, and an eerie purple-brown dimness crept across the sky. He drank his last water tube, feeling the liquid dissipate through his body and knowing he needed more. He wondered how much water a body lost while it slept. Though the air was cooler than midday, it was still horribly hot. At least he could breathe, though—better, anyway. His face was achy with the sunburn he had received in only fifteen or so minutes of exposure. His lips cracked with the dry air. Unless he stumbled upon some unlikely water source, he needed to find his emergency kit or he was done.

Eventually, he forced himself upright and limped from the crevasse.

His calf had cramped while he slept, so he pulled himself along, limping while using the strut to help him walk.

The near-dark landscape was even stranger to his eyes now than it had been in daylight.

Its vast emptiness was colored in deep violets and burnt oranges. Stars glittered from the mostly clear sky, but what few clouds were there bent the thin rays of Alpha Cen B to make vivid pink and red scars at the edges of the dark dome. He looked at them in wonder. The models he and Kitchell created from meteorological reports said the drain on Alpha Centauri A shouldn't have been enough to change things so quickly. So where were the rest of the clouds? Everything he knew said they would be thick and omnipresent, yet instead here were stars, and here was a night that was rapidly cooling.

If those models were right, or at least close to right, Eden would have a brief period of intense warming followed by a plunge into an atmospheric ice age.

He wondered if they had gotten the time compression wrong.

How long before the planet went cold?

As he moved along, night cast an edge of danger over the area.

Lizards were here, after all. If there were lizards, there would be predators. Survival instinct rose. He suddenly felt eyes staring at him. The strut bit into his hand, and pain everywhere turned his stride into a lopsided lurch. Each step was a labor. He muttered and pressed forward, though. "You've come too far, damn it," he said. "You've come too far."

He would find his kit. That was the only answer.

At the edge of his vision he saw someone.

It was Kitchell, young and all assholey as he had been on *Everguard*.

"Goddamn it, kid," he said. "Don't just stand there, come and help me find the water."

No. What the hell was wrong with him? Kitchell couldn't do anything for him because Kitchell was in his hospital bed after Torrance had gotten him shot.

He shook his head.

Crap. That was wrong, too.

Hallucination?

Suddenly he was terribly afraid.

He tried to follow the shuttle's crash path. The ground was dark, and the rocky floor was slippery where it was smooth. He made it into a depression, and found what he was pretty sure was part of the ship's computer panel lying over a field of small rocks. The crumpled tail assembly lay in another.

The wind picked up, and nearly blew him over.

Jesus, he was tired. He shivered in the breeze, trying to bring back information about black holes but realizing his brain wasn't able to reconcile anything.

The first howl startled him.

It was deep and long, but in the distance. A wolf's bay crossed with a bear's grunt. At first he convinced himself his imagination was playing games with the wind. "Kitchell," he muttered, not sure why. But the sound came again and then again, seemingly closer.

Then he heard a thin scratching, and dark movements came from within the shadows.

The planet was waking up, animals were stirring.

Torrance suddenly felt hunted, understood exactly what it meant to be truly afraid.

A crack came from behind him, and he twisted around, imagining some kind of horrible wolf at his back. Too fast, he spun too fast and fell to the ground with a thud that took his breath away.

Nothing there, though.

He lay still for a moment, panting and gathering his wits before he stood and pressed on. It would be hours until the suns rose. He needed that water.

He came to another fissure. A dark lump of spacecraft lay broken at its bottom.

It was too dark for Torrance to identify what it was until he picked his way down to it, but once he got there he saw it was an instrument panel—and, to his blessed amazement, the right-hand seat. The entire assembly was bent in a V and pierced by the copilot's navigation yoke. Wires hung from it like plastic spaghetti. A wicked crack split the windscreen, and the display panel was shattered, too.

But, there, still intact under the seat, was the bundle he had prepared.

He almost fell in his rush to get to it.

He hugged it to his chest, fighting tears of unabashed joy.

Water.

Dear God, water.

His fingers were numb as he untied the package.

He ripped the blanket out of the way, throwing it to the ground in haste. He would use the blanket as a robe against tomorrow's heat, but

it didn't matter now. Now all that mattered was the water. For whatever reason, he thought about Commander Du standing in full camo at
survival school and tearing sections of a blanket to use as moccasins.

"Your feet are your life," he said when the guys laughed at him.
Torrance remembered the sad little shoes the commander had made,
half blanket, half plastic composite sole.

The sound of water tubes sliding from the pack broke his memory.

Yes!

Water tubes! They were smooth to his touch. He wrapped his hand
around the first, and literally cried as he cracked the seal and drank it
greedily.

The contents were halfway down when the growl came.

Impact happened a blink later.

Torrance choked as he fell to the ground, his leg twisting underneath him.

The animal smelled of black asphalt and sounded like a Bengal
tiger. It may have been just as big as a tiger for all Torrance could tell. It
fell on him, teeth crushing his shoulder with a blazing pain.

Torrance hit it hard with his elbow and heard a sound he thought
might be teeth breaking.

It let go, but twisted around so Torrance could see it.

It was like a big dog, but leathery or scaly, and hot as an oven.
Others were here, too, a ring of them waiting for the lead animal to
make his business. Teeth flashed. Its eyes were feral in the starlight.

Anger rose up from somewhere deep inside. An adrenalin-powered
flash of raw survival kicked in, and Torrance pushed himself up to hit
it with his titanium stick.

The creature yowled, and bit down on Torrance's forearm with
crushing pressure, but the EVA suit didn't puncture.

Its jaws clamped together, its head thrashed to and fro like a shark
trying to rip meat.

Torrance gave a savage scream and dropped his stick. For an
instant there was nothing in his life but pain, the heat of the animal,
and the crushing strength of its jaws. He felt anger. He felt rage. He felt
the sense of life's harshness, its unfairness. His fingers scrabbled over
the stony ground to find his walking stick. Then the strut was in his

hand again and he was beating the thing, swinging at it and beating it and swinging harder again. The beast screamed with its alien throat.

Dark blood spattered the night.

He hit it again as it turned and again as it ran, feeling the impact give him a solid sense of power. He swung again, missing and sprawling to the ground, then spinning around to sit up and defend himself again.

But the animal was gone, as were the others.

He panted for breath in the heat of the night, grasping the strut and waving it before him like a laser weapon. His shoulder and arm ached and he thought he was going to pass out for a moment, but several minutes passed and Torrance calmed enough to remember the pack.

He went back to it.

It was surrounded by a dark patch.

The water tube he was drinking from had drained into the parched ground.

The rest had broken when he fell on them, each adding to the pool of dampness that was soaking into the rock as he stood there watching.

Torrance screamed in despair. He dropped to his knees and lapped at the ground, sucking at the stone to get any moisture he could, clawing at it with his fingers as if they might become sponges.

There was nothing there, though. In ten minutes the stone was dry.

His water was gone.

CHAPTER 11

Torrance sat back against the rocky surface of the crevasse, defeated. He could quit here. He could lie down and give up. Maybe the wolf-things would come again, and then it would be over more quickly.

Yes. He could quit.

He thought about his girls, then. Ana and Mercy. He wished he could see them.

For reasons he couldn't put into words, the idea of them made Torrance stand up.

He grabbed the blanket and fashioned it into a poncho-like drape. It would cut the heat when Alpha Cen A came out. Working on it made him feel better. He peeled the EVA suit off and tossed it over the broken second seat, then ripped part of the blanket away to form a belt, and looped the survival kit onto it.

He couldn't think of anything the helmet he had salvaged would be useful for, but it was familiar. He liked it. Its unmarred surface made him feel better, and it was light enough to carry without much of a problem. So he clipped the helmet strap onto his belt loop, and left it dangle.

By the time he was done, a hazy orange light was beginning to color the eastern horizon.

He headed toward the volcano, giving up a pretense of finding water, and instead pretending that he would find aliens, pretending he could find intelligence out here in the desolation of this weird desert. He talked to himself, pretending to be a real explorer, no longer caring how crazy he sounded.

"Your feet are your life!" he barked into the air at one point.

Progress was slow.

His shoulder and arm throbbed from the beast's attack. His bad leg was merely a steady ache now.

Alpha Cen A rose and rode across the sky.

The "poncho" helped keep him cooler, if you could call it that, but the pair of suns burned down hard on him, sizzling against any bit of skin he left exposed. He tired quickly despite resting every few minutes. The helmet swung from its loop in a strange pattern that he found gave him an odd sense of comfort because its sway was predictable, and the shell was something of his in this strange world that was most definitely not his.

Lizards, rodents, and oddly shaped insects skittered across his path, making him laugh out loud. He managed to avoid larger beasts, though he found four-toed footprints and the desiccated carcass of a strange animal that worried him. Still he found no sign of aliens capable of sending messages through space.

Just the idea seemed crazy-insane now.

"Where's a goddamned hallucination when you need it?" he called.

The sun pounded on him. The walking stick scored his hand. His tongue swelled. His stomach knotted into a shrunken mass that he thought might be eating itself.

His body was breaking down now, slowly destroying itself.

Cramps twisted his muscles to burning coals with every other step. His vision blurred and his thoughts jumbled. As wind raked his parched lips, he spoke to Kitchell, and he spoke to Ana and Mercy.

At one point he pulled the covering off his head and let the skin on his cheeks burn just so he could see the peak better. The volcano loomed closer, he thought.

Still far away, though. Too far away.

He remembered a day in high school physics class when he and his classmates threw an entire set of calibrated weights out the window of the third-floor room, then had to spend the next period digging in the soft ground until they found them all, their teacher looming over him. He remembered cool earth between his fingers, damp and slippery and smelling of worms.

He heard Marisa's voice, but couldn't make out the words.

He turned to look, then laughed at himself when he saw he was alone.

"Probably 'I told you so,'" he tried to say, but his tongue stuck to the roof of his mouth.

One foot went before the other.

"Why this?" he finally croaked. "I'm doing my best."

But that was the thing for Torrance Black.

His best had never been enough. He wasn't bright enough. Never talented enough. Not strong enough. He had a distinct lack of courage. He was never the last man standing.

He was a failed husband, a failed father, a failed diplomat. Hell, he was even a failed hero when you got down to it. What the hell did he do with himself? Wasn't even strong enough to do what Kitchell did and focus on the damned Eden files.

At the end of it all, he had always made it exactly as far as the people above him allowed, and no farther.

He was pitiful.

What better way to live the last moments of his life than to be alone on a remote planet, failing to find the intelligent life he had believed in for so long?

His mother stood beside a growth of thorns, shaking her head.

"I'm sorry, Mom," he mumbled. "I'm sorry."

He stumbled and fell then, his cheek bruising against hard rock, the dusty flavor of his own blood filling his mouth as it ran across his tongue. It would be good to just lie here, he thought. Yes. That was good. Just lie here and let the sun get to him. The intensity of the radiation burned his cheeks.

"No!" His voice was a croak.

The black hole.

He had to warn someone about a black hole.

He pried his eyes open to see a pile of thorny brush inches from his face. The scratch of claws on rock came from the distance, then the cough of a wolf beast.

He glanced around as best he could, but didn't see anything.

Could the beasts disappear? Just teleport away? Had they had been following him, waiting until he died for fear of his white strut? He peered toward the horizon with nearly blind eyes.

He had to find the aliens. It was all he had left.

Had to.

Somehow he found the strength to stand.

The helmet brushed his hip and he almost fell over with its sway.

Useless piece of crap.

He pulled his belt loop, almost falling over as the clear shell fell away to tumble against the uneven ground, then rolled to a stop against the wild brush that grew here.

"Hope you're happy now," he said without knowing who he was talking to, or even if his tongue was forming words properly. "What more did you want?"

It was hot. So goddamned hot.

He took a step, then another. He fell on the third, collapsing to the ground, worn and exhausted, his breath coming in birdlike gasps.

He closed his eyes then. He tried to lick his lips.

This time, Torrance Black did not get up.

CHAPTER 12

Alpha Centauri A, the star known by the quadarti as Eldoro, hit highpoint. Katon was not far behind.

The air shimmered in distorted waves over rock that lay exposed and baking in the heat.

Rays of light bent through the atmosphere to fall upon the still form of the only human being on the planet known to those in the Solar System as Eden.

Other rays found the curved surface of a helmet that had fallen first from the sky and then again from the man's belt. The beams curved with the shape of its clear dome, some collecting to a tight focus on the gnarled roots of brush that grew in the cracked surface of the lava bed.

The temperature rose at the root's surface.

Smoke came.

Just a wisp at first, then a thick rope that wafted upward.

The root darkened. Fire formed.

Flames spread from the root to the branches. Thorns curled in combustion, and oily smoke rose into the wind to twist and writhe like a desert snake.

Or, the man might say if he had been conscious, like an emergency beacon.

CHAPTER 13

The smoke brought Karshi to the burning bush and the fallen form that lay on the exposed mesa. She had never seen anything like it.

The creature had arms and legs like a quadar, but its proportions were different—its bones thinner, and its hands showing only five fingers rather than six. Its skin was bright red. As she bent over it, the creature made a noise of some kind. Incomprehensible. Its primaries opened long enough for her to see they were dark and milky white and crisscrossed with crimson, then closed again. It had no central.

Karshi stepped backward in case it struck out.

The creature did nothing, though, so she bent to examine it further.

The wind picked at the hair on the thing's head and face.

Carefully, she reached to touch it. It didn't respond. She put her hand around one of the creature's arms, and pulled it away from the smoldering brush. It grunted again, but still didn't move on its own.

Karshi shielded her gaze from Eldoro's heat and peered at the mountain.

This was a strange gift, she thought. It was nothing she knew what to do with. It seemed to be barely alive.

Perhaps she should kill it.

This is what she would do with an injured *kax*, but something about that brief gaze the creature gave her and the sounds that it made caused her to dismiss that idea outright. The sky had granted her this gift. It felt wrong to kill it. It also felt wrong to leave it sit. Besides, it was like no other animal across all of Esgarat, and it was trying to communicate. She was sure of that. It was trying to make itself known.

What was it saying?

What was it doing here?

For an instant she considered the idea that another quadar might pay a reward for such a creature, but smirked the thought immediately away. What did she care about rewards? What good were currencies outside the ring?

Karshi looked at the creature again.

Yes, she thought, there *would* be a reward in saving it, but the payment would be in the form of understanding something she hadn't understood before. The only question was who, on the whole of the Esgarat, could help her discover what that message might be? Where could she find someone who could understand what such a creature had to say?

She pulled her water bladder out, and dribbled liquid over the creature's lips. It drank absently, but at least it drank. She gave it more, then driven by her decision to save it, Karshi spread a blanket from her satchel over the ground. Putting an arm around the creature's back and another under its legs, Karshi hefted it up, centered it, and laid the creature on the makeshift sled.

It weighed less than she expected.

She tied the ends together and slipped the creature's walking stick into the hole, twisting it until it was tight.

Turning her back, hands behind, Karshi Fael grabbed the handle and began her long journey.

ARE YOU US?

Eden: Quadarti Council of the Clans
Local Date: Convergence, Year of First *Piela*, Cycle 57

CHAPTER 14

Baraq Waganat sat at the back of the council chamber, doing his best to keep from letting his anxiety come through. It was warm here. The air was stale. The chamber was expansive and broad, built and refurbished over many cycles, carved originally of rock from the great Esgarat mountains and polished by some of the quadarti's finest artisans. Given that the council was in special session, the chamber was only half-full, a state that meant the sounds of squeaking chairs and clearing throats echoed in the hollowness of the hall's open space. It was nearing Eldoro-high, meaning the heat was rising. The council would break soon to avoid the peak.

The Family's box was set in the back section of the ring, having been chosen for its clear line of sight, and because the technologies the Waganat Family had created, peddled, and controlled gave it leverage to be able to make such selections. The box was easy to slip into and out of, a quality Baraq wished he could advantage of, but knew he wouldn't.

He wanted the session to be finished so he could get on with the rest of his agenda, but Councilor Pelorit had called this meeting specifically to deal with problems created by Lelo's efforts. To miss it would be dangerous.

Whereas everyone else considered the revolutionary renegade as a weak-willed coward who went so far as to hide behind a mask, Baraq knew him as someone else—his son, Brada.

The role of spy was one Baraq had come to grips with over time.

His father, Ranya Waganat, had forced him to make his choices, and he had made them.

Quietly, Baraq had been supplying Lelo with as much information as possible, just as he had been doing for Louratna, though that was a different problem all together.

With Baraq's help and Brada's own inherent charisma, Lelo had become the most effective voice among those who had been stirring up younger and more independent quadars. His efforts were specifically aimed at making the power structure uncomfortable, relentlessly exposing moments where the Families caused pain, and as such constantly proselytizing a new order. It was a dangerous path, of course. Baraq schooled his whelp often on how to treat the Families with proper distance.

So, yes, Baraq knew what his whelp was doing, and he knew something else, too.

The forces lining up behind Lelo, while not powerful by themselves, were immense in mass. And they were upset—which made sense. The Families lived well, but the average *hedgie,* the independent quadars who had been born of parents outside the Family structures, barely made it from one heat to the next. Now the burning rain was falling often, and black sickness was coming over the quadarti. Crops failed. Water mining was being monitored.

The population was hungry, tired, and more than unhappy.

The council, of course, remained blind, but Baraq knew exactly how big of a problem they had on their hands.

There had been a crime now. An attack.

While the rest of the committee argued over the details, Baraq already knew what had happened because he had helped plan the operation. Several of Lelo's followers had raided a Family and stolen currencies.

"We took what was theirs," the raiders said in a statement.

Theirs, of course, meant the *hedgies..* The Otara Family had not paid for work the *hedgies* had completed because the Family had complaints about quality—not an unusual case. Lelo's followers had broken into an Otara business and extracted the exact amount the *hedgies* had been due.

No more, no less.

The amount stood as a protest in itself. The currencies would go to provide proper housing to the families involved.

Baraq was not surprised, however, when these details were not presented to the council at all.

Hedgie families would hear the whole truth, though. They would know the Otara head was short on a payment. These were the kinds of happenings that had been building Lelo's following.

Baraq was growing tired now.

He fidgeted with the frayed liner of his Waganat robe.

Since the council's early morning commencement, speakers had rambled on and on, most pounding the podium, demanding justice, and demanding that Family whelplings receive additional education on how the structure kept the quadarti operating—as if they weren't going to get that at home, anyway.

Baraq did his best to hide anxiety behind a façade of boredom.

He ran his knobby fingers across the lap of his robe, trying to smooth wrinkles that did not exist. The air was so stagnant he considered breaking protocol and shouldering his robe to give his back plates better access to the airflow. That would be crude, though, and it would get back to his father. He closed his primaries instead, and used his central to examine residual heat patterns that came from the rest of the council members, noting the cooler, high arcing walls that rose to the chamber's open dome.

Council Member Olan of the Festia Family sat in his Family's area to Baraq's left.

The Banit's box sat empty in front of him.

Ceri Tah, perhaps the only quadar with any energy in the chamber, filled the Amat'tesh box on the diagonal. She was still young, and she scribbled notes with vigorous excitement at each turn in the conversation. Baraq knew of her affinity for Lelo, a backing that was controversial but which he obviously admired.

It made him angry, though, made him think of his own cowardice when he was her age, and Brada's age—or if not cowardice, at least his oblivious nature and his excessive concern for caution.

So much wasted time.

Olan leaned across the barrier that separated their boxes. "What do you think of these conversations?" he said.

Baraq shrugged.

Olan's Festia Family was focused on construction, and had been made wealthy by performing work across Esgarat City as well as several other projects the council had authorized for failed expansion efforts outside the ring of mountains protecting the quadarti homeland. These were all items Baraq had backed, which made him a favored compatriot in Olan's eyes. Like most of the greater Families, the Festias controlled several lesser families, parceling activities and choosing which clans received which currencies. Like his own Waganats, who controlled hundreds of technologies through outright ownership as well as several others via coordinated partnerships, the Festia Family controlled a large portion of the quadarti economy.

The whole of Family politics was a delicate balance at the good times, and bloody conflict at the worst. It was a balance Baraq had become intimately familiar with, and which let him understand that Olan Festia had little patience for the topic in question.

Baraq understood Olan's question was really an attempt to see if the Waganats would support quashing the discussion of Lelo in favor of taking votes to authorize plans for updating the city's pathways— plans that would result in the Festia Family delivering smoother, rock-hard surfaces that motorized carts would find less damaging, and that the Families could then use to create a more advantageous economy.

"I think," Baraq finally replied, "that I will take *havra* for dinner this evening."

Olan gave a perplexed expression, but he sat back.

Baraq smiled at the result. There were considerably bigger issues to deal with than the idea of smooth motor cart pathways. Beyond that, he felt satisfaction as he thought of Crissandr, his pair-mate. She had been working earlier this morning to make the broth he liked so much.

She was too good for him.

They had been through much together.

Baraq closed his central and tried to follow the conversation.

Yendar, a priest, went to the podium.

Baraq adjusted a wave talker mounted in the Waganat box. As usual, his father was listening through it, and he would want to hear Yendar's commentary clearly. Or, better put, if Ranya Waganat could not hear what he wanted to hear, Baraq would be the subject of his wrath.

The priest was tall and growing toward her elder seasons. She held herself with regal posture, looking resplendent in the purple and mauve robes of the Northern Churches.

The chamber buzzed in anticipation.

They, like Baraq, understood that Yendar had been building her case against the revolutionary concepts of youth groups such as Lelo's over the past few sessions. In this talk she would make a formal Petition of Focus—meaning she would request that all the clans' resources be put to building a huge church to circle the great mountain's upper reaches. She would ask that the Families send their troubled whelplings to work on the construction for mandatory stints of two seasons each, thereby removing much of Lelo's audience, and thereby teaching the value of productive labor, not to mention the teachings of the Holy Esgarat.

This would please Eldoro, she would explain, which would result in Eldoro bringing back the clouds and their protections from the burning rains.

Baraq stifled a grimace as Yendar took her position in the center of the chamber.

A glaring shaft of Eldoro's light knifed from the ceiling's open ring to fall in a dramatic column beside her. Dust motes danced like *sheka* flies as the hall quieted down.

Finally, Yendar spoke.

"There need be no debate of the problems we have faced over the past years," she said. "We need not speak of quadars stricken with the fever, or felled by the frequent occurrences of melting rain. There need be no debate that the *havra* root that once sustained our civilization is now being baked in place before it can be harvested, and that in addition to heats strong enough to burn these crops, Convergence now brings nights so cold that our water turns to rock."

She paused for effect, gazing over the ranks.

"And, since we are all aware that Lelo struck again last night, we now have no need to discuss whether we have hoodlums growing within our ranks. The time has come for the quadarti to recognize that changes must be made."

"Aye, aye, aye," Councilor Labek spoke out immediately. "Lelo is a delinquent. We have to stop him now."

Chief Councilor Pelorit halted Labek's tirade with a sharp click from his throat.

"Please hold your commentary," he said. "We have no definitive proof of involvement by the quadar known as Lelo."

"You've heard him speak," Labek said, ignoring protocol.

Pelorit's face constricted. He stared at Labek until the quadar finally sat back. "I suggest we leave the floor to Yendar, whose turn it is to speak," the council leader said.

Yendar gathered control of the floor again.

"I note appreciation for Council Member Labek's views, and ask: what can be the cause of all of this? And, of more relevance, I ask what should we do?"

Ag Liean raised his commentary flag and spoke before being formally announced—another breach of etiquette, but forgivable in that Ag represented math workers in Northern Esgarat, and that everyone in the chamber knew it had been coming because mathematical expertise across all quadarti was not in unison when it came to Eldoro's influence on the burning rains.

"Our science isn't finished," Ag Liean said. "Blind leaps lead to unpredictable consequences. Without firm understanding of what's happening we're likely to make bad decisions and create situations we may never be able to recover from. We need to continue our studies."

Baraq stifled a glare.

He knew exactly what was causing these changes, but he also knew he wouldn't live long if he discussed them openly. Even if he did discuss them, however, it was unlikely anyone would believe him. No quadar across the whole of Esgarat, other than Louratna's community, of course, would accept a story of civilizations from other worlds stealing Eldoro's heat—and even if they did, the argument of the Esgarat heating up because Eldoro was fading seemed nonsensical.

That is, until you did the math that Louratna's quadars had done.

It was over a full cycle ago that Louratna, a renegade philosopher and perhaps the quadarti's most effective mind, had deduced that the Taranth Stone was a device that drew energy from Eldoro. Baraq's covert work for the council on that matter is what had landed him in this form of Waganat exile in the first place.

In a way, he was lucky to get off that easily.

The demotion hurt, but he accepted it because the alternative was to be exiled from the Family, and because it gave him a platform from which to gather information. Louratna was still working on the problem, so Baraq listened to discussions inside the council and helped her whenever he could. Unlike Yendar's request, which he was convinced would do nothing, Baraq felt certain that Louratna and her philosophers were the quadarti's only real hope.

None of this had anything to do with Lelo, of course, but Yendar was politician enough not to miss the opportunity to build on it.

"We have been studying this situation since before I was birthed," Yendar replied to Ag Liean using the formal *we* in order to raise the power of her response. "Yet, each year the sky grows clearer, the daytime warmer, and the nights colder. Indeed, this very session will soon be interrupted because the heat will become too strong for comfortable discussion. I need not remind the council that it once met for as long as necessary when resolving such important issues."

Baraq tried not to yawn. The two had argued this point publicly for the past three seasons, and probably in private for far longer.

"I am aware of our ways, Priestess," Ag replied. "But our science is important specifically because it will tell us what we, as a civilization, must do as the world changes around us."

"Tell that to the quadars who have children scarred by burning rain," Yendar said much more for the benefit of her audience than as an argument. "Or to the farmer who stands amid her crops as they flake and blow away in the wind. These hardships are why the messages of criminals such as Lelo take hold. Some say Lelo's words cause young quadars to turn against the Family structure because that structure is unfair, but we know this is not true. They would have us believe Lelo's complaints fall on willing ears due to some economic grace he has suddenly shown them, but we can see that, too, is false. Our quadarti culture has lived for generations without strife or conflict, so this is not about economics. It is about false reliance. Young quadars see that our words and our actions do not align when it comes to following the ways of the Great Heat. In this, Counselor Liean, we do not need your science to give us guidance. We have our eyes and we have our memories. And, mostly, we have Eldoro and Katon's word, spoken in the stones, that tell us we must pray for forgiveness. Now is the time for us to focus our energies on what has been important to us since our very beginnings."

"And that would be?"

Those words were ragged and raw, and came from a new voice behind Baraq.

The chamber turned almost as one to view the quadar who stood at the chamber's entrance.

It was a bent figure, robed and hooded against exposure in such a way as to hide its face.

It walked down the central aisle as if each step was more painful than the last, and was followed by an aroma filled with the sharp odors of desert dust and expended effort.

The sound of weight on the floor was thick.

The quadar was dragging something behind, but despite edging forward to get a better view Baraq couldn't make it out. His knees ached and his back complained as he stretched further. It was some kind of sled, a tattered blanket, folded over to protect the contents. It left clouds of dust in its wake. The sling's handle was weather-beaten and made of metal that at one time might have been painted white, but was now stained, mottled, and worn through.

The visitor walked until it was beside Yendar, then let the handle fall to the floor with a startling clatter. It straightened as if the movement was painful beyond time, then knobby hands pulled back the hood.

A gasp circled the chamber.

It was an older female, gnarled by time.

Karshi Fael.

Baraq recognized her from perhaps two full cycles back when she was a very young whelpling.

Karshi spoke in a voice as raw as cave stone.

"Eight heats ago, a light crossed the sky. It was farther south than you might have seen, but I saw it, and I went to discover what it was."

Her central focused on the older council members.

Some nodded without speaking, a few understanding her undertone and remembering in their own ways that another light had fallen from the sky in the past.

Baraq, however, had a much stronger reaction.

His blood chilled, and he couldn't help but recall the many nights he had spent in the outskirts of the desert after stealing his brother's ancient wave talker, sending its signals up into the sky and hoping someone might be listening. They kept the old thing working longer than he thought possible and kept it secret for even longer, scrapping it in parts only a few years ago after the desert eventually claimed it. And he couldn't help but remember how, as the clouds cleared away, he had seen other lights fall, how he had worked with Louratna to send expeditions to retrieve several of the rocks that had fallen, each time hoping that his clandestine work to send wave talker rays to other worlds might have worked, that there would be another gift like the Taranth Stone at the end of the surveys. Or better, that members of the species who had created the Taranth Stone to begin with would arrive and help them.

The results had always been disappointing, though.

"When I got to the wreckage I found parts of a machine. Metal and burned things," Karshi said. She turned stiffly toward the sling, then bent to pull the cover off her prize. "And I found this."

Mumbled voices rose in a wave that echoed across the chamber's ancient floor and rebounded off its rounded walls.

The thing was formed like a quadar, but it appeared to have no central. Its skin was bright red, fading to pale. A patch of desert-clotted hair covered its head. Its hands, rather than six long digits, showed only five stubby fingers. It had been attacked, also, clearly sporting wounds of some sort that Karshi had dressed in field fashion.

A creature, Baraq thought as he felt his hearts beat.

It was a creature from the sky.

He pressed his lips into a straight line, and looked at the exits. He had to get this information to Louratna.

Councilor Pelorit quieted the gathering.

Yendar regained her composure.

"What is this creature that Eldoro brings to us?" she said.

Karshi squinted at her. "That is for you to tell me. All I can say is that it is still alive, but suffering. It does not seem to bear Eldoro as well as a quadar. I have fed it water at many stops, but mostly the liquid just runs down its face and into its fur."

Councilor Pelorit spoke then.

"I suggest we take it to the medical center, and bring it back to whatever health we can."

"I concur," Yendar and Ag said at the same time, both clearly piqued.

"Attendants, please take the creature to the medical grounds," Councilor Pelorit said.

Quadars in pale robes hefted the blanket sling between them and took the creature away.

"Karshi Fael, you are a treasure that our histories will tell of for many years to come. We thank you for your effort, and would like to see you justly compensated."

Karshi pulled her lips back in a grim smile as she scanned the council with an expression that Baraq read as quiet mirth.

"I request only to understand its message."

Surprised voices murmured.

"I will see it done if it can be done," Pelorit said.

Karshi turned, and left the chamber.

"I suggest," Ag Lean said, "that we adjourn to further consider the day's events, and convene again tomorrow to discuss what—if anything—should be further done in regard to this new Light That Fell from the Sky.

"Arguments against?" Pelorit asked.

All eyes turned to Yendar.

Beside him, Baraq felt discomfort in Olan.

Yendar assessed the state of the room. This had been a strong moment for her push, but now it was clear that the power of her argument had been stolen.

"I concur so long as the council's agenda is modified to include this important topic at its soonest possible occurrence hereafter."

"So heard," Pelorit said. "I call this session of the council complete."

The chamber echoed with voices and with the shuffling of feet and robes. Baraq slipped quietly away.

He had several reports to make, and little time to make them.

CHAPTER 15

To avoid suspicion, Baraq went straight to his Family's complex.

The Waganat home was a sprawling collection of buildings and houses built originally of Esgarat's red stone, but now extended to include additions of brick and clay. Three well-tended gardens sat just inside the grounds, serving the dual purposes of providing cool shade and displaying Waganat wealth and power. Huts and cottages were built in several places, most serving as homes for members of the Family and close Family supporters. Tangled *halta* brush covered the wall surrounding the compound, threatening intruders with long, bonelike thorns that broke off in hands and legs if the walls were ever scaled.

The manor was built in three levels above the ground, with a taller tower at the north corner.

A catacomb basement of multiple rooms, chambers, and hallways lay underneath and were connected to an indefinite number of caves that ran together and connected with much of the Esgarat if one were willing to follow them to their farthest reaches.

The guards at the gate let Baraq pass without fanfare.

Eldoro's light made everything bright. Its heat made him uncomfortable as he walked across the stone-lined path to the central building. The smell of the nearby gardens, usually sweet and refreshing, seemed heavy and dead, the usually vibrant stalks of the *stalla* vines that covered the late-heat shade side of the entrance was faded and dusty. Even though he wore sandals, the stones were hot against his feet.

"Greetings," Hester, the Family cook, said as he stepped through the back door and into the large open-air kitchen. "Can I get you something?"

Baraq raised an acknowledging hand. "No. Thank you anyway."

Hester had been old when Baraq was a boy. Now she was bent, wrinkled, and barely able to see a root to cut it, but Father kept her here out of his firm concept of loyalty, as would Tierra, Baraq's brother, who would most certainly inherit Waganat control upon his father's passing.

She may be a *hedgie*, so the saying went, but she was almost a Waganat.

Baraq descended the narrow stairway.

His footsteps echoed in the tight space, and the air brought a chill to his neck that felt good. As he approached the lower platform, Baraq ran the backs of his fingers along the wall to increase the cooling effect.

Castaada, another of the Family's personal staff, sat behind the control station. The security zone had been cut partially out of the rock here, the desk itself made of stone, but finished with a composite cover that the Festias had designed as a gift for some other favor. The station was sparely decorated but clean, the walls polished to a deep sheen that showed the mineral content of the stone. The pairing of finished stone and Festia composite was oddly attractive. The area was lit with an expensive, battery-driven system that had come from Tierra's research, an invention that, alone, would have been enough to feed an entire Family for a generation.

The ability to store and move power to wherever it was needed changed much about quadarti life.

Castaada wore loose robes and rolled a pen over his spindly fingers.

He had been working on reports.

"Greetings," Baraq said to the servant. "How is he?"

"The same," the guard replied. "He may be running on just the one heart, but he can still strip my skin at *ona*."

Baraq laughed. "Never underestimate my da."

Two of his father's three hearts were malfunctioning now, so it was likely that Ranya Waganat would never go to the surface again. A single heart could push enough blood to keep a quadar alive, but not enough to keep him cool. This was a favorite plank of several retro-philosophers, especially those who were making the "back to the caves" arguments that were gaining favor in some of the more extreme wings of quadarti society. The whole of the quadarti came from the caves, they said, and the burning rains were a sign that it was time to return.

They weren't totally wrong.

It seemed likely that any real solution to the heat included a reason-able usage of caves and a stronger system of excavating the thick rivers of water than ran in their down-deep veins. The radicals, however, pitched the arguments so fervently that no one could agree with them. This is one reason he appreciated the rhetoric of Lelo—which was certainly militant in its approach to social issues, but was more reasoned in its view of progress. Small steps in the right direction made a difference.

Not that any of that mattered today.

Today he had to finish this conversation as efficiently as he could, then get to the exchange point to ensure Louratna knew of the creature.

Baraq pulled his outer robe from his shoulders and placed it on a hook beside the doorway.

He shook nerves from his shoulders, then he went in.

"Good day, Father," he said.

The Waganat patriarch was splayed out on a couch.

The chamber smelled of the half-eaten remains of his lunch, which sat on a plate that, in turn, lay on his chest. The wave talker he listened to the council with was now turned off, and wedged into a gap between the mats he was resting on. It was cool here. Very comfortable.

A steady movement in the air spoke of a ventilation opening from deeper in the mountain.

Baraq sat on a chair across from the couch, then plucked a stick of sweet *kandata* from the bin Ranya's staff kept filled because it was the elder Waganat's favorite snack.

It was fresh. Very good.

"That must have been quite a session," his father said, his voice rough-hewn.

"Quite so." Baraq sat back. The gaze of his primaries flicked to the doorway. "I would have expected Tierra to be here to discuss the result."

The elder quadar clicked from the front of his throat, then waved the fingers of one hand. "Tierra has more important things to deal with than this. Tell me about the creature."

Baraq did his best to ignore the insinuation that Baraq himself did *not* have more pressing things to deal with than briefing his father. It wasn't hard to do. He was familiar with being diminished and dismissed, but this time it was also in his best interests that Tierra miss their discussion. His brother's absence would help limit information flow.

"It was small," Baraq replied. "Maybe the size of a whelpling, dressed in something like a blanket. Karshi dragged it across the desert for days. I'm surprised it still lived."

"But it does live?"

"Yes, Father. It lives. Or at least it did when it was removed to the medical grounds."

Ranya Waganat waited with patient impatience.

Baraq chewed more *kandata*, and continued.

"Its skin was red and scaly. Probably heat-baked. It was similar to us in that it had hands, feet, and a head, but odd in that it had only two eyes and a face covered in fur."

His father took that in with a grunt. "What did it do?"

"Nothing I could see. At first it appeared to be dead, though after a time you could see its breathing patterns. Karshi mentioned its thirst had no end."

His father was quiet.

"May I suggest I go watch over the medical grounds?" Baraq said.

"Why should I do that?"

"Come, Father. The Family should stake a claim in his knowledge, correct? Perhaps even lead the salvage of whatever craft he came in." Baraq took a centering breath, then leveled his full gaze at his father. Baraq's work with the Taranth Stone had been exposed years ago. Both of them understood the context of the moment. "There is, of course, some precedence here."

His father gave a grunting nod, pursed his lips, and scratched an ear, a gesture that had become familiar over the years. "Oh, I certainly agree with that precedence, Baraq. We want a hand in whatever is going to happen with the creature, but my question was why I would choose *you* for this detail?"

Baraq swallowed.

Appearing too eager would trigger suspicion, being too lackadaisical would bring his father's ire. Anxiety rose inside, but his body would still be flooded with heat from the surface. That profile should hide any but the worst case of nerves.

"I was being presumptuous," Baraq replied. "By all means, we should choose the best available candidate. That said, if the creature is connected with the Taranth Stone in any way, we both know I have some specific experience to draw upon."

His father's central probed him for several long moments. Then its gaze fell away and he scratched his chin. "I want you to concentrate on Lelo," he said.

"I don't think—"

"I know you can't see that Lelo is a problem. But mark my time, Baraq, I know he is. The rest of world will get itself sorted out. This creature will be examined. Lessons will be learned. Heat will rise and fall, rain will come or not come. Businesses will die, others will rise up. All those changes will affect the Family, but we will survive them without difficulty.

"Lelo and his group are different, though. They want to destroy the way the Quadarti do things. Some of the other Families don't see his strength as clearly as I do. They discount Lelo as if he is just another grouser. But I see the truth. If Lelo keeps growing in power, he might well find himself in a position to overrun the council someday, and that would change everything."

Baraq gave a gentle click of agreement.

Speaking with such passion tired Ranya Waganat quickly, though. He sat back and rested.

Baraq waited, thinking.

It was the first time he had heard his father raise Lelo to this level, and he wasn't sure what to make of it.

If his father knew Baraq was supplying information to Louratna and Lelo he would have Baraq banished, or worse. If he ever found out that Lelo was actually Baraq's son, he would probably have them both killed. But until now, Ranya Waganat, like most people in Esgarat City, had only the vaguest idea of what exactly was really happening in the depths of the quadarti. His commentary suggested he had shifted his position. Baraq fought the urge to twist his hands together as a final thought made its way through his mind. Was it possible that Ranya Waganat already knew what Baraq was doing? Was it possible this was a setup of some kind?

"I understand, Father. I've come to your side on this entire Lelo situation. He is a renegade, and must be stopped. But I don't think I am the right person to track this rebel down."

"Then you should stop thinking."

"Yes, sir."

They sat in awkward silence that Baraq realized might continue indefinitely.

"Is that all?" he said, making to stand.

"Tell Tierra I want him to get someone to the medical center to watch the creature."

"I will."

His father nodded, and Baraq rose fully.

"Oh, there is one other thing, Baraq."

Baraq waited.

"Please tell Crissandr that I am pleased to accept her offer to bring my dinner tomorrow, and that her *jah* is most excellent."

"Yes, sir. I'll let her know."

"And give her my regards."

"Yes, sir."

Baraq left then, stewing as he climbed the stairs, exited the manor, and reentered the heat of the day, a heat that seemed suddenly less oppressive than the chill of the basement he had just left.

Baraq gazed at Eldoro as he walked away.

His stomach grumbled.

It was time to eat, he thought, shading his gaze. Yes, it was time to eat.

He went to a hutch that he often frequented, a ramshackle place that served *havra* nearly as good as Crissandr's, though pricy. He read notes as he ate, standard business papers he carried with him from the council. Product agreements, mostly. Some zoning questions.

Nothing important.

He jotted ideas on the margins of some requests, paying attention to patrons as they came and went, noting their disinterest in his work.

On a clean page, he wrote a few words, then doodled an outline of the creature.

With a showy grimace, he folded the page in half, then half again.

When he was finished with his food, he placed his business notes into the satchel he carried, then laid enough currency on the table to pay his bill. A final check of the table showed that none of the folded page he slipped under the plate showed.

As he left, he gave a courteous nod to a young quadar seated at a table in the opposite corner of the dining area.

The quadar replied with the proper signal.

CHAPTER 16

Xian's Tower was a magnificently crafted structure of redbrick and volcanic rock that had been perfectly fitted, then ground together to make it appear to be one piece. Its stage was wide. The walls around the amphitheater were sculpted to allow a speaker to be heard over long distances. Standing at the exact center of Esgarat City, the tower was also the true center of the Ring of Esgarat.

Brada admired such exacting stonework and had always dreamed of speaking here, so when this day came there was only one option.

After donning the *Shensi,* he gave Ezi a hug, then stepped from the staging room to walk across the platform, a lone figure, appearing as always without introduction. His robes flowed with his stride, bringing a breeze that gave him a moment's refreshment. The mask clung to his face like it knew this was its last time out. Ceramic edges pressed against his cheeks and scored his central ridge. Straps pressed against the back of his skull.

A throng of quadars clicked and clacked as they noticed him. Voices called out, flat and indistinguishable over the hum of the gathering.

Across the distance, Eldoro blazed red as it approached the horizon. Katon's thin light cast a pale golden glow that brought softness to faces of the audience and made the colors of their clothing seem to vibrate. Anticipation burned in their gazes. Energy crackled through the ranks.

As he neared the podium, Lelo raised his hand to quiet them.

Ezi had been right—of course she had. The quadarti were ready for this.

He cast a glance at the Orange Army who lined the theater walls, each bearing rifles and wearing padded armor, their traditional warrior's garb. He never asked them to come to these events, but they called themselves the army of the Orange Ring, and considered themselves his security. They were bold in their approach and militant in their dedication to defense of *hedgies* and other quadars on the lowest rungs of the ladder. But they were as disciplined as they were fervent, and they had always been morally right in their occasionally overzealous use of force. Brada may never have asked them to attend, but he would never ask them to leave.

Director Oast'el, another officer in the Ring, stood stage left, Director Vareta stage right. Their teams would pick up the pieces of the session when he left, distributing the plan in the form of fliers and word of mouth.

As always, Family security ringed the gathering's perimeter, basically *hedgie* goons the Families hired to report on his public gatherings, a hiring that, given his message, was blind to any sense of irony.

The Orange Ring had been fighting Family controls since Ezi and Brada had birthed it.

While he often found the goons annoying, their attendance now pleased him. Everything depended on them reporting events of this gathering properly. The Ring needed the Families to understand how big this group was and that it intended to operate peacefully unless provoked.

Everything was perfect.

As was his practice, Lelo started on point.

"I see a future, sisters and brothers, where we will *all* be able to live together. That is true. But we do not live in that time now. Instead, we live in a present when we have to face the fact that we are living with a disease."

A lone quadar in the crowd called out in support.

"That's right," Lelo said. "We have a disease, but it is not our bodies that are sick. Instead, it is the whole of our community, the *whole of Esgarat*, that is in bad shape."

A wave of clicking throats grew deep.

Voices called out.

"Most of us are hungry," Lelo continued. "Most of us are tired. Most of us can't manage to make it to anywhere beyond our next meal, and if a sickness comes to us…well. It's time to shine light on the truth that our sickness is a disease brought on by the greater Families and by its crony council, time to say that spending our lives climbing that sheer cliff face is hard enough when it's vertical, but nearly impossible when the Families cover its face in oil."

Clicks began to rise.

"I say it's time for the whole of Esgarat to stand up and show them this is not right."

"Say it right!" Another voice came.

"You know who I mean when I say *the whole of Esgarat*, right?"

"We do!"

"We do too. We know because, unlike anyone from any Family, the sisters and brothers of the Orange Ring have spent time with you. And we know because we are you, because we've worked with your whelplings, your teachers, and your doctors. We know who *the whole of Esgarat* is because you've had us in your homes. We've seen how all of us live. So when I say *the whole of the Esgarat*, you know I mean every quadar, everywhere. You understand that all our ancestors crawled up from that same mountain cave together, and you know that now the burning rain falls on all of us the same way. When we say *the whole of the Esgarat*, you know we don't separate because when we do that all we accomplish is to spread our hate."

The crowd clicked and clacked, some speaking parts of the phrase back.

"Lelo! Lelo! Lelo!" the chant grew. "Separate will spread the hate!"

Lelo raised his voice over the din.

"You could be a quadar of the Esgarat fringelands," Lelo said. "Or a hardened free-ranger. I don't care. A Family member. Doesn't matter. Because we don't care where you're from, it's where you're going that matters. And all you need to be part of *the whole of us* is to get your three hearts lined up with the three hearts of your sisters and your brothers."

Hands rasped together in a wave of noise.

"Are you us?" he said over the growing crescendo.

Voices roared in support. *"I am us!"*

"Are you us?"

More voices, louder.

"Are you us?"

More voices, louder still. *"I am us! I am us! I am us!"*

"That's good." He paused to let emotions settle. The heat of his breath was damp inside the mask. He sweated as he waited for the crowd to calm. "That's good, sisters and brothers, because I say it's time for the revolution to begin."

The word *revolution* sent a wave through the crowd.

The Family spies perked up.

"I know some of you fear that word: revolution. You say we need to take small steps. That we need to work with the Families to get our way. But how many cycles have to pass before we admit that kind of collaboration isn't working? How many cycles before history moves past that point? I say it's already been too many. That's the answer. And I say now that any quadar who thinks we can cure this disease we have by joining up with that disease has become part of the disease itself."

Cheers came.

"They're afraid!" a voice called out, creating a stir. "We're all afraid."

"Yes," Lelo said. "I understand. We're all afraid. But when we ask 'what are we afraid of?' I think it always comes down to violence."

The word *violence* created another stir.

Members of Family security groups were suddenly paying intense attention.

He glanced at the Orange Army guard, his fists clenching into balls.

"None of us want violence, sisters and brothers, but we can't fear it. When violence is in the toolbox of oppressors, those being oppressed cannot remove it from theirs." The crowd grew more intense. "But I understand that fear. I understand how we can look at quadars like the Orange Army over there with their guns and their bravado, and become afraid. I'm not stupid, all right?" A bitter form of laughter came. "These quadars who are afraid of conflict, they're not dumb either. We all know what happens when a council guard gets upset with a *hedgie*. That's the problem, though, you know that, right? That's the disease showing itself. Quadars fear Family guns and clubs because the Families use them. And it's right to fear that. It's right to fear Family control because we know it comes from the edge of a blade and the barrel of a gun. But what we fear, sisters and brothers, is exactly why we're here."

Throats clicked in agreement.

"This isn't a question of violence, though. Not really. Once we separate the question of violence from the idea of revolution, we find the real question is whether together we cure ourselves of this disease together, or individually we choose to get swallowed up by it."

More clicks filled the area.

"I know some others are afraid we can't win, though. They say the Families are strong and ruthless. They kick us and beat us. If we fight they say we risk everything. To those I say that if you don't risk, you don't win. But worse than that, if you don't take that chance, if you don't risk losing, you don't *deserve* to win."

The accusation buzzed through the gathering.

"You wouldn't face a pack of *neantha* beasts without fighting back, then wonder why you got eaten up, would you?"

"No!"

"That would be insanity, am I right?"

"Yes!"

"Besides, I'm here to tell you that we *can* win," he finally said. "Look at us here today!" The words resonated. "Look at our numbers. Look at our passions. Look at who we are, young and old, and of all the independent families and even some of the Upper Families: farmers and builders, cooks and carpenters, masons and weavers. Look at us, I say! Really look at us and see that together we are strong. Yes, we should be ready to defend ourselves with blood if we need to, but we fight with our numbers because wherever we have one quadar, we have power, but wherever we are all together, we have more power than anyone can understand."

Voices rose, fists raised. Clicks crossed the expanse in flowing waves.

The crowd was sizzling now.

He could see it in faces and expressions, the bonding happening, something firm and obvious, almost a physical thing itself. Eldoro's light seemed to paint the air colors that didn't exist, sharpening every feature. Lelo came to the edge of the platform, energy from them lifting him like a warm wind. As voices rose, Lelo ran his hands over the edge of his mask. He could already smell the sweetness of fresh air.

Yes, he thought as the voices settled. It was time.

"There is one more thing I need to discuss," he said, "one more truth that I need to face before I can ask you to follow the Orange Ring."

The gathering grew quiet, then a few throats clicked.

"I've said before that our problem is not with Families, all right? Our greater Families are quadars, after all, even those who have not yet come to our views. And truth is we have Family members here today, and they are all clearly part of 'us.' They love their parents and their siblings just as we all do, right? And I love them all. I need you to know that our fight is not with Families themselves, but instead it's with the systems they've used to forge themselves into the hammers that pound us down. We are here for justice and change, not vengeance and retribution."

The response was more reserved.

He opened his hands, feeling questions forming in the minds of the audience.

"I know this for the same reasons I know we can win, sisters and brothers. I know this because I have survived the heart of the disease myself and come away from it stronger. I know we can win this fight because I have been in Family boardrooms as they parceled out their profit schemes. We *all* know how this works because we all see the results, but *I* know it even better because I have seen it firsthand."

Lelo felt pressure from every direction.

He was vulnerable now. Alone out here on the podium.

He felt Ezi watching from behind, and the Orange Army on his flank, but this was the moment he had been building to and now he was alone. No one could stop anything from happening.

Lelo held the mask firmly against his face, then pulled the straps.

Hushed astonishment rolled over the crowd as they realized what was happening.

"I have been a faceless leader for a long time," he said as the bottom strap came loose. "That's been proper in the past, because truth has no dependence on its origin and because I have never asked for sacrifice. But now I'm asking you to be a revolution, and I don't think a revolution can be driven by a faceless leader."

The sound of clicks were questioning now. Anxious.

A final fastener loosened, and now only the force of his hand was holding the mask on.

He took one last breath, and pulled it away.

Gasps came from the closest rows.

"Sisters and brothers, my name is Brada Waganat, whelp of Baraq, grandwhelp of Ranya, one of the most powerful of the Families in the Esgarat. And I am us."

The information crashed from quadar to quadar in a rippling cascade of waves. In the distance of the periphery, Family observers scurried for their skippers. Two quadars in the front seemed upset. The guards seemed okay.

Brada tossed the mask aside and perched at the very edge of the podium.

"I know our numbers, sisters and brothers. I know our histories and I know our communities because I am both us, and born as a member of a greater Family. I say that if we stop working for the Families they will have to join us, and I know this is true because I am Brada Waganat, and I am us."

The collective seemed to take a combined breath.

"It's time for the revolution to begin, sisters and brothers. We have time to spend but no time to waste. Together we are *going* to make that future where we can all be together happen. We're going to get our quadars fed, going to fix the burning rain. We're going to get every quadar a fair opportunity to scale that sheer cliff."

He paused to stare across the gathering. They were coming together again. He could see it in their eyes, feel it in the way their expressions had bent from glowing and enlightened to deep and resolute.

"So here's what *the whole of us* are going to do *now*, all right?" he said. "When Eldoro rises again, we're going to stand up together, and we're going stop working. Rather than going to our offices and our factories, we're going to gather to stand strong against the council and the Families. We'll show them the medicine is here."

Voices began to rise up.

"The Families can't work if we don't follow them, so we're going to tell them and the council that we own ourselves. We're going to say we want our share—but nothing more than our share."

Clicks became stronger.

"Together we will not fear." Silence began to settle. Heads began to nod. "Together we aren't going to slink away quietly anymore. Together we will use our bodies, our minds, and yes, even our guns, to remove the disease that is killing our community."

A single voice, cracked with age, called out. *"I am us!"*

"Are you us?" Brada said.

"I am us," more responded.

"Together we're going to make this happen," he replied. "Are you us?"

More joined.

"Are you us?" Brada said.

"I am us!"

"Are you *us*?"

More voices, louder this time.

"Are you *us*?

Thousands of quadars joined together then, cheering, chanting *"I am us! I am us!"* Their energy sent chills through him. The muscles of his back crawled with inspiration. He spoke the phase again, and again, interspersing pauses to give the quadars below opportunities to raise their voices.

"Are you us?" he said one more time.

"I am us!"

"All right," he said. "I'll see you again at Eldoro rising."

Then, his words spent, Brada walked into the crowd.

They gathered around, touching him and chanting. "Lelo, Lelo, Lelo." The Orange Army led him through the press until he went around the tower and found Ezi and the motor cart she had promised. He ducked into it.

The door closed.

Then he was gone.

———

In the farthest regions of the crowd, members of the Families dispersed, each riding off to their leaders, each carrying news that the most feared renegade in the whole of the Esgarat was Brada Waganat, son of Baraq, grandson of Rayna.

CHAPTER 17

Simply breathing sent peals of pain crashing over every point of Torrance's body. It was if his skin had been flayed. He flashed cold, then hot. His stomach twisted like a knife was turning in his gut. His leg burned, and his shoulder felt like a wall of fire. He wanted to throw up, but nothing was there.

And it was still goddamned hot, almost too hot to breathe.

As Torrance came to consciousness, things grew more concrete.

The room. Small.

Electric lights strung up like Christmas wire.

A box that reminded him of an intercom, mounted on the wall.

A long counter. Built into the wall. Covered with instruments made of stone and metal and wood. A window open to the air. It was daytime, though he had no idea what part of the day it was. Maybe afternoon.

A bowl made of red clay sat on a nearby table.

He moved his hand, and recoiled with pain. His skin felt too small for his body. A cough ripped his throat up like razor blades. He winced again as he instinctively brought his shaking hand to his lips. They felt like cardboard and burned at his touch.

A presence draped in yellow appeared before him.

It was large and hairless, with pebbled, leathery skin and a pronounced forehead. A glittering green eye was embedded in the center of that forehead, two more of gold sat to each side of the face. The being had arms, hands, and fingers.

Like his dream, he thought.

It was like the thing in one of the dreams he had out in the desert before everything started getting weird.

Or afterward, maybe.

The thing said something that Torrance couldn't understand, and two more of them came into view.

Aliens.

The truth came to focus with the impact of a baseball bat. These were the message senders. Edenites or whatever the hell they would call themselves.

He suddenly realized he was naked and tried to cover himself, but the pain of movement made him suck breath. He realized then that his leg and shoulder were both draped in soft padding, his shoulder deeply bruised and his leg open and once again healing. Were they were tending to him, then? Nursing him back to health? He didn't know what to think, but he didn't really have any energy to consider things further.

The aliens chattered excitedly.

One reached to the table and brought the bowl forward.

It had six fingers, all six of which were wrapped around the bowl that appeared to contain water.

Water.

Suddenly he was as thirsty as he had ever been in his life.

Christ. He was alive.

His lips stung with needle-like pain, still Torrance managed to open his mouth to let the alien drain a slow trickle. The first swallow hurt, the second, also. But as his throat dampened, the pain grew less. Water ran down his face but he didn't care, it was water, sweet, glorious water.

The bowl was empty too soon.

The aliens spoke to each other, then one took the bowl away.

"No," Torrance said, nearly crying.

Lying back on the bedding sent shivers through his back. It occurred to him that he should be worried about what the aliens might do to him, but just the idea of trying to get away made his brain scream.

One of the remaining aliens scratched notes onto a slate and spoke.

The other responded by mimicking the sound of Torrance's original cough.

"That's right," Torrance said. "I coughed."

The aliens—though he realized now that *he* was really the alien here—exchanged another round of discussions.

The third returned through an arched doorway, and poured more water down Torrance's throat.

He drank gratefully.

CHAPTER 18

t was late when Baraq slipped out of their bed. Both Eldoro and cold Katon had long ago passed under the horizon. He donned a pair of comfortable *kami*-skin pants, and a green wraparound.

"Where are you going?" Crissandr said through her grogginess.

"Go back to sleep," he replied. She needed her rest.

"Where are you going?"

He made the motion for *I can't tell you*.

Her expression turned sour. It was the response he gave any time he was doing something for Brada or Louratna, though Baraq was certain she was wondering if he didn't take advantage of the practice whenever he just didn't want to talk.

His shrug said the late-night excursion couldn't be helped.

If he could have spoken, he would have explained that Louratna had replied to his note by saying she needed to know for certain that the creature was attached to the Taranth Stone. Wanted to be sure it was "Heatborn," as she called it, because she had convinced herself that any creature who understood the Taranth Stone would have to be from Eldoro or Katon or any of the other pin-dot heats that now filled the night sky. Baraq was the only agent both close enough and with experience enough to make that determination. He was glad he couldn't speak now, though. Since his father had already assigned the task to someone else, it meant he would have to disobey a Family order, something that would cause Crissandr unnecessary distress. Baraq understood that Louratna was aware of this danger, too. He could imagine the expression on her face as she developed the plan. The skin around her eyes would go slack, and her lips would grow warm. Her gaze would become deeper than the dark skies at night.

The mere fact that she asked him to do this meant it was important.

The medical center was across the city. He had to go now or risk being seen.

Crissandr nodded with the resigned patience that Baraq had come to count on. They had grown old having half-conversations like this. The Family didn't monitor *everything* they said, but neither Baraq nor Crissandr was willing to take a chance when it came to their child or anything else they thought was important.

"Take care."

"I will."

He pressed his hand to her cheek, then left.

He pulled his skipper from its cubby, noting the battery light glowed in the darkness to show it was ready. He grabbed the handle, hit the starter, and pushed off, stepping onto the platform as the machine began to roll. The smell of the battery was faint, but the sound of rolling wheels was sharp in the nighttime quiet.

The pathways were dark and empty.

His primaries were nearly useless in the dim starlight, but his central showed heat shadows fading across the city. Its monocular vision caused him to take the pathways slowly, which was probably better given his need for stealth, but which let stress build. Traffic was sparse. Only the few quadars who collected waste were out at this time, and, of course, the council guards who were posted at various corners of the city's overview grid. He took a longer path to avoid contact there.

A few windows burned with electrical light.

The smell of fires filled the alleys, cutting the chill.

There had always been a few cooking fires in the alley, but fires for warmth was different. Not unexpected, but new. Louratna's equations showed that as cloud cover left, the planet's heat would eventually drain away, too. He understood the basics because she explained them in terms of the resistors and capacitors he had once used to build little bits of equipment in his shop. The details were beyond him, but the truth was that the equations seemed to be working, if you wanted to call it that. It was colder in the dark than he remembered it. In the past it had been rare to burn root for heat.

Nighttime burning twisted at his gut for other reasons, too.

There was only so much root fiber and he hated the idea of it going to waste. The ores that carried fuel content were hard to mine, though, and heat was heat. The council decided to keep quiet the fact that combustible material was growing sparse because they wanted to prevent mass concern and because no answer to the problem appeared forthcoming.

Prudence would say conservation in burning was in order, so Baraq realized that in making that decision the council had put themselves into a bad box. If they announced the problem now, it would leak out that they had known of the issue earlier and done nothing. So even now, with the situation growing dire and the possibility of disaster becoming more and more realistic, the council refrained from revealing the problem. Instead, they choose to persecute those—like "Lelo" and Louratna—who tried to bring such things to the public's attention.

Baraq ground his teeth together, his hearts redolent with the weight of quadarti excesses.

He had been doing his part for two full cycles, more than forty years—as had Crissandr.

They had given much, and they would continue to give more as they were needed. They had made that commitment even before Baraq made the decision to turn agent on his Family. But their burden was wearing on them both. Perhaps, he thought wistfully as his destination drew near, the creature at the medical center would bring it all to an end.

He parked his skipper, and entered the medical center through a door that should have been locked but wasn't. The entryway was dimly lit by a growth of luminescent moss. He closed his central, knowing the inner hallways would have artificial lighting. The quadar behind the desk looked anxious as Baraq entered the hall where the creature had been taken.

It was Hazelta, outwardly a member of the Denari Family and the Hlrat clan. She had been with Louratna for three years, however, and was just now being activated as an operational covert resource.

That was Louratna's way: patient, and calm, let her people train until they were ready.

It was one of the many things Baraq loved about her. Louratna was quick and intelligent, but she also understood the game itself was long. Brief victories held no value to her.

Baraq gave the guard a simple hand sign to ask for status.

Hazelta returned the proper symbol for "all is well," and pointed to the doorway.

Baraq stepped into the room and went to the thing's side.

It lay on a hospital mat that was raised on a standard examination table. The smell was heavy and foreign. The creature made sawing noises as it slept.

A sense of fear chilled Baraq's chest.

Was this creature Heatborn? Did it know what they needed it to know? Was it tied to the Taranth Stone? There was little time, and he had to be certain.

He touched the creature high on its shoulder.

It jumped, then groaned in obvious pain, then blinked warily at him through the darkness.

Shielding the creature's eyes from the light, Baraq clicked it on.

Its face bunched together as it blinked against brightness. Dry criss-crosses scored its upper cheeks. Patches of thick hair over its eyes clumped in the middle, and its tongue, a thing of an odd pinkish color, ran over chapped lips. It pointed to the bowl of water and spoke an odd word.

Baraq tried to mimic its language, pointing to the bowl.

"Wa-ter?"

It didn't sound the same to Baraq, but the creature gave a movement of its head that seemed agreeable enough. He picked up the bowl and brought it closer.

The creature took the bowl. Its hand shook as it guided the liquid to its lips. Water ran down the creature's face as it drank deeply. When it was done, Baraq took the bowl back, then dabbed its cheeks with a dry cloth.

This close, a sudden kinship came over him that made his chest hurt.

He was standing in a room with this thing from the sky, a being so powerless, so alone, and so out of its environment, but a creature of some obvious intelligence, something so different, but that somehow felt so much the same. In a normal moment, or when he was younger perhaps, Baraq would have spent time being amazed at the probabilities of such an occurrence. Instead, he shelved his thoughts to make them another time.

Baraq took a nerve-settling breath, then retrieved a slip of paper from his belt.

It was a drawing he and Louratna had worked on together many years prior, a guess at what the Taranth Stone must have looked like before it fell from the sky. He unfolded the page and held it in his hands, staring at it one more time before turning it around, noting the drawing's elongated shape and the odd configuration of fins along its body and tail end.

Let this be it, he thought. *Let this be it.*

Baraq turned the drawing around.

The creature looked at it, then glanced at Baraq, then back at the drawing.

Its lips pulled back to show flat white teeth, and it began to talk in an animated voice that was still rough. It raised a hand, one of its fingers pointing at drawing.

Then it looked up at Baraq.

Its eyes were blue and wide, the muscles around them soft. It was an expression that Baraq understood—a universal essence of longing, the deep expression of desire, of unadorned hope. It was a gaze that told Baraq everything he needed to know.

This creature knew about the Taranth Stone.

A noise came from the door.

Hazelta stood in the open doorway. Her face was drawn and dark. "It's Lelo."

Baraq grimaced. His son was supposed to speak to an audience earlier in the evening, but he hadn't heard from him afterward. "What has he done now?"

"He's just been taken by your family."

Baraq could not have been more surprised if she hit him with a paddle. "When?" he said.

"Earlier tonight. I just heard."

He saw it then. There was something more to her expression. Something she didn't want to tell him. "What is it?"

"Lelo exposed his identity."

"He did what?" Baraq clicked his throat. "Why?"

"I don't know details. But he revealed he is a Waganat. Your Family has taken him someplace inside the compound."

He blinked all three eyes. At least that part made sense.

Brada and Ezi had planned to do this earlier, but Baraq, Crissandr, and many others argued them out of it. The revelation was important, but the timing was even more so. Both Baraq and Louratna needed Brada to stay quiet right now. She was nearing some kind of breakthrough, though she wouldn't tell Baraq what it was.

His whelp was young, though. Both Brada and Ezi thought that since they knew how the quadars around them *should* work, they knew how they *would* work. Neither understood exactly how firm the Families would get when pressed, neither understood the depths to which Ranya Waganat could go. They wanted their issues resolved now, though, and Louratna's suggestion of playing the long game didn't appeal to them. Only concerted lobbying had shut them down the first time.

"We're in the right," Brada said at the time. "If it takes a revolution, then that's what we'll have."

The truth dawned hard on Baraq.

This time, Brada and Ezi had not asked for either permission or concurrence. Lelo had told the world who his Family was. The Family reacted exactly as Baraq expected they would.

The creature made a noise and motioned to the empty water bowl.

Baraq ignored him for the moment, folding the drawing and putting it back into his belt. He clicked off the light.

"Get word to Louratna," he said to Hazelta as he stepped briskly to the door. "Tell her this creature is the one. Tell her it's Heatborn. Do it now. Tell her I don't know how much time we have, so we'll need to move as quickly as possible. Tonight, even, if she can manage it. Tell her that she needs to get Crissandr as soon as she can, too. My father will not stop with Brada and myself. I want her safe. Tell her that. And, finally, tell Louratna that I'm going to my father's compound to see what I can do to get Brada freed."

"Is that wise?"

Baraq faced her.

"He is my whelpling," he said.

She put her hand on his shoulder.

"Don't fail at this," Baraq said. "We need that creature."

"I won't," she said with almost too much sincerity. "We already have quadars here to take it away."

"Good," he said, almost chuckling despite his tension. "Louratna is always prepared."

"Yes," Hazelta said. "Louratna is always prepared."

Baraq straightened up and rubbed his tired forehead. A resigned click came from the deepest part of his throat. Ranya Waganat knew the truth about Lelo's identity, which meant he would know Baraq had withheld that information. If true, both Brada and Baraq were likely dead quadars, but if he could keep the Family occupied he might be able to save Crissandr and give Louratna the time she needed to steal the creature away from the council before they did something both stupid and horrendous.

Baraq went to the doorway, then glanced back into the creature's room.

It called out after him.

He clenched his jaw and left.

CHAPTER 19

Torrance had been dreaming of falling through space when the alien woke him. The pain always muddled things, so his first thought was that he was on the shuttle, but that wasn't right. The light from the bare bulb had been dim, but was still stark relative to the total darkness he had been in. Still, there was no doubt in his mind that the alien who had so carefully turned on that dim light and given him more water, had also just shown him a picture of a wormhole pod.

The two aliens exchanged animated conversation in suddenly clipped tones.

Then, before Torrance could react, both their footsteps rumbled away in a great hurry.

Seeing them leave the room broke the spell.

"Come back here, damn it!" Torrance called.

He tried to sit up but only managed to bring himself a wave of agonizing pain. Even with the water the alien had helped him drink, his throat was raw.

"I want to talk to you."

A few moments later, a flurry of sound came from outside the room. The door burst open and another gathering of the aliens stepped in, speaking in high-pitched bursts.

"Wormhole pod," Torrance called. "Wormhole pod!"

It brought the room to a standstill, but didn't make any other difference.

Of course not.

They couldn't understand a damned word he said any better than he could understand them. Torrance looked for a paper or pen of some kind.

Nothing.

He looked at the closest of the tall, three-eyed aliens.

"Can you get that man back here?" Torrance said, pointing at the doorway, then tried to create the shape of a pod with his hand, failing magnificently but causing himself another agonizing kaleidoscope of pain. "He showed me the wormhole pod. You know? The pod?"

One of the aliens held up its hand with its six fingers. Yes, six fingers. They made Torrance think of a kid's drawing.

Calm down?

Or maybe *wait.*

Torrance fell back against the pillow and waited. This seemed to appease the thing.

Two more aliens carried a wooden pallet between them, ties spaced along its side reminding Torrance of emergency equipment used to carry people with spinal injuries. The aliens chattered in hushed whispers and positioned themselves around his platform before grabbing the bedding.

"Wait a minute," he called. "What the hell are you doing?"

"Grazzdonnont!" the alien said firmly to him.

Torrance stopped.

He looked around in confused silence.

Suddenly, the aliens made some kind of count, and lifted his bedding, sliding it onto the board.

Christ! No!

He fought them as they tied him down, but he was worn out and weak and every movement made him think his skin was going to tear.

His mind ran a hundred directions. What were they going to do with him? Why were they tying him down?

He imagined pokes and prods.

He imagined vivisection.

His body splayed on a table, chest cut open and organs exposed.

He yelled, and one of the aliens put a ball of gauzy wrap into his mouth and tied it down. He strained, pain searing against his wrists and ankles, but nothing moved. Nothing changed.

A moment later they picked him up, and with some effort carried him out of the room, through a series of hallways, and into the chilly night.

CHAPTER 20

Baraq gripped the skipper's handlebars as he raced along the most direct path to the Waganat compound. The night air bit into his knuckles and clawed at his cheekbones, so he closed his central to keep it from burning dry as he rode through the night.

His wheels gave a raw growl that clawed its way over the city.

The sensation of speed in the darkness, which normally would scare him, served like music had in those quiet times at his shop—the shuddering rush of the nightscape passing around him was an ever-present sensation that numbed him to the point that his thoughts crashed around his mind until they became clear as the night sky.

He had been happy once.

He thought about that as the skipper zipped through the dark pathways.

Baraq had been an engineer, or, since the term *engineer* implied a certain discipline he never really had the patience for, it was probably better to say he had been an inventor. He had run a shop where he sold Waganat devices, tools, and other hardware. The shop had been his place to do as he wanted, so, in addition to selling standard Family fare, he also dabbled in creating his own devices, silly though they were at times. And he sold sticky treats that whelps came in to purchase with their parents' currency, sometimes giving it away without charge if it made him happy. Occasionally he'd pay a reed player or a strummer to pick tunes outside. He told Crissandr that he did that to entice business, but it was really because the music made time glide by and because he found that rhythmic sound in the background made it easier to get into that glorious state of mind it took to do serious dabbling.

That was a long time ago, though.

Since then, he had learned it was best to do what was expected of him, or at least he had discovered exactly what happened when he did not.

He throttled the skipper up as far as it would go. The vehicle rotated left as he turned.

His father would accept no arguments this time.

The entire family would be aware of everything. That's what he had to assume, anyway.

And if Brada had let his identity go that could mean only one thing —that sometime soon the *hedgies* and whatever other ragtag group of followers "Lelo" had gathered would be moving on the Families.

It was going to be a bloodbath of unseen proportion.

The only good news here was that at least Baraq knew his father well enough to be fairly certain Brada would be alive when he arrived.

Family ties wouldn't be enough to spare "Lelo's" life in the end, but this night was as much personal it was business. Ranya Waganat would wait to exact his vengeance on Lelo until Baraq was available to watch. Beyond that, keeping Brada alive was the right play from the business end of it, too. His father would leave the traitor alive for as long as it took to discover how far this went—which is exactly what Baraq had to cover. Once the trail began to form, there was little he would be able to do to keep his father from learning the basic facts about his connection to Louratna, but Ranya Waganat could not be allowed to understand exactly how far this went.

He couldn't learn how much Baraq had given her.

If Baraq could keep that silent, perhaps he could keep the Families and the council from actively working to destroy her efforts, though to be honest, he wasn't sure there was anything that would stop the Families if they caught them in the act of stealing the Heatborn away.

The creature understood the Taranth Stone.

If Louratna could work with it there was a chance Esgarat's problems could be stopped. If true, the creature was the most powerful bargaining chip on the table and what the Waganats didn't know right now could make a difference in the end.

Given Hazelta's comment, Louratna's team was probably already descending upon the medical center. If they got to the foothills of the mountains before the creature was found to be missing, they could make it. Baraq and Brada were almost certainly now on borrowed time themselves, but the longer he occupied his father and the Waganat security teams, the better it would be.

He arrived at the compound, and slammed on the brakes. The skipper skidded to a stop.

Guards paced at the entrance—fully alert now, and more of them than usual.

Fear rose in his throat.

"Baraq!" a voice called out. Probably Jee El, his brother's muscle and primary adviser, but he was too excited to be certain.

"What's with all of you out here on such a lonely night," Baraq replied. "Is there a party going on?"

"We know why you're here, Baraq." Yes, it was Jee. He stepped forward, exposing a black Yangu rifle in one hand. It was a blunt instrument. Not as refined or glamorous as a Tegra like the one Baraq once owned before the Family required him to get rid of it. The trigger mechanism fit into one of Jee's palms, the butt of the weapon levered from the nook of his elbow.

"Come on in," Jee said.

"What's wrong? I'm just here for a late-night visit."

"No games, Baraq. Just come in." The darkness covered Baraq's grin.

Instead, Baraq hit the throttle.

The rear wheel whined then caught. The engine screamed as he raced away in a cloud of rocky dust.

Jee yelled.

The rifle cracked, and a bullet hit the ground ahead of him.

It would take longer to reload than Baraq needed to get away.

He turned down an alley, his wrap flapping behind. Another alley came, and he turned again, then another. He needed distance now—as much space as he could manage. The Family would release their stable of speedy *kax* and send others on skipper boards of their own. Every piece of equipment he could engage was a piece that wouldn't be available if news of Louratna's raid came now, so he took the next long road and let his skipper run.

He blew past a post of council guards, waking them as he raced between buildings, and laughing out loud as one fell off his chair.

The night air blew cold against his face.

The machine vibrated below him, the engine's power sending ripples through his body as it torqued the wheels. *This is my time*, he thought. *This is my city.*

For the first time in years he felt totally free. Totally on his own. Powerful.

Let them take him. He was tired of playing *piela* lizard.

Just don't let them stop Louratna, and don't let them take Crissandr. Would Louratna's people get to her before the Waganats did?

A pair of *kax* riders seemed to materialize in the street before him.

He leaned the skipper hard to turn around. Wheels screeched against loose stone and the smell of burning compound filled the air. The engine was hot beneath him now, its battery draining fast due to the stint at max speed. He turned twice more, then cut the motor to save charge and to let it run quietly as he coasted down a hill. He bent his knees to take a sweeping right along the center circle, ducking down to reduce drag.

As his momentum carried him, his brain latched onto a thought.

If, by some stroke of luck, he managed to hold off his family for most of the night, then escape with his son, *and* find a way to slip into the wilderness, he, Crissandr, and Brada could live there and avoid the worst of the situation that was going to come to the Esgarat no matter what now.

The idea of living away from the council made him smile.

Riding silently, he ducked into a darkened alley and shut off the skipper.

The buildings to either side were decrepit lean-tos. An empty market lay across the street. The smell of garbage seeped in through the alley as he stood in silence. The clop of *kax* hooves rang out nearby. Skippers sounded distant. An occasional voice echoed in the streets that were so empty, Baraq couldn't tell what direction the sounds came from.

"You are very slick for an old quadar," a familiar voice said from behind him.

Baraq turned slowly and raised his hands.

"Jee," he said.

"Very good to see you again, Baraq. I'm sure you and your father will have a lot to talk about."

Baraq didn't need to see through the shadows to know Jee had reloaded his rifle.

The lights were on around the entire Waganat compound this time.

Baraq sat on a *kax* in front of Jee, bouncing with each of the animal's strides. The barrel of Jee's gun pushed hard against the base of his skull. All it would take was a single slip and Baraq would be missing half his head. He looked to the east and thought he saw the very beginning of Eldoro's pre-arrival glow. It seemed early, though. Perhaps he was imagining it. Dreams are for idiots, after all.

Jee brought the animal around to the main gate.

Baraq slid down when he was told to.

"We can cut him loose here," Jee said. "He's got nowhere to run now."

Baraq held his bound hands up when commanded, and the restraints were removed. It wasn't surprising to find that having his hands free did nothing to make him feel better. The rest of his father's guards led him down the stairs. Baraq didn't fight them, nor did he rise to their rough handling. The chase he led them on had raised their anger, and he saw no reason to give them even more reason to let it loose.

They led him into his father's sitting room.

Algar and Timboro, his father's dark-shift "butlers," stood to each side of his father, both carrying Tegra handguns. Jee covered the doorway. Tierra, Baraq's brother, sat primly in the chair to his father's left, his face set in a *how could you do this to us* grimace.

Ranya Waganat was seated in the same place on the same couch as he had been earlier. He looked smaller tonight, though, defeated and frail. He wore a black robe that folded about him in empty swathes, and his skin was washed out. The folds of his face spoke of troubled sorrow. Perhaps Baraq should feel shame for putting his father though this, but this man had ceased to be his father back when he took the Taranth Stone away from him.

"There was a time when blood held this Family together rather than tore it apart," Rayna Waganat said. He looked at Baraq, and for a moment Baraq actually thought his father might cry. *Pitiful*, he thought. *My father is pitiful.* "You could at least have told me that Lelo was my grandson."

"I thought you knew everything, Father."

"Bring him in," Ranya said, waving a hand at Jee.

Jee brought Baraq's son in.

His shirt was blue, and made of a heavy cloth. He wore loose trousers, more befitting a desert guide than a leader of quadars. Brada stood tall, though, and his face emitted a warm glow of confidence. As they led him into the room his stride seemed fluid and smooth, almost so perfect that Baraq thought that maybe he was gliding on air.

Despite a growing sense of pride that prickled Baraq's neck, he wanted to kick the boy.

Crissandr had always been the strong one, Baraq thought, and his son was very young, tall and slender, with both the physical expressions of his mother and more of her emotional fortitude. Baraq's only strength consisted of being born into the Waganat family, but now that single factor would tear his whelp down.

His father spoke. "All I ever wanted was to pass the results of my labors to my Family, so that they could pass it on to their Family."

"At the rate things are going there won't be anything left for my children," Brada said.

Ranya Waganat glared at him, unaccustomed to being interrupted.

But Brada was no longer a Waganat. Baraq saw that now, and, in seeing that, his hearts were filled suddenly with a rush of that pride that had tickled his neck a moment ago. His boy was a true quadar, not of the Waganat Family or the Terilamat clan, but a quadar of the quadarti above all else.

After all this, perhaps *that* was Baraq's one true accomplishment. He had raised a child who was not a Waganat.

His father glared, then glanced at Jee. "Crissandr?" Ranya Waganat said.

Baraq's stomach dropped at the mention of his pair-mate's name, but he almost sighed with relief at Jee's response.

"Gone when we arrived."

Louratna's team had made it in time. Crissandr was probably on her way to the foothills of the great volcano.

Ranya's fist clenched and his gaze grew to a red-hot glare. He turned his gaze on Baraq.

"Have you *no* shame?"

"I—"

His father gave a weak gasp, and his head fell back and he slid to the side of his chair.

"Are you okay, Father?" Tierra reached over.

Ranya Waganat's primaries clenched shut, and his central rolled to gray.

"Get him to the medical center," Tierra said. He pointed to Timboro. "And get these two locked up someplace."

Timboro wasted no time.

"That way," he said, waving his weapon under Baraq's nose and shoving Brada ahead of him. A few moments later they were locked in a half-full storage cell.

Baraq looked at his son. "I guess this is how it ends."

"No, Father. This is just the beginning."

"What do you mean? The Family will—"

"There is no Family, now," Brada replied, his smile radiant. "There is no council. After tomorrow, everything will change."

Baraq clicked in mock agreement.

"Yes," he said. "That is what I'm afraid of."

CHAPTER 21

The creatures carried him through darkness to a vehicle that resembled a flattened jeep with an open platform trailing off its back end.

Torrance was fully awake now. He wanted to get up but was lashed to the board. His heart pounded in his chest, and now that it seemed the aliens weren't immediately planning to put him under the scalpel, the restraints served to piss him off more than anything else. The gag felt and tasted like twine. Worse, it was so huge he could barely breathe.

What in hell was going on?

The air was almost cool now, and smelled only thinly of sulfur. It had to be in the rock, he thought, trying to recall his chemistry. Sulfur in gaseous form would resolve to liquid when combined with oxygen. At least that's what he thought. How bad was it to breathe a mix of sulfur? Obviously not bad enough to kill him, yet.

He took the fact that he was thinking about this as a good sign, but none of it helped him get in tune with what was happening.

Alien voices whispered in the darkness as they tied his board to the jeep.

Hard boots clopped against the jeep bed as others hopped in. Three of them. Two to the left, one to his right. They stabilized the board. The engine revved with an electrical whine, and the jeep jerked ahead painfully.

A cloud of dust billowed behind.

For the most, the aliens here were thin, which made them seem young.

Their skin was mostly unlined, and reflected light as the jeep passed fires that burned at places where the streets intersected. They spoke with hand signals despite the rumbling of the vehicle and the crunching of its hard wheels over the hard-packed pathway. Each time the ride jogged him to one side or the other, they pushed him back to the center.

It didn't take a genius to realize these things didn't want to be caught.

He tried to picture some unfathomable underground resistance on this alien planet, which suddenly made him feel like part of a story-book vid.

He was being kidnapped, though. That much was clear.

Just the idea made him laugh—which made his ribs hurt.

Many minutes later, the road, barely better than a cow trail to begin with, grew even more rutty and bouncy as the jeep climbed up into hilly terrain. Despite the darkness, Torrance made out harsh rock, thicket, and rugged trees. Vibration jostled his arms and legs, making the blankets and the boards feel like sandpaper against his skin.

He used the nighttime sky as his only focus.

It was a familiar thing, that sky with its stars and its infinite darkness.

It reminded him of when he was a kid in Wisconsin, standing in his backyard and picking constellations out of the darkness. The sky, he thought. It was his connection with reality.

Torrance cried, then.

Two thin lines of salty tears rolled down the side of his head, one from each eye.

After what had to be hours, the vehicle came to a merciful stop.

He lay on the pallet, gasping for breath.

They were in a clearing, high in the mountains. The air was sweeter here, and cooler. Torrance was almost comfortable.

To the east, Alpha Centauri A threatened to give enough of a bloody sunrise that he could see the stone was dark brown. Black openings of caves and shelters spotted the area, some glowing with low illumination of various soft tones.

Below him, a city sprawled.

It was beautiful, Torrance thought in a strangely lucid moment— the whole scene was like an exotic jigsaw puzzle of stone and wood that made him flash on ancient Egypt or the great American southwest.

He blinked.

Was he seeing things?

Down in the city they had come from, large masses of aliens seemed to be gathering to both east and west of the city.

He frowned.

Why would they be doing that? It reminded him of demonstrations he had seen. But that didn't make sense.

What did make sense about this place, though?

Nothing, Torrance thought. Right now nothing made sense.

He wished he understood what the hell was going on.

CHAPTER 22

The holding cell room, no bigger on each side than an average quadar, was too small to pace in, so instead Baraq sat on the stone floor and burned his nervous energy by twisting his fingers together. There was a lot to think about. His father had collapsed. What did that mean? He worried about Crissandr and Louratna. There was no way to know if his work had helped them get hold of the creature. And then there was Brada.

Beautiful, and somewhat naïve Brada.

"By 'everything changes tomorrow,'" he said to his son, "do you mean that you're going to get a lot of whelplings killed?"

Brada gave another beatific smile—another trait from his mother. He was slumped in an unfinished chair, which he had leaned against the door with his arms crossed. Despite their situation, his very skin seemed to glow with energy.

"Everything is in place, Father," Brada replied.

"In place for what?"

"We're tired of the council. And we're tired of the Families. The Kandar and Hlrat clans have joined us—they are massed at the border of the city. At daybreak, we will force the Families to listen."

"Kandar and Hlrat?"

"Inclusion gets you everywhere," Brada said, smiling. "We have directors from each of those clans included in the planning. Brother Oast'el and Sister Vareta. The Terilamat will come when they see our success."

Baraq waited for his son to continue.

"This Eldoro rising will see sheer numbers of dedicated soldiers break the chains our council uses to maintain their superiority."

Baraq looked at his son quizzically. "Where did the Kandar and Hlrat receive their weapons?"

"Of course we have weapons, Father. You know what they say about the Orange Army. And we're not afraid to use them. But those on the side of truth have little need of weapons."

Baraq couldn't help but scoff. "I don't think you've thought this through, son."

"We are not blind to the danger. But no one would dare face down the will of the entire community combined in one. Kandar and Hlrat will fill the streets, and when they do, the rest of Esgarat City will join us."

"You expect your own Family to sit idly by while your uprising takes their power away?"

Brada gave another smile.

"We will win, Father. The light and the weight of our numbers will expose the evil of the Families and of the council, and they will crawl away like *dooka* exposed to Eldoro's heat."

"We need to find a way to get you free," Baraq said, ignoring these fanciful ideals of his whelp.

He stood up and looked out a window in the doorway. Perhaps they could use surprise. He looked at his sandals, noting the bindings. If he disassembled the sandals, there was enough material there to make something of. "What tools did they leave you with?" he said as he began to disassemble his footwear.

"We will win," Brada replied to him.

"Let's say you win," Baraq said, removing one sandal to examine it further. "Let's say the council and the Families do something they've never done before and give up. What are you going to do?"

"First," Brada said, "we will listen to the quadars. But mostly, we'll work on the project."

"The project?"

"You should spend more time with Louratna, Father."

Baraq glared at his son.

"While she won't tell anyone directly, I've been listening to her and learning, and from what I've learned I've determined she's very close to building the one device that will save us."

"And that would be?"

A noise came from outside.

Keys rattled in the lock, and Brada dropped his chair back to the floor.

Baraq wondered which of the guards it might be. Jee? Algar? He moved to one side, and put his one free sandal behind his back.

As the door swung open, he clenched his fist.

It was Crissandr.

"Brada!" she whispered, smiling at her whelpling and opening her arms to give him a hug while at the same time suggesting quiet.

"Mother," Brada mouthed as he hugged her. "I've got to go."

"I know," Crissandr replied. "I have a ride for you."

"Is Ezi safe?"

"Yes."

"What's happening?" Baraq said, still trying to gear his mind for this turn of events. "I thought you went with Louratna."

"She tried to take me away, but what kind of *kalla* would I be if I let someone slip me out of the city while my son and my pair-mate are still at risk?"

Baraq stammered.

"Come," she said, grabbing her son by the hand and motioning Baraq.

She led them through the underground passages, and into one of the rough caves that ran beneath the compound. Baraq remembered playing down here when he was a whelp. It would be easy to hide here, for a while anyway, and if they wanted to he could even image going further, finding the wild caves that he used to explore on his own against his mother's wishes when he was a true whelpling.

Crissandr bypassed all that, though, and after some time they climbed the natural stairs that led into a warehouse filled with Waganat stores.

A sliding door was open. A vehicle waited outside.

"I don't understand," Baraq said. "How did you know where we were?"

Crissandr glanced over her shoulder.

"Males are not the only quadars with ties inside the Family," she said with a smile as she took the driver's side. "And where did you think I went every afternoon on my constitutional?"

Baraq grinned. His pair-mate had been doing her own intelligence gathering.

"And here I thought I was the only turned Waganat."

She raised the flesh above both primaries. For a moment she looked a full cycle younger.

"Get in," she said, looking at Brada. "I'll take you where you need to go."

Baraq understood then that Brada was intending to stay in the city, and that Crissandr was going to get him to his position to lead the Orange Ring.

He wanted to argue, but the words stuck on his tongue.

Instead, Baraq and Brada climbed into the back.

Crissandr engaged the gear train and turned the power on.

The motor cart gave a lurch, and the three of them were traveling toward the horizon where the earliest rays of Eldoro rising were giving off a perfectly orange glow.

CHAPTER 23

t was as if the mountains themselves had released some hidden cache of quadarti.

The clan of Kandar joined *hedgie* quadars from the east, Hlrat came from the west. As planned, they all walked calmly through Esgarat City, led by quadars hand-selected by the charismatic leader whom, until yesterday, they had known as Lelo.

They came by foot. They came by skipper and by *kax* and even a few *tal* beasts.

Some came bearing rifles and guns, but most had sticks and clubs.

They came holding hands, singing softly, chanting "Lelo, Lelo, Lelo," or another of the dozen slogans the Orange Ring had made popular, or walking in dignified silence, some dressed in colorful tones of orange and red and yellow and blue.

They came with their sons and their daughters suckling.

They came hundreds at a time.

Thousands.

They walked through streets and alleys, giving Eldoro's blessing to those they met, and marking signs of tranquility upon the doorways of those who were not yet awake.

It took only a short while before the city was filled with milling quadars from across every region.

"Sir?"

Pelorit, the leader of the Quadarti Council of Esgarat, woke with a start.

It was Risco, one of the council stewards.

"What is it?"

"You are needed."

Pelorit sat upright. He was old, and his joints ached with the movement. The earliest rays of Eldoro's light cut through thin slits between the blind and the windowsill. The sound of a wheel creaking came from the street below. He thought he might have heard voices.

"Is everything all right?"

"I cannot say," Risco replied.

The councilor slipped out of bed and rose to meet the first of today's unknown challenges. He went to the window and looked over the city.

What was this?

Risco helped him into his clothes.

It was slow going in the motor cart.

Members of the march called to Brada and touched him as Crissandr drove him into position behind Xian's Tower. The quadars got in her way, and made her crank the wheel right and left. The first heat of Eldoro was near when Crissandr finally halted the motor cart.

Brada slipped from his seat. "Thank you," he said.

"Be careful," Crissandr replied as Brada stepped away.

"I should go with you," Baraq said.

"This is my struggle," Brada replied too quickly.

"You're afraid of my name," Baraq said, the truth dawning. It was his name—Waganat—that was the problem.

"More your position," Brada admitted. "Or, at least what others will think of it right now. I can explain better when everything is finished. I promise, though, that when we have that moment, your past title in the Family and your work with Louratna will give you a proper voice in the whole of us. But right now I think your presence will burden my message."

Baraq clicked reluctant agreement.

He understood what his son really meant.

Perhaps when you cannot do any more harm, we can find a way for you to make a difference.

He didn't like that, but he understood. When a quadar chooses to work under cover of darkness, he loses the option to be trusted in the daylight.

"Be careful," he said.

They clasped hands, and Brada turned away.

Baraq shared a glance with Crissandr, and saw tears glittering in her primaries.

"Let's go," he said.

She pulled the vehicle away, but did not head directly to the outskirts toward Louratna's mountain hideaway. Instead, they doubled back to watch their son in action, both worried, but both unable to miss seeing their whelpling in what might be his moment of triumph.

Brada raced through the crowd, speaking to quadars as he went toward the podium at Xian's Tower once again. He had spoken as a masked leader just yesterday. Today he was who he was, and as he raced through the crowd he found himself touching each quadar around him, feeding off their presence in ways he always imagined.

"Are you us!" he called as he ran.

And the quadars answered back with a firm *"I am us!"*

"Are you us?"

"I am us!"

He made the stairs, and climbed upward two and three steps at a time until he reached the platform.

From here he could see the extent of the gathering as it drew near, the full collection of quadars who were all calling for the Ring of Esgarat to be listened to, for the bend of quadarti politics to twist in another direction. His father had been wrong. He saw that clearly, now. The throng of quadars was huge. They were strong. In a moment he would lead them to the council chamber and they would make their presence understood.

Together they would win the day.

As he ran farther up the stairs to the podium, he realized he was no longer Brada, no longer a Waganat.

"My name is Lelo!" he called out as he climbed, "and I am us!"

The quadars around him roared "Lelo!" from deep in their throats.

Yes, he thought. Lelo would be his name from now on.

It was the person he had been born to be. The person he had been the most comfortable as.

"This is a new day across the lands of all quadarti," Lelo said to his crowd. "It is a day of unimaginable beauty. A day of reckoning. It is a day of providing for those who cannot."

The crowd cheered again.

Tierra Waganat stood on the rooftop of his Family compound, watching the crowd gather and, like his father would, listening to the handheld wave talker he had put on the table behind him. The masses had been gathering in an eerie process for the past hour.

"They're breaking into buildings, sir," one of the shopkeepers who paid the Waganats a share to operate her store said over the wave talker.

"Don't let them in," he replied.

Though he knew it was what his father would have said, he did not feel good.

Ranya Waganat was dead now, his third heart giving away for good late last night, sometime just before or after his traitorous brother and nephew had somehow escaped. Now the Family was under Tierra's control, and now that the job of making decisions was his, the need to make them seemed to roil in his gut. The weight of eyes felt heavy upon him.

The sound of breaking glass crashed in the background.

"It's not like I have any choice but to let them in," the shopkeeper replied.

"They can't have our stores," Tierra said.

The shopkeeper did not reply.

Tierra turned to Jee. "Did you hear that?"

Jee nodded, but said nothing.

Tierra glanced over the crowd. Eldoro had risen fully now, and the masses were beginning to press in toward the compound and the central zones of Esgarat City.

"We can't give them our shops," Tierra said. "They can't have our technology."

"I understand," Jee replied, adjusting the straps on his rifle. "Should I take care of it?"

Tierra looked across the crowd again, feeling the steel-hard edge of this moment.

This was his decision. It would set the tone for his Family rule.

"Yes," he finally said to Jee. "Take care of it. No one gets in."

Jee clicked an affirmative. He called for his rifle and turned away.

Tierra picked up his wave talker and called Chief Councilor Pelorit.

His diplomacy would have to be quick, and it would have to be direct. But currency had always spoken before, and it would do the same this time.

He knew the councilor would agree with him.

Lelo fed off the power that radiated from the crowd.

Now was the time.

"Let us take back our land, my sisters and brothers. Let us take back our labors. Now is the time we will visit with the council and our Families, to give them our friendship, and invite them to join us. It is time we become family with all Families."

He smiled and raised his arms.

The crowd clicked and rasped hands together.

From a distance, a motor cart rumbled through the crowd, traveling quickly.

Then more. And more again.

Larger vehicles. Riders. Foot soldiers, all carrying colors of Families. Quadars with guns stood on the platform behind the drivers of each vehicle.

A burst of gunfire tore through the crowd.

Return fire came from an Orange Army guard before he was rapidly mowed down.

Gunfire erupted from everywhere.

Quadars fell.

"No!" Lelo said, his hands raising. He moved down a step. "Stop it!"

More vehicles entered the circle to cut off escape. Fire spewed from guns mounted atop platforms. Quadars screamed. Those of the Orange Ring who had brought guns returned fire. Others attacked with knives and clubs and anything else they could find. Still others ducked and covered their ears and their eyes.

Bullets tore through the crowd.

Blood flowed.

Bodies fell atop bodies.

Lelo watched as a young whelp holding his father's hand was trampled.

"Stop!" he called at the top of his voice.

Then came a blast of gunfire, and it felt like he had been hit in the chest with a mallet.

He spun with the impact and fell to the ground, seeing then that it was Jee El standing on a motor cart bed with his long-range rifle who had hit him. The crack of Jee's weapon ripped the air again, and it was like something kicked Lelo's ribcage. A dark pool of blood ran over the stone of Xian's Tower.

Another blow struck.

He lay there on the stage, exposed for all to see as bullets rained over him.

No, he thought.

He raised his good arm and felt the hole in his chest. His final call to arms gurgled in his throat.

No.

Another gunshot rang out among the hundreds.

Then there was no more.

CHAPTER 24

Torrance lay in a daze, still strapped to the board at the back of the aliens' jeep. Despite the fear he felt in the earliest moments of his removal, he had dozed on and off during the trip, unable to keep his brain from shutting down but also unable to muster the strength to remain fully conscious. Now, though, his thoughts were beginning to congeal into something more than a sloppy mess.

Alpha Centauri A was just cresting the horizon when a group of aliens emerged from the caves and gathered around the jeep. They wore tight-fitting shirts of a rough fabric, and some kind of dark trousers. Guards, Torrance thought as he looked at them. Or foot soldiers. They carried what appeared to be guns slung over their shoulders, weapons that were something between ancient revolvers and short rifles. The mechanism appeared to be loaded through large-bore barrels.

He tried to talk, but his tongue was stuck, tried to twist from the restraints, but pain inflamed his leg and his shoulder was worse.

His groans made the guards' voices rise and press closer.

He picked out males and females—or at least that's what he thought at first, then realized he had no idea what gender might be for this species. There were at least two body shapes, however, and while there were similarities in them, the proportions were different. He was keying on size and muscle mass rather than angles and curves, but did that make sense? Did these creatures even have gender? How did they procreate?

How anthropological of him, he thought.

The aliens stepped to either side of his jeep, and grasped the board he was tied down to.

He smelled warm spices coming from something one of the aliens had been eating, and was suddenly hungry. With a heave, the group slid him out of the vehicle, then lifted him over their heads and carried him through a curious gathering of even more of the creatures. The board's jostling hurt, but he had become accustomed to the pain. Mostly he was worried that the restraints would give and he would be dumped onto the floor.

The whole thing made him feel like a circus exhibit.

What were these things doing? Where were they taking him?

The answer to the second question was one of the caves they had come from.

Electric light glowed from inside a craggy cavern. The aroma was clean here, the air almost damp. Between the altitude and being inside the rocky mountain, the temperature was cooler to the point of being almost pleasant.

It stuck him that he should try to escape, then he laughed.

He tried his best to remember the turns they were taking, though. When the time came, it would be important to know the lay of the caverns.

As they got deeper, the passages grew tighter and darker, and pretty soon he was insanely lost. The aliens seemed to know where they were going, though. The caves were often lit by mossy lichen that glowed with neon phosphorescence, and the occasional battery-powered electric light. It made him wonder about the aliens' three eyes. Did that configuration give them better vision? Could they see in the dark like cats, or maybe they saw a different spectrum.

Their footsteps echoed in the enclosed space.

The pallet hit a wall at one point, and Torrance grumbled.

A clean airstream flowed from somewhere inside the rock, and for the first time since falling to the planet, he almost enjoyed the act of breathing.

They came to a rounded chamber with benches of carved stone that were arranged in concentric circles. The light was electric and brighter here. It made the stone almost inviting. They proceeded down another pathway until they came to a chamber with a thick door made of thatch and heavily woven root built into it. The material made a dry rasp as it opened and then closed behind him. They laid him down beside a bed pallet toward the back of the chamber. There was light here, given in the form of a soft green glow from moss growing on the walls, a light that made everything feel like it should be underwater.

Two of his kidnappers then very slowly removed the ties from his board.

He lay still as they worked, his heart calming considerably.

Blood flow made his hands tingle, a sensation he found hopeful.

He was tired now, tired and hungry, but the sensation of being freed from his restraints made him happy.

Another pair of aliens knelt beside him, speaking in low, trilling tones. One carried a bowl with a thin liquid inside, the other a tower of folded cloths. The one with the bowl took a cloth from the stack, then dipped it in the liquid before draping it over Torrance's shin.

The pain slipped from his leg.

Sweet mercy. Sweet mercy. No pain.

He didn't know what was in that bowl: Maybe some hellacious kind of narcotic, maybe something that would destroy his brain, but it stopped all his pain and that made it a fine tradeoff in his book.

"Thank you," he said.

"*Osto*," the nurse said, holding up the rag, then continued up both legs and over his chest.

He grew numb, and his mind seemed to wander, but his pain continued to recede.

"*Osto*," he said. "*Osto*."

Robes rustled from down the hallway, and the nurses stepped back.

He twisted his head to see a tall member of the species entering.

She seemed female and older, draped in a light gray garment that was part robe, part dress, and accompanied by an entourage the likes of which Torrance hadn't seen since the days he had been assigned to advise the self-appointed mayor of the ten colonies of the asteroid belt. She didn't need the entourage to grab Torrance's attention, though. There was something about her—the way she carried herself, or the way her eyes glittered with confidence. They were bold, yet unassuming eyes. Her examination of him reminded him of a captain's gaze, controlled and steady, like something was always going on inside her mind. A patchwork of leathered wrinkles crossed her skin. She smelled of something that reminded Torrance, oddly, of peaches.

"Who are you?" he said.

His question caught her attention, but she said nothing. Just squatted beside him and examined his wounds.

He sat up, and she didn't attempt to stop him.

The movement took most of his strength, though, and he found the medicines made his head swirl.

Remembering protocols, he put his hand on his chest. "Torrance," he said. "You?"

One of the woman's attendants handed her a slate and a block of chalky material.

She turned the slate so he could see it, then drew a right triangle and labeled each of the three sides with a symbol. Then she drew a vertical line. On one side, she marked two instances of one label, and two more of the other. On the other side of the vertical line, she marked two instances of the third symbol.

His jaw went slack.

"Pythagoras," he said. "Yes."

He motioned her to give him the chalk. It was waxy in his hand, or maybe the painkiller just made his skin numb to any other feeling. It had a citric aroma. The effort it took to write hurt even with the help of the *osto*, though not as much as it had previously. He marked out an equation. "A-squared plus B-squared equals C-squared."

The alien examined his notation. She marked another vertical line. On one side she marked two of her first symbols, on the opposite side she added the notation of Torrance's C-squared.

"Yes," Torrance said, nodding harder. "I follow. That means C-squared."

He rewrote the equation using an equals sign rather than a vertical line.

She made a sound he took to be affirmative.

"Equal," he said, pointing at the symbol.

"*Krazit*," she replied, pointing at both symbols for equality.

He smiled.

They had just learned the first real word of each other's vocabulary. Suddenly he wasn't hungry or even tired.

He marked a circle. The chalk slipped, but he pressed on.

She followed the determination of pi without any difficulty.

Torrance became giddy.

He had been alone for so long that he had almost forgotten what it was like to be understood. Now here he was, having a "conversation" with an alien species.

He sat against the rocky surface of the chamber and closed his eyes, suddenly drained, and suddenly famished.

"Food?" he said. "I'm hungry." He pointed to his mouth and rubbed his stomach.

The alien made an expression Torrance decided might be a smile, then spoke to an attendant, who then left the chamber. She turned to Torrance and spoke another string of something he didn't stand a chance of understanding.

The attendant returned with a large decanter made of stone and filled with water, and some crusty form of bread Torrance had never seen before. There was also a greenish thing he decided to call a fruit of some kind.

They broke the bread for him.

He was no biologist, but he understood DNA structure was important to human compatibility. Earth-born DNA was "right-handed." Right-handed DNA would interact with his. Left-handed would not.

Flip of a coin, he thought as he ate.

The bread was chewy, but filling. The fruit was something between an orange and a lemon, on the bitter side, but quite good. The water was warm, but it seemed clean enough and tasted sweet.

The woman watched intently as he ate.

He offered her some, but she declined.

When he finished, she stood and smoothed wrinkles from her robe. She said something that Torrance thought might be "I'll be back," or maybe "sleep well," and she left. The rest of them followed suit, the last of which locked the door—as if he was going anywhere.

Then he was alone.

He was full, and tired, and his muscles were too relaxed to fight off sleep even if he wanted to. Torrance lay back and stared at the ceiling. It was natural rock, broken in places, with fissures running down the domed wall. His head swam with a trippy sense of just being. Surreal, he thought. What a surreal end to a surreal day.

He wondered what these aliens were doing, and why he was here.

Mainly, though, he realized he missed the female he had just been talking to.

He drifted off to sleep, wondering where she had gone.

CHAPTER 25

After a long, painful drive through darkness and across rugged terrain that caused bone-jarring drops and annoying double-backs, Crissandr brought the motor cart to a halt outside Louratna's security clearing. She shut the engine off, then placed her head dejectedly against the steering column.

Baraq sat still and silent beside her, his back aching, his throat clogged with dust.

The sharp smell of ozone oozed from the motor cart's overheated battery.

Both Eldoro and Katon burned high in the clear sky now, making them visible even from the tight confines of the clearing, which was built in an open crease of rock on the opposite ridge from Esgarat City. The clearing was in the foothills and lined by steep cliffs of harsh rock that housed armed sentries at several locations, accessible only on foot or via a rugged drive of the type that had battered and bruised the two of them and taken nearly all the power of the vehicle.

Knowing they were being watched made Baraq self-conscious, but he knew they couldn't have gotten even this far if Louratna's security hadn't already recognized them. Regardless, after the events of the past heat, both he and Crissandr would still need to be inspected in order to enter.

They sat together, though, dealing with the sudden silence.

For either of the two to speak would be to admit what they had seen was real.

Their son was dead. His revolution was over.

Not that the revolution mattered anymore. Everything was over for them, now. Everything was done. Esgarat City smoldered on the other side of the mountain, and if he used his imagination Baraq could still smell the harsh scent of its smoke and hear the firing of guns and the piercing screams of dying quadars mixing with the smell of rock and the vast emptiness of the desert wind. He didn't want to know the tally of dead.

He understood exactly what was going to happen next, however.

The Families would use this uprising to tighten security. They would move quickly to step over the council, now making no pretense of following it.

He looked into the arid sky, heat rising within him. His shoulder plates grew damp with moisture.

How long before they came for Louratna? Could they find her here in the mountains?

Voices came from a distance: Louratna's people waving them in for review.

"We have to go," Crissandr said, her head still bent against the steering apparatus.

Baraq breathed deeply and clicked absently. Yes. They had to go.

Crissandr raised up, then touched his arm.

When he pulled away her primaries darkened. Her central was open and wide. *You are all I have left,* her expression said. *We are all that remains for each other.*

And that was true.

They had lost Brada now, just as they had lost his sister before he was even born, little Hara who would be old enough now to be making her own way through the Esgarat if she had lived. For a moment, he was glad she wasn't here to see this, then immediately felt a fresh stab of remorse.

What kind of fool was he, thinking like that? What kind of father? He felt Crissandr beside him, and felt the weight of their lives together. She was suffering, too. She needed him to reach out and touch her, but Baraq was too angry and worn from both the long ride and from the fact that he had not slept. His hands felt nailed to the seat. Words backed up in his throat.

If he could talk he would tell her…what?

What would he say to her?

That he was a failure?

That he was weak—that he had been used by his Family for his entire life, used by Louratna, he thought, remembering Brada's words to him before Crissandr had broken their conversation. Louratna had used him like the rest had, hidden something important from him, and maybe even used his dead son to do it. Would he tell Crissandr this was his fault? That his failures all combined to leave their boy dead, but that he wished now that he had died in the shootings, too, because at least his son died doing something he believed in while Baraq himself had been too afraid to stand up to his Family when they were so obviously wrong?

"I'm tired," he finally replied, as if that was enough.

He left her, then. Slid from the seat, and walked alone into the opening of Louratna's caves, his mind broiling in a cloud of thought.

The main hall was once a natural vent for a volcano, and had been cleared by Louratna's quadars. They recognized him. One made an off-hand comment, but Baraq just clicked something resolute and smirked as he passed them.

How many supporters did she have?

Three hundred? Six hundred?

He had wondered about the size of her following for a long time, but never enough to question her about it.

She was a philosopher. Philosophers gain followers.

What was to question?

He walked farther down into the network, into the cooler air, each step bringing him more anger as he recalled the look on Brada's face as he spoke of "the project."

How had he been so stupid?

What were they working on so secretly behind his back despite what he had given them?

What did it matter?

Betrayal lay like a branding iron in his gut. He had trusted Louratna, and what had it gotten him? A dead son and withheld secrets. To make it worse, he almost couldn't blame her.

It was early. Louratna would be in her meditation room. He knew the way. Guards stood outside the door. Reedy music filtered from inside. He pressed past them before they realized what he was doing.

He pushed and the door flew open.

Louratna sat on a woven mat before a burning brazier, an open flame snaking toward the ceiling from an oil-soaked chunk of coal ore. A piper sat opposite her, holding the brittle instrument to his chest like he would die before letting Baraq destroy it. The chamber was lit by the fire as well as a few mossy glowsticks placed around it. The configuration cast much of the chamber in shadows, making it feel both smaller and larger than it really was.

Baraq stormed forward.

Hands clasped his arms from behind. He tried to twist from the guard's grasp, but the quadar was stronger than he was, younger and certainly better rested. The guard dragged him back toward the door.

"Leave him be," Louratna said.

The guard grunted and clicked, then slowly let him loose.

Baraq had seen him before but never asked his name.

Louratna motioned to the piper, and he, too, left them alone in the chamber.

"You've had a difficult night," Louratna said thinly after Baraq calmed and the guard left. The controlled tone of her voice inflamed his anger again.

"I trusted you with the Taranth Stone, and I get this in return?"

"Yes."

It took all of his self-will to stand still. He clenched his fists instead. "Why?"

The question hung in the air like mist after a melting rain. *Why?* That single word could serve infinite purposes. Why was everything so wrong about him? Why had his life turned inside out like this? *Why?*

"What would the Waganats have done if they learn of our efforts?"

"I would never have said anything."

Louratna leveled her gaze at him. "Every room in your home has a wave talker directly linked to your Family compound. Every step you take is watched by your Family's guards."

"That didn't stop me from running information for you," Baraq spat. A bitter taste crawled over his entire body. He felt the chill of the mountain deep inside his empty stomachs.

She sat as if expecting something more.

He had been so stupid. Clicks came from the deepest part of his throat. He turned and pounded his fist into the wall. The impact felt good. Louratna made no motion, a fact that only served to heighten his own desperation.

"You've never trusted me," he said.

"I've always trusted you."

He laughed.

"The information flow had to be one way because your father would have killed you if he found out about us."

"My father would have killed me if he found *any* secrets." He glared at her, all three eyes blazing. Coming here had been a mistake. He turned and put his head against the raw stone of the mountain, not caring that Louratna was there or not there. The room remained silent until Louratna finally responded.

"To provide you information would have multiplied contact, and therefore increased the probability of your becoming ensnared."

He breathed in through his nostrils.

"I think my head is going to explode," he said mostly to himself, then he stepped to the doorway. Yes. He had to leave.

"Regardless of the past, however," Louratna said. "Your situation is changed. Now you are free to join us."

He glared at her through his primaries, and his central wandered to indicate separation and disbelief. All he had left was his pride, and now Louratna wanted that.

"No," Baraq said, meaning the word more fully than he had ever meant it before. "I don't care anymore," he said. "I would sooner slice off my hands than work with you now."

He stood calmly, as tall as his frame provided, and brushed wrinkles from his soiled robe.

"I'm leaving," he said.

He turned and strode back through the hallway.

For their first evening in the wild, Baraq chose a small crag dug into the western section of the mountain, specifically because it was not part of Louratna's complex. Crissandr tried to get him to reason and go inside, at least for the night, but for reasons he didn't fully understand, he wouldn't.

Couldn't.

Just the idea of staying in Louratna's complex brought wells of anger up inside him.

"You stay where you want," he said to her.

She stayed with him.

"We can't live here forever," Crissandr said as they lay together under borrowed blankets.

He did not respond, though he did grasp her hand when she took his.

They lay like that for a long time, together under the stars but both feeling deeply alone.

Louratna came to him early the following day. Baraq and Crissandr were sitting on open rock and eating raw *havra* that Crissandr had packed away before leaving the house. The root was stale, but it was the first thing he had eaten in two days and it tasted as good as anything could taste at this point. The philosopher hesitated, squinting into the light as Eldoro rose over the horizon. She looked older in the natural light.

"I need you, Baraq," she said.

"You did not need me yesterday."

"Don't be foolish."

"I'm not," he said.

Louratna waited until the mood calmed. "Crissandr has asked permission to move into the mountain," she said softly.

He glanced to his pair-mate. The truth sat on her expression. "Then let her."

"You will come with her?"

"No."

"Baraq," Crissandr said.

"No."

The pair of them were silent, then Louratna spoke. "I'm sorry about Brada. You raised him well. He was a good quadar."

Baraq closed his eyes. *Yes*, he thought. *And yet I am* not *a good quadar.*

Taking time, he stood and put the last of his *havra* on the place he had been sitting, then turned and began to pick his way down the mountain.

Crissandr knew him well enough that she made no move to stop him, yet he saw his action hurt her.

"You can't go back, Baraq," Louratna argued as he made his way. "The Families control Esgarat City. You know that's true. You can go back if you think that's best. But they will never give you the freedom you need."

"I don't care about the city," he said, a statement he found suddenly freeing.

It was true. He didn't care about the city.

He didn't care about the Families or the council, and that made him feel suddenly powerful. How ironic. To gain ultimate freedom he only had to lose everything. *Life is a horror, sometimes*, he thought as he stomped further down the trail.

"You never asked about the Heatborn," she called out behind him.

He scoffed then. Baraq Waganat stopped and scoffed again, and then turned back to Louratna with a caustic click of disgust in his throat.

"The Heatborn can starve for all I care."

UNDER THE MOUNTAINS

Eden: Esgarat Mountains
Local Date: Convergence, Year of First *Piela*, Cycle 57

CHAPTER 26

Mostly, Torrance slept.

He wanted to get the hell out of this place. Wanted to get up and move, but resting was all his body would do: lie here on this pallet, sleeping and dozing or whatever it was he was doing in this thing that might or might not have been a drug-induced haze. It helped, he supposed, that his cell was cool and his bedding was a pile of blankets and pillows thrown over a hard surface, which made for a good, firm plane. The chamber had no view of the sky, so he measured a "day" as the time between the applications of the medicine his nurses applied to his sunburned skin, though in reality that span could have been just hours.

They left him a robe made of a coarse material. Maybe processed root, he thought. It was rough against his skin, but not in a bad way. There was food waiting when he woke—a pair of hard green fruit and a bowl with fresh water. At first, moving enough to eat hurt him, but he did it anyway. The first time he had to relieve himself, he found what he took for a chamber pot nearby. It was cleaned the next time he woke.

As he recovered, Torrance began to notice sounds the aliens made outside his chamber. Their voices were flat, their language filled with dips and sharp sounds that came from the back of their throats as well as some kind of squeaky clicking that at first he thought was coming from a mouse or a rat.

After two meals he felt strong enough to explore, but got only as far as the locked door before deciding the pain was too great.

The fact that there was a barricade in place to begin with was all he really needed to know, anyway. Its unyielding click told him that he was a prisoner, a lesson that made him angry.

What did they want from him?

What harm could he do?

He woke to find himself alone in his chamber.

His mind was stronger now, his thoughts clear. His body still ached, but it was a low pain that wasn't too hard to bear.

Torrance rolled to a seated position and, for the first time, examined his chamber in some intense detail. It was rock and more rock, lined in a few places with a moss that glowed with a neon green aura that cast just enough illumination to see by. He found nooks and small cracks, thick veins of minerals in the walls, and other formations that seemed to grow from the ceiling.

What he didn't find was another way out.

The activity tired him.

Almost panting from exertion, he sat on his pallet and tried to get a grip on himself. What was he doing here? What was going on? A noise came from the lock, and the door scraped open. A nurse entered with a bowl of medicine, his face contorting to an obvious expression of anxiety at the sight of Torrance sitting up.

"What's happening to me?" Torrance said.

The nurse stepped back, the bowl sloshing. For a minute Torrance thought he might leave.

"It's all right," he said in what he hoped was a conciliatory tone. He raised a hand, and gently motioned to the nurse to proceed. "It's not your fault."

The alien came to his bedside and cautiously dabbed the medicine over Torrance's skin. It felt good.

"This is frustrating as hell," Torrance said softly.

The nurse replied with a string of gibberish and clicking that Torrance's high school German and Spanish didn't help with.

When the medicine was administered, the nurse rose and got out of the room.

Torrance lay back on the bed.

He felt lost.

He wanted to learn more about this place. Now that he knew he could survive, he wanted to see the land. Wanted to know what was going on here.

Between these thoughts, Torrance found his mind wandering to his old job, to Marisa and the girls, Thomas Kitchell, and, of course, his time on *Icarus*. He thought about the message he had received from Kitchell that had confirmed an intelligent presence in signals from Eden. He imagined Kitchell, direct-wired into interstellar listening posts and madly deciphering codes and wave forms, dealing with signal-to-noise issues and frequency amplifiers, and running the signals through multiordered filters or other data cleansing routines.

The signal had come from Eden, and it was done in some form of language.

He was sure of it now.

If it was true, it meant these aliens had transmitters, which then meant that if Torrance could find one he could send more messages. And if Kitchell was still listening, maybe the kid could use the message along with the ones Torrance had sent from the shuttle and get a rescue mission launched.

Probably not, he supposed.

Even if such a mission happened, he would probably be dead by the time it arrived.

But he had thought that before, and here he was.

One problem at a time, right? Could he get another message to the Solar System from here?

He got up and paced. All these thoughts made him feel even more powerless.

They made him grit his teeth and consider things he might do the next time the door opened. Where should he start? He glanced to the lock. Could he get away? Could he fight them if he needed to?

Maybe he could fashion a weapon out of his blankets or pillows?

Did the aliens breathe as he did? If he covered their mouths and nose for long enough, would one of these things expire, or did they have other parts to their respiratory systems?

He didn't know.

To be honest, he also didn't know if he could bring himself to kill one of these aliens. They hadn't done anything to harm him so far, anyway. In fact, it seemed to be just the opposite. They had him in lockdown, but they had also brought him back to health.

All he could say for sure was that after all this time wondering about life on this planet, being a prisoner here on Eden made him feel like the entire universe was having one gigantic laugh at his expense.

He damned well didn't like it.

CHAPTER 27

The woman visited him again later that day.

Woman, Torrance quickly decided, was the proper label.

She seemed to be a female where others appeared to be male. Or at least hers was definitely of the smaller of the species' two body types. Rightly or wrongly, he considered that to be female. And since she was definitely older than others, he thought *woman* would be her correct descriptor.

As she entered the chamber, he sat up and pulled the robe over his chest.

His exertion from earlier had knocked him down a peg, and he had been dozing. It took a moment for his mind to snap completely back.

She was dressed in a flowing tunic and a pair of loose-fitting pants that made a scratching noise as she walked. Her footwear was a pair of cross-knit sandals made of some kind of animal skin. She looked as sharp as he remembered from earlier, and her movements were controlled and precise as she came to him.

Another of the aliens brought a stool into the room, which she sat on.

"Hello," he said, perking up even further when he noted she was carrying a dark green drawing slate and a bowl of waxy, chalklike writing utensils.

She clicked in return, then got straight to business.

On the slate, she drew a circle, then a stick figure standing on top of the circle.

As she worked, Torrance marveled at her fingers. They were long and graceful despite their weathered appearance against the smoothness of the chalk. When she finished, she motioned to the figure, then herself.

"That's you," Torrance said.

Then she pointed at the circle, and the ground.

"That's you and the planet," Torrance said, repeating the motions.

The alien drew a second stick figure on the circle, then pointed at Torrance.

"That's me." He put his hand on his chest.

She made two more circles higher up on the slate, one considerably bigger than the other. "Eldoro," she said, pointing at the larger. "Katon," at the smaller.

Torrance grimaced. Did she mean the suns?

"Alpha Cen A and B?" he said, also using his finger to suggest movement.

"Eldoro," she replied with a confirming click as she pointed at them. "Katon."

He nodded, then picked up another chalk stick and placed a small dot where he thought Proxima might be. "Proxima," he said, pointing at it. "Alpha Centauri A, Alpha Centauri B, and Proxima."

"Eterdane," she replied, pointing to the third. Perhaps he was wrong, but he thought he heard a bit of respect coming through her voice. "Eldoro, Katon, Eterdane."

Torrance couldn't help but grin.

They were communicating. Truly sharing.

Then she drew a line from Torrance's stick figure to Eldoro, and spoke a phrase that also included a raised ridge above her biggest eye.

It's a question, he thought. *She wants to know if I'm from Alpha Centauri A.*

"No," he replied aloud, "I'm not from there."

He drew a line from his stick figure out past the edge of the slate. "I'm from a long, long way out there," he said.

Her eyes grew wide, and she whispered a phrase under her breath, then she clicked and cocked her head to one side as if she was thinking to herself.

Slowly, she stood up.

The assistant took her seat away.

She clicked at Torrance one more time, then turned to the assistant and made a word. The assistant seemed to either defer or agree in some fashion.

A moment later, she was gone.

CHAPTER 28

The air was cold as Baraq entered Esgarat City.

Stars scintillated as he stepped silently from shadow to shadow, and down alleys toward the Waganat compound. Back when the skies first began to clear and the stars had originally appeared, he had often stood outside with Crissandr and Brada, staring at them, pointing upward and wondering what they were. Then Louratna explained her theory that each was another world, and it suddenly made sense. Even knowing the other secrets they shared, however, the idea had stunned him.

Yes, he had fully absorbed the idea that the Taranth Stone had come from another world, so the idea made sense.

But so many new worlds?

The thought that each tiny dot could house other places like Esgarat had made him feel suddenly very big. It helped him understand there was a future, and that working to make his city viable was the most valuable thing he could do, which in turn made it so much more possible to bear the pressures of being an agent under his father's dictatorship.

Back then, though, Baraq and little Brada had made games of

creating pictures with those stars: *Jah* and *pax*, and, once, an imaginary creature that only the child could see.

Baraq didn't even notice them now.

Instead, he focused on the scent of smoke and burning fires that settled over the city, the smell of dead bodies massed in corners, waiting their turn to be removed. Freed from social pretense now, and given the opportunity to flex their strength unmitigated, the Esgarat Families would make the entire area a different place.

He was worn now.

It had taken four complete heats and much of a fifth to make it from the mountain home of Louratna's complex on foot, a path he had taken with poor preparation. If the distance had been even a heat longer, he may not have made it. His body was parched and beaten, and his legs felt nothing but the ache of the dead as he made his way through the dark allies of Esgarat City. His fingertips were torn and scabbed from climbing, his knees bruised. The chill of the nighttime made the heatburn of his skin that much worse.

He wondered if he might grow the dark spots and die like many so others had when exposed too long.

Stupid, really, but he no longer cared.

If he was still alive when Eldoro rose next heat he would teach himself to be more cautious with his wanderings. Maybe he would chase down Karshi Fael or some other free-ranger to teach him proper survival in the deserts. It could be done, he supposed. Even at his advanced age he could become a free-ranger.

If he lived, anyway.

He reached to his belt and retrieved the Tegra revolver that he had kept hidden away for so long after his father forced him to be rid of it. Of course, rather than dispose of it, he had merely hidden it away in case a day like this came. Now he found its existence ironic. It was a weapon he once kept under the counter of his shop at the urgings of his father, Ranya Waganat, who made his living out of being cautious and who, when Baraq argued that no quadar in their right mind would take from a Waganat shop, commanded Baraq to be silent and do as he was told. "Enterprising quadars will stay away from Waganat shops specifically because they will understand that all Waganat shops will exact their own justice," his father said.

Tonight, that would finally come true.

The weapon felt heavy as Baraq hefted it. It absorbed nighttime heat in a way that made it appear to be a void in his central.

It felt ugly, but ugly in a way that made him feel good.

Baraq would kill his father tonight.

He would kill his father, and he would kill his brother, Tierra, who had directed the attack on his son's gathering. But first he would kill Jee.

Then, one way or another, he would leave the city behind him forever.

CHAPTER 29

From that point on the woman visited often, staying longer as Torrance grew stronger.

Their ability to communicate got better.

Torrance picked up phrases from her, and she from him. Perhaps a linguist could have moved faster, but he was pleased. He looked forward to her visits.

Her name was Louratna.

When he taught her his name, she repeated it until it came out almost right.

Something in the alien's tongue didn't allow her to get the soft hiss sound of the "ce" quite right, but the sound of his name on her lips grew on him. After that, the aliens all called him something that sounded like "Torranze," a fact he found more pleasing than he thought it should. She also taught him the term *quadar,* which he was happy for because he didn't like thinking of this species as "aliens."

The sweet root that now made up a part of his diet was called *havra.*

Beasts that he could sometimes barely hear howling someplace outside were *neantha.*

The fruit he loved so much was *janga,* and grew on ranches that were west of mountains such that they got the morning shade.

He explained "human being."

She seemed to appreciate that.

Torrance drew an image of the wormhole pod similar to the one the quadar he had met in the city before had drawn for him.

Louratna paused. Her two outside eyes drew to points, and she seemed to debate something insider her own mind. Her answer was noncommittal, or at least he didn't understand it. She moved on from there, though.

Over the next few sessions they shared more math and picked up a few more words.

She understood geometry and trigonometry best, but there was clearly more there.

Progress was slow, though, and Louratna seemed more comfortable speaking in the symbols of mathematics than in language. So, for the most part, that is what they did. On the whole, the whole process felt a lot like his work in the ambassadorial field, a profession where frustration came from the fact that every conversation between people from different places had been filled with linguistic noise, where words were contorted with different things among human beings of different tribes. It made him consider how languages, even among those on the same space station, often served to separate people rather than connect them.

"I want to get out of here," Torrance said after a session.

He wasn't sure what to expect, but it was time to push. He didn't seem to be a prisoner so much as someone in some form of protective custody. He wanted to find out how far he could go.

Louratna looked across the tablet with the expression he had come to know meant she was uncertain about what he was saying.

"I feel good." He flexed his leg carefully, searching for words that seemed to have positive connotations. "*Mata*," he said, using the creature's word that seemed to be positive. "I feel *mata*."

She smiled. "*Mata*."

He pointed to the hallway, then himself, and hoped his gaze had a glimmer of expectation rather than demand. "Outside," he said.

"*Mata*," she said, scratching her shoulder. In a louder voice

Louratna spoke a stream of language that included several clicks and guttural sounds.

"Woah," he said, raising his hands against the current and trying to take it in.

But the lock to his door opened and another quadar stepped in.

Louratna exchanged conversation with the guard for a moment, then turned to Torrance.

"*Adiago nar*," she said. It was the phrase she had been using for something he thought was *next iteration*, in their other discussions.

He smiled.

"Yes, *adiago nar*. Tomorrow should be fine."

The next time Louratna came, she was accompanied by two males and a female.

Standing up, Torrance looked instinctively to the door behind them. They left it open this time. The idea of escape hit him like a sledgehammer. Could he make it?

The flesh around Louratna's eyes relaxed as if she was sympathetic to his situation.

She spoke, but he couldn't interpret any of it.

She turned, though, and motioned to him to follow. Torrance hesitated, his heart racing. The others parted for him. He took a step and Louratna led him out into the hallway, which was pitch dark and where the chill in the air felt suddenly hostile.

He stopped and put a hand on his head on pure instinct.

"I can't go on," he said.

So much for escaping.

A crack came from beside him, and the second female was suddenly handing him a chemical glowstick of some kind. When he was settled, they proceeded to follow a path ahead.

The muscles in his legs were weak, so he nearly stumbled but still it felt good to move like this, with long and uninterrupted steps forward. He followed them, half by voice and half by the vision of their shadowed forms reflected in the green light of the glowstick.

It wasn't long before they came to where a beam of natural sunlight sliced down from above with enough power that he blinked back tears of both pain and joy.

The mere idea of sunlight stole his breath.

He squinted as they passed by.

The air in the cave soon grew warm, almost too hot. His movements worked up a sweat, and his breathing became labored.

Where were they taking him?

Then, almost without warning, the cave opened to a view of rugged terrain outside the mountain that took his breath away.

The land before them was full of sweeping browns and oranges, dusty grays and hardy greens. It was huge and expansive, higher up than he had seen it from before. To his left, the mountain chain seemed to go on forever. Straight ahead and to his right, rocky land sprawled into the distance with some patches of ground covered in some kind of hardy growth, others just cracked spans of rock. Formations rose up here and there, and a spiderwebbed series of cracks ran through the ground in the distance.

Far away, a patch of rain was falling.

After he had been caged for so long, the view was the most magnificent thing Torrance had ever seen. Even though the cave mouth was protected from the direct sun, the air here was almost too hot to breathe, though.

As he stood there, Louratna spoke to the other female, then returned the way they had come. He recognized the passing of command.

The new quadar came to Torrance's side, then sat on the ground, lifting her robes to let them settle over her crossed legs.

Not knowing what else to do, he joined her, sitting lotus style to look out over the landscape. The quadar was impassive beside him. Or perhaps *resigned* was a better word. She seemed unworldly silent, the sighs of her breathing coming in heavy gasps on more than one occasion.

They were showing him this for a reason, he thought.

Were they telling him he wasn't a prisoner?

Or maybe that the lock and key were for his own good?

They sat there for a long time.

Eventually, his legs began to hurt. He stood, ready to get away.

That was apparently the signal to take him back to his chamber, which was fine with Torrance. The air was too hot and too dry to be comfortable.

Ten minutes later, he was back in the cave, totally exhausted, and washing down a meal of fruit and roots with a bowl of water.

CHAPTER 30

t was still dark when Baraq used his key to slip through the
compound gate and slink first into the gardens, then around
sentry buildings. The Family's takeover of Esgarat City was days
old, long enough that the edge was off the guard. Baraq knew their
assignments. Understood where they would be. He took his time,
feeling a sense of greater destiny come over him the further he
progressed.

The image of Brada's face loomed before him.

His whelp's smiling expression gave him a sense of sadness deeper
than he could express.

In a short while, he arrived at Jee's cottage and pressed himself
against its rounded wall to stay as covered in the shadows as he could.
The sky was still full of stars, but it wouldn't be long before Eldoro
would lighten the horizon. The night chill was sharp. A slight wind
was the only sound.

The cottage was small, but clean. Skins lining the roof were
stretched so taut that star shine glistened in the oils that covered them.
The aroma of those oils seemed omnipresent. They repelled any
burning rain that might fall, but they had to be steadfastly maintained.
Jee had obviously refreshed them recently. Ahead, a clutch of *katja*

grew over the eastern round, blooming fully now so it could feed off the colder morning air.

Katja did well in this new world: closing up as it did protected it from curling in the peak heat, and drinking as it did in the evening hours meant harder chills gave it more to live on. The flowers were green in the darkness.

The path to Jee's door was swept clear of debris and lined in striated rock that had been perfectly placed. The hut's rounded walls had been painted in the past season. That was Jee's way. He was meticulous about everything he did, which is what made him so good at his job. And he knew his business, too. No detail went untouched. When it was collection day, he returned with what a Family partner owed, no more, no less.

If Baraq was counting correctly, today was that day. If so, Jee would be waking soon.

He laid his head against the stony concrete of the building's wall.

Jee had been Tierra's heavy for the past three years, and had bragged of his approach often enough. "It's best to hit them before they get too tired," Baraq remembered Jee saying with a hint of glee to his voice. "Before the heat makes them think crazy things about trying to hold out." The Waganat security quadar never had any complaints about taking extra steps to ensure payment. Jee was big and strong. Usually, he intimidated the hell out of Baraq, but now Baraq was oddly pleased to realize he wasn't afraid of this confrontation at all.

Baraq drew the Tegra.

Jee wasn't pair-mated, so he was likely to be alone.

The window crease to the south of the cottage was open to the air. Baraq could go that way, and hope to avoid any unforeseen barrier that might be placed inside, or he could force the main doorway and announce his presence. One would tax his grace, the other his strength. Either would leave him briefly exposed.

Putting the gun back into his pocket, Baraq chose the window.

A glance showed the path was clear.

He gave a nearly silent click of confidence, then stepped out of the shadow. The sill felt hard under his hands as he reached up and wrapped his fingers over it. With a grunt he hoped was quiet enough, he pulled himself up.

A moment later he was seated in the frame.

The window led to a small common area. Jee's sleeping pallet was in the back corner.

A glance inside said the landing area was clear.

"What is that?" a quadar spoke in the distance behind him. "Hey?"

Baraq glanced over his shoulder and saw a guard coming his way.

Instinctively, he pulled his legs up, swung around, and slipped into the cottage.

Blood rushed through his body. The sound of footsteps came closer.

"Jee El?" the voice asked.

"Who is that," Jee said, waking.

Baraq stepped hurriedly toward the still supine quadar, fumbling to get his Tegra out. The barrel of the weapon caught on the cloth of his robe. His throat tensed as his fingers fumbled. The robe finally let go of the gun as he came to the bed. Jee was rolling away, but Baraq fell on him, managing to get the gun to Jee's temple.

The sensation of cold metal on skin stopped his target in his tracks.

Jee peered upward. The quadar's face was barely discernable in the starlight that came through the window.

"Who are you?"

"I am Baraq Waganat," he replied, grinding the gun against the head of the man who murdered his son. "You killed my whelp."

Nothing moved for a moment, and for that moment the only sound was the clomping of the sentry's steps as he came to the window.

Jee's face split into a wild grin. "You're going to kill me then," he said. "Is that it?"

Baraq leaned in. He felt powerful now. Certainty built inside him. It was right for him to kill this quadar. His eyes were wide and his body felt strong. He swallowed and clicked, and focused on the moment rather than the noise at the window.

"I'm going to kill you," he said through teeth he had suddenly clenched. "Then I'm going to kill Tierra, and then I'm going to kill my father."

"Good luck with that."

"You think I won't?"

"You want to kill Ranya Waganat, you're going to have to move a lot of rock."

Baraq frowned.

"You don't know?" Jee continued, his smile getting more self-serving. "The old man's dead."

"What?"

"Put him under stone two heats back. Your brother runs Family Waganat now."

Baraq froze. His father was dead.

"I'm coming in," the guard said outside.

"Looks like you best be getting on to your business," Jee said, the tone of his voice taunting Baraq.

The two of them sat as if locked in place. Baraq's mind processed the news, and as he did he saw himself as if he was outside his body, kneeling over Jee, the whelp of his aunt three spaces over, the quadar's huge muscles roiling under his knees and his shins. The image was horrifying. Grotesque. Who was he? What was he doing?

He lowered the gun.

"You drop that thing, and maybe your brother won't have you killed straight out," Jee said.

Behind him, the guard entered the window and came through the common room. A cold revolver clicked.

An explosion of pain blossomed along Baraq's back like none he had ever felt.

He turned and shot back, rolling off a stunned Jee El, and bouncing off a rounded inner wall. He shot at the guard again. The quadar screamed and went down, clutching its leg.

Baraq took a step, screaming in pain as he moved.

His back was on fire but he had to go.

A warm trail of blood ran down his leg as he took two more steps, limping and dragging one leg, pain shooting through his back. Jee said something behind him, but the sound of the shots was still ringing in his ears.

Baraq threw himself out the window and hit the ground so hard he bit his cheek raw. He rolled as he fell, though, drawing breath and using his momentum to get back onto his feet. He found shadow, and slipped as silently as he could against another cottage, following it around a corner and back to the garden.

Behind him, voices raised and footsteps scuffled.

He pressed himself behind a woody bush and lay against a stone fence to avoid being seen. The need to pant was a physical thing. He fought it, listening with intensity as Jee's voice echoed in the nighttime, and the Waganat security crew came to full alert.

If the shots had been the only disturbance he might have had some time. That's what his plan had been based on, anyway. But now he was in trouble.

He put his hand down and felt the wound.

The bullet had torn up his central plate and penetrated at a lucky angle lower down in his back. If he could staunch the blood flow he would probably survive. He edged around the brush, and considered the lay of the compound. The disturbance meant he would never be able to get out the way he came in, though.

Probably best to go further into the complex, find a cave and get lost there.

If nothing else heading deeper into the complex might surprise them.

Gritting his teeth, Baraq straightened and rounded the brush.

"Hello, brother," a familiar voice said from behind him. "Imagine finding you here."

He turned to see Tierra flanked by a pair of guards, both with rifles pointed directly at Baraq's gut.

"Take him to the cells," Tierra said.

CHAPTER 31

f he was ever going to see the Solar System again, Torrance was going to have to find a way to call home. It would help, anyway. If Interstellar Command received his first transmission, they might be intrigued. But if they didn't get a second, there was every chance everyone would assume Torrance had died in transit. Why come to Eden for nothing more than a dead body?

A second transmission would change the game, though.

Given the message Kitchell had decoded, it was clear this species understood radio communications. Torrance wanted to see how much Louratna knew.

When she came next, he diagrammed the planet with two stick figures on it—their default symbol for the two of them. He pointed to the figure that was himself, and said "Torrance." Then he pointed the other figure, and said "Louratna."

She nodded.

He pointed to the planet. "What is?" he said, using a phrase he used to ask an identity.

"Esgarat," she said, starting with understanding. She pointed to the three. "Torranze, Louratna, and Esgarat."

"Outstanding." He smiled, drinking from his water bowl. It was good to have a name for where he was.

"Outstanding!" she replied with a phrasing that was almost right. She seemed as excited as he was.

He proceeded to diagram Alpha Centauri A and B.

"Eldoro and Katon," he said.

Louratna clicked in her positive way.

He drew a representation of another system on the far edge of the slate. "Earth," he said, pointing to the planet. "Sol," he said, pointing to the sun. Louratna studied him and then the diagram.

"Eldoro," he said, pointing to Alpha Centauri A. "Sol," he said, pointing to the other.

She clicked a positive.

"Earth," he said, pointing. "Esgarat."

All three of Louratna's eyes got huge. She grabbed a chalk and made a figure on Earth, then drew a line between that figure and the Torrance figure on Esgarat. "Torranze," she said. "Earth," the last word coming out *Eart*.

Torrance nodded. "Yes, yes! Torrance is from Earth."

He picked up a rock, then took it to one side of the chamber. He hesitated a moment, hoping his example of putting abstract concepts like messaging into simple terms would work, then spoke to the rock. "Hello, Louratna," he said. After that was done, he marked it with chalk, then gently tossed it across the room. After it clattered to the floor, he walked to the rock, picked it up, and put it to his ear, repeating "Hello, Louratna!"

He looked up and smiled.

He repeated it, going the other way.

Louratna was still deeply engaged, though perhaps she just thought he was going desert crazy. She twisted her lips as if she was thinking, then went to the slate and methodically drew a horizontal line, then several intersecting lines that made it look like a fishbone diagram, or a numerical table without the border. She put a cap on the upper right table leg, then the lower leg of the next vertical line, then on the upper of the next, continuing back and forth until each vertical axis was marked. When she was finished, she looked at him with an expression he thought was expectation.

Was she saying that she understood wave oscillation?

He went to the water bowl and put his finger in the middle, causing ripples to cascade to the sides of the bowl.

Louratna chalked a quick diagram in the form she always used to represent an equation: vertical line for an equivalency, each side weighted. The wave equation was a partial differential, and it didn't seem like she had the specifics down right, or at least not in a way he understood, but it was obvious her concept was there. What she had drawn was clearly a power function that used time and distance in an attempt to define the wave.

He nearly laughed in glee.

He wondered if Louratna understood amplitudes and phases, and assumed she had to. If they actually made radio work, quadar mathematics had to go beyond the high concept.

Torrance had to be sure, though.

He went to the slate and drew a fishbone line between Esgarat and Earth, then capped it as she had. He put a hand on Earth, and the side of his ear onto his hand. "Hello, Louratna," he said in the direction of Esgarat.

Louratna went to the diagram and did the same thing with Esgarat.

"Hello, Torranze!" she called.

He grinned.

Amazing.

Yes, the quadars clearly had radio.

Now he just had to find it.

He went to the slate and circled the figure that represented himself several times, then drew a wave line to Earth. He put the rock back to his ear.

"Hello, Earth?" he said, his gaze glued to Louratna's.

She hesitated.

He grasped the rock harder, and pointed to the figure of himself again. "Torrance call Earth?"

"*Ohna*," Louratna said, using the quadarti term for negative.

Her face clouded. She picked up the chalk and went to the slate.

After a few moments of thought, she drew a boxlike formation beside Torrance's stick figure. From that she made a wave form.

"That's a transmitter," he said. "Take me to the transmitter."

"Transmitter," Louratna said, then added her own word.

"Yes, transmitter," he replied, holding the rock to his ear again. "Hello, Earth?"

Louratna clicked in a gentle fashion. "*Ohna,*" she said. Then she leaned over and drew lines over the image of the transmitter. When she was done, she used the meat of her palm and cleared the whole image away.

Torrance swallowed hard.

"I see," he said. "The transmitter is dead."

"Dead," Louratna replied.

It was clear she didn't really understand the words he used, but it was just as clear that his assessment of her message was correct. Whatever equipment the quadars had used to hail the Solar System was no longer in existence.

He sighed and took a seat, staring at the slate with its messy diagrams.

Torrance felt hollow then. The skin across his whole body tingled with a sensation that he hadn't felt before. The room was oddly silent, and the dim light and dark shadows added to the disjointed sensations that were playing over his mind.

The quadars understood radio, but if Louratna was telling the truth, they didn't have anything powerful enough to provide for interstellar communication.

He put his head in his hands.

Despite Louratna's presence, he felt oddly alone.

CHAPTER 32

Baraq lay on his belly, stretched out over a flat table, his hands and ankles tied.

A medic had tended to his gunshot wound, but mostly to ensure he didn't die. He had been only lightly stitched, the wound fresh and still open to the air. It hurt just to breathe.

The interrogation room was in the second floor of the Family's secondary tower, a distance away from the central nervous system of the compound. He was positioned so he could see out a small window and take in the city as Eldoro rose—a fact Baraq assumed was on purpose. Xian's Tower stood in the distance. Smoke rose from fires around the area, probably *hedgies* and others of lower families still working to burn bodies. The air was already growing hot.

Tierra sat on a chair beside the window, draped in his Family robe and drinking from a bowl. He had a new guard with him, a huge and unnervingly quiet quadar who loomed above Baraq at an anxiety-creating angle.

"Where is the creature?" Tierra said, his voice sharp and direct.

"I don't know," Baraq replied.

"I hope you'll understand why I don't believe that's true, Baraq."

"I can't help what you think."

Tierra nodded to the assistant.

The quadar pressed a metal probe against his wound. Baraq groaned and clenched his body against the pain.

"That's how it's going to be?" he said once he had recovered.

"Not if you tell me what I want to know. The creature was stolen by outside forces. We know that much."

Baraq said nothing.

"Does the name Louratna mean anything to you?"

Baraq took a breath, but again said nothing.

Tierra nodded, and Baraq suffered again. The vision in all three eyes blurred.

"How is Father?" Baraq asked.

Tierra smirked and clicked in a way that indicated disinterest. "I'm sorry about Brada," he replied. "It's a tragedy that had to be."

Baraq recoiled. The acid in his first stomach ate at his throat.

"It makes sense that you were protecting him, Baraq. We understand that, even as we see it for the lack of loyalty it was. It had to be hard to see your own whelp bending so far from the Family." Tierra rose from the chair and went to the window. He sighed, taking in the rising plumes of smoke. "But you were the adult, right, Baraq, and that means…?"

Baraq refused to tell Tierra what he wanted to hear. He clenched his fist and pulled against the restraints.

They did not give, and the effort hurt.

"Brada was his own quadar," Baraq said. "It was something I admired him for." The statement made him feel stronger. Even though it was too late, it felt right to stand behind his boy.

Tierra turned from the window, clicked sadly, and bent to address Baraq.

"Brother," he said. "You are going to tell us where the creature is. The only variable is time."

Then the pain came again.

CHAPTER 33

Torrance heard shuffling and voices outside, so he was already standing as the quadar entered. He was wearing a set of odd-fitting pants and a wraparound shirt the quadars found fashionable. The ensemble was comfortable enough, and made him feel more like he belonged here.

"Hey, it's my tour guide. Is it time for my walk?"

Torrance learned the second in command's name was Crissandr, but he had taken to calling her his tour guide because after the third time it was clear that her job was to take Torrance to the surface—which made him feel a little like a dog, but not so much that he was willing to bite the hand that fed him.

"*Teckto,*" she said, bending her knees.

"*Teckto,*" he said. It was a word she used often, a phrase accompanied by a hollow click from her front teeth. "Does that mean walk?" he said aloud. "Or exercise?" It felt strange to talk to the quadars this way. He knew they couldn't understand him, but it felt better to speak.

She took him to the opening again.

It was cooler today than the other days, but that wasn't saying much.

He was feeling stronger now. His wounds were healing, and *teckto,* whatever it was, was helping his frame of mind. Torrance's sunburns had peeled and grown back, then peeled again. Its constant pain had faded to a low ache before eventually being replaced by incessant itching that was almost as annoying as the pain. The skin left behind was marked with brown splotches that looked like connect-the-dot patterns he used to play with as a kid.

Alpha Centauri A's radiation was clearly intense.

Everything here kills you, Torrance thought as he sat at the edge of the cave's mouth, staring out over the landscape. *The official travel slogan of Esgarat.*

Despite that cheerful thought, Torrance considered walking away. The drop to the ground was only three or four meters, and he could mostly slide down. He could easily survive that. His guards weren't really guarding him, either. What would Crissandr do if he just got up and walked away?

Without thinking, he pushed off the rock, and slid down the cliff face.

The landing was rougher than he expected. A cloud of dry dust made it difficult to breathe again, but he made it.

Voices came from above.

Crissandr and another of the quadars scowled at him from the mouth of the cave, both obviously unhappy, but neither taking any action to stop him. In fact, after the scolding, Crissandr stood with arms crossed, glaring at him more like a mother than a guard. Above him, the cliff face rose like a heavy gate and seemed to grow even taller until he thought it might fall over and squash him any minute. The heat of suns pressed in on him.

He understood then.

He was "free" to go here, but really, there wasn't any place around where he would be able to survive on his own.

The guard lowered a rope made of some heavy root-twine. He grabbed it, and pushed against the wall as the guard pulled him up. He pulled himself over the lip, and sat again. When he turned to apologize to Crissandr, he found her looking at his forearms, which had become uncovered and bare as his robe fell away. She reached over, and pulled the arm of his sleeve back to reveal dark freckles.

Crissandr clicked and clacked and looked up at the guard.

The two exchanged conversation which ended in the word *Louratna*, and the guard immediately turned to leave.

It felt like he was being sent to the principal's office.

Louratna was in Torrance's chamber when they returned. She spoke a sharp phrase and came to his side. Crissandr reached Torrance's arm and raised it. His sleeve fell back.

"What's wrong?" he said, as Louratna drew near and scanned his arm. She twisted it around to let her see the opposite side. Then she scanned his face, which was lined, too, but not as marked as his arm. She raised a hand to run through his hair.

Torrance pulled away.

"What's wrong?" he said.

Louratna made the word for *dark*, and pointed at his arm. He raised it up, and she traced lines between his blemishes.

"Freckles," he said.

She repeated the word, then spoke to Crissandr, who went to the door and brought in another quadar Torrance didn't remember seeing before. He was a staff worker of some type—the most obvious element of his appearance was a set of three dark bulbs that were growing on his face, two on the side of one cheek, the other on the bridge of his nose.

Torrance then saw the rest of the quadar's face was covered in blemishes.

Louratna spoke, and the quadar raised his own sleeve to show his arm was also covered in "freckles," only much, much worse.

"Skin cancer," Torrance said, the facts dawning on him.

He locked eyes with the quadar, and saw fear.

He glanced to Louratna and saw a similar expression.

"How many?" he said to her. It was a phrase in their shared vocabulary.

"Many," she replied.

Torrance sat down and leaned back against the cold rock wall.

It made sense.

The meteorological models he and Kitchell had run said that as the wormhole drained material from the quadars' sun, the planet would cool at first, causing the cloud cover to condense out in rain, then without its reflective base to protect it, the surface would heat up for a while as its atmosphere changed. Kitchell's most sophisticated models had predicted it, and this was what was happening now. If his process was right, then most likely, the atmosphere would soon begin to blow away in a fashion similar to what had happened with Mars. Eventually, Eden—Esgarat—would wind up a cold, tundra-like desert.

But they hadn't considered the short-term effects on life-forms in anything more than the abstract.

Neither Torrance nor Kitchell had considered what unfettered light from Alpha Centauri A would do to life on a planet that had never seen the intensity of the raw ultraviolet spectrum. The quadars hadn't evolved the kinds of melanin or whatever natural protections they would need to protect themselves. If this worker was a standard example, they were suddenly being burned up.

All he had really been thinking about was trying to save the quadars before the sun got too cold to support life—which in theory was a generational kind of problem. But the fact was, the quadars probably didn't have that kind of time.

Torrance looked at Louratna, and for the first time realized that she knew what was happening. She understood that if they didn't do something soon, the entire population of the Esgarat could die.

CHAPTER 34

Tierra provided food. Baraq ignored it, drinking water only. It wasn't because he wanted to die that he kept himself from eating. Instead it was only that his intake of food was one thing he could control. It also helped that his abstinence made Tierra angry. His brother tried to get Baraq to eat, force-feeding him at one point.

Tierra questioned him each day, berated him, had his anonymous guard inflict pain of multiple flavors.

"Please stop the silliness," Tierra pleaded with him on the fourth day, or was it the fifth? "We can do this forever."

Baraq lay limply on the bare tabletop, the straps still burning raw circles around his wrists and ankles, the hard surface like a rock on his chest and his bleeding cheekbone. He missed Crissandr. That was the only regret he had left now. The punishment his brother had enacted on Baraq's body had helped him atone for the blind support he had given his father, and if Baraq died, that debt would finally be paid. But there was nothing he could do to atone for reneging on his promise to always be there for her.

He couldn't let Tierra know that, though.

It was all he had left to live for.

"You're the one being silly, brother," Baraq finally gasped, spitting blood. "You think I'll break, but I have nothing to break over. You've already taken everything I care about."

Tierra grimaced.

"Just imagine what Father would say if he were here now?" Baraq added, then laughed. It was a dry laugh, the only kind he had left. It helped him bring up the image of his father and see his Family in its whole light.

For the first time, then, Tierra took the metal bar from his assistant, and beat Baraq himself.

It was a short violence.

Three poundings across the back and buttocks that brought wincing pain, but resulted in his brother storming out.

When the attendant also left the room, Baraq laid his head down and closed his blood-drenched eyes.

Victory had been painful, yes, but it was still sweet.

There was poetic value in it being Jee who carted him away.

Baraq was probably twelve rocks lighter than he had been the night he had been shot, maybe eighteen. It made Jee's job easier—lift him up and throw him on a cart, then wheel him away in the dim light of near-dark. Not that it really mattered now, Baraq supposed. Unlike earlier, when Ranya Waganat would have used darkness to cover Family discord, Tierra had fewer such cares and the Families were running things now anyway. He used darkness only because it was here. Jee did nothing to hide his actions, didn't work to reduce the squealing of the cart's wheels or take any steps to cover his movement. Just pushed the cart through the tower and wheeled him through the manor span to the elevator shaft, then managed the controller that took them down.

Baraq lay on the cart, arms dangling, body bleeding and exposed for all to see.

He knew where he was going.

Though it had always been held secret, Baraq has seen his Family operate.

He understood that when commerce was being disrupted his father would bring partners or rivals or subjects, or any other quadar required, into one of these rooms to have a "conversation." Assuming that conversation resulted in the agreement he wanted, Ranya Waganat would straighten his Family robes and leave the room alongside his "collaborator." Things would be fine.

If it did not go so well, however, there were more steps—a scale of coercion that could include pain, extortion, being put in a "guest room" of the kind Baraq had been in for as long as it took, or, worst of all, sent to the catacombs of the caves below the compound. That last happened rarely because, as Ranya Waganat would joke while lifting his favorite *katja* wine among compatriots, "it was generally unnecessary."

But it happened.

And when it happened, Baraq understood exactly how unlikely it was for any quadar to return to the surface alive.

Today he was being moved to the catacombs.

Which was exactly where he had wanted to go.

CHAPTER 35

Torrance straightened up. His head cocked itself to the side. As his gaze bounced back and forth between Louratna and the sick quadar, a truth began to dawn. It made sense that they would keep him for observation and even examination; that's what the United Governments would do if an unknown species from another system dropped into the Solar System. But Louratna wasn't really examining him, now, was she?

She was spending time on him. Working with him.

Almost training him.

He looked at the sick quadar and flashed again on others he had seen. Was the entire planet sick like this?

"What are you doing," he said to Louratna, but she clearly didn't understand.

He went to the slate.

"This," he said, picking it up. "And this," he said, motioning with his hand to indicate the two of them. "Now this," he said, moving toward the cancerous quadar so quickly that the poor thing shrunk back. Torrance showed the quadar his open palm, which seemed to calm him, then slowly reached to touch one of the dark lumps.

"What is?" he said to Louratna, arcing an eyebrow. "Why?"

The quadar's expression set in a way Torrance hadn't seen before. Anger? Resolution? Determination? Resignation? After several beats, her face relaxed.

"Come," she said in her language.

She led him through a set of passages that twisted into the mountain, Louratna ahead, Torrance next, Crissandr behind.

The going was tougher here, the rock rough-hewn, the walls covered in patches of luminous moss. They pushed through splits and teetered on a natural bridge, Torrance growing fatigued and panting with more exertion than he was used to.

"I don't know if I'll be able to make it back," he said out loud.

Louratna smiled and used a word he figured meant *old man*.

Whether he was right or not, he laughed and she seemed to appreciate that.

At one point, the passageway grew dark, so they sandwiched him to walk forward, his chest pressing against Louratna, Crissandr pressing from behind.

It was a strange feeling, like floating in the darkness, alone, but connected to these two other beings in ways he had never felt connected before. *"Close your eyes and let yourself fall,"* he remembered a faceless instructor telling him at an Academy team-building class. He was supposed to trust that the people behind him would catch him—which he had, but only because the instructor was there. This, however, was different. He felt Louratna's concern for him and heard the caution they spoke with as they shared progress points.

Maybe the quadars' eyes saw infrared or maybe a spectrum of ultralow energy given by all matter. Maybe they saw the strong force, or some other radiant energy spectrum. He didn't know how they saw, but he was certain they *did* see because they guided him well enough to make it through the cave. As they moved together, Louratna's pulse came through heating plates that pressed against his chest, and the protective shield of Crissandr's arms wrapped around his shoulders.

Finally they came to a dimly lit finger of the cave, and took it.

After total darkness the illumination seemed bright.

The caves grew colder as they descended. He was happy for the robes, and wished they weren't cut high in the places that quadars had their back plates.

"Where the hell are we going?" he said out loud, but Louratna just led them further.

———

Eventually, they came to a shaft where the floor grew wide enough for several quadars to walk side by side. A warmer breeze of fresh air blew from somewhere ahead of them, and electric lights were now spaced widely along the way, green lichen growing in fan-shaped patterns on the wall above each.

Louratna stopped in a small chamber with scalloped walls.

"*Anjinoba tra*," she said, around the area. The phrase seemed important.

"*Anjinoba tra*," Torrance repeated.

Louratna picked up a rock and handed it to Torrance. It was veined in green, dull bronze, and black.

"*Anjinoba*."

"Copper?" he thought out loud, or maybe silver. He would have to test it to be sure. Chemistry had never been his strength. Too much like magic, not enough like math. Whatever it was, though, the walls showed signs of a lot more ore.

"Copper," Louratna repeated with an uncertain angle to her expression. "*Anjinoba*."

He shrugged. Maybe that was right. Maybe not.

Communication was frustrating.

They went on. Not knowing what to do with the rock, he slipped it into a pocket. She led them down a set of stairs cut from the rock, through corridors, and down more stairs.

The smell of something burning wafted upward. The pass bent around a shallow depression where the odor became even thicker and laced with the tang of ammonia and metal. Mechanical grinding came from the opening. Clangs of pickaxes rang out, and mallets against rocks. Voices called, too. It all melded into a single symphony of industrial effort.

Torrance forgot about his aches and pains.

"*Adiago nar*," Louratna said, pointing to the end of the corridor. Next one.

They stepped through the opening, Louratna first, then Torrance, then the attendants.

The doorway opened onto a walkway built about halfway up the wall that overlooked a chasm below them, a chasm that was easily as large as a football field. A strange array of lighting of various types were jammed into crevasses and holes along the walls and ceiling— electrical systems, huge chemical glowsticks, and natural mosses that glowed with luminescence—a mix that made the place look like an old adventure vid. The overall effect was disorienting, almost oddly Victorian. He kept expecting to see some kind of weird sailing vessel hovering in open space, but what struck Torrance the hardest was how the feeling of standing on the platform brought him an eerily familiar sense of standing at the command station in *Everguard*'s Systems Command all those years ago.

Unlike Systems Command's perfect order, though, the chamber was a dark and dirty mess.

A dusty haze hung in the center of the area. The walls were of striated stone running with dark veins. The floor appeared to be divided into six sections, each being worked by quadars who were sweating in the heat. Three sections were separated by walls. Off to one side, a blackened tank the size of a small school bus dominated the largest work area, a pair of doors opened to reveal a raging fire.

It was a boiler, Torrance realized. An oven of some kind.

A ramp fed the tank from above, and hoses appeared to bring other liquids into the machine. A quadar worked to scoop material into the doors. The sounds that came from the thing were raw against the ears.

The output was a straight tube of molten metal.

Three aliens stood at the output end of the tank, arguing and pointing animatedly at what could only be a mold.

Torrance's jaw stood agape.

It was some kind of smelting and casting operation.

Once he saw that, other pieces began to fall into place.

The station closer to him was clearly an assembly area. Benches and tables were littered with equipment and instruments. Grinders, polishers, hand tools, and an interesting device that he realized would probably work as an industrial-grade vise filled a section of their own.

"Jesus Christ," he muttered. "What is this place?"

Louratna clicked and grunted, then led him down to the work floor. Her gait and her posture as she crossed the open space reminded him of a captain's or an admiral's. Working quadars noted her passing, and she greeted them, apparently by name.

They clicked and nodded back.

She brought them to a large "shed," open on one side, but built up with set-rock on three others. The shed was maybe three stories tall, without a ceiling of its own. Louratna led them around the corner and to the open side.

It was a roughly rectangular space, marked off by tables.

No quadars were in the area at that moment.

At each corner, support structures held spools of cable that looped around huge pulleys then rose to the cavern's ceiling to roll over a collection of additional pulleys before falling together at the central area of this room to connect up to a harness that held a large device suspended in midair.

Torrance stepped forward, his heart pounding.

Hair rose on the back of his neck.

It could only be one thing.

A rocket engine.

The quadars were trying to build a rocket engine.

CHAPTER 36

The sound of footsteps was so slight that Baraq, as he lay in a fetal position on the cold floor, thought he felt their vibrations rather than heard them. As always, the basket was placed in the slot. It smelled of hard bread and mashed *havra* root. There was meat there, too. Probably *kax*. A bowl of water was set beside the basket.

The food's presence made Baraq's stomach twist.

"I wish you would eat," a thin voice said. "It makes me sad that you don't eat."

The server was a whelpling, Baraq realized. Probably one of what had to be hundreds of *hedgies* who found themselves without parents or siblings. The Family would pick through them, selecting the healthy ones and the ones who could work, and leaving the weak and diseased to whatever natural result would come.

The idea that the whelpling was alone hurt.

Whelplings had no context of the world to fall back on. Nothing to push ideas against. No way to understand why they were in the situations they suddenly found themselves in. They couldn't understand why one heat they had a da and ma, and the next heat they did not.

On the other hand, Baraq thought with a stab of cynicism, maybe it was better to not know.

No. That could never be true.

Anger rose in him. He could hear Brada scolding him. "A quadar needs to understand things if they're going to make a difference," his son would say if he were here in this cell. "And a quadar has the right to know what things make a difference."

Baraq would never doubt that again.

That was why he was here, after all. He looked at the basket and decided it was time to start.

"What is your name?" he said, pushing himself to a sitting position.

"Pella," the whelpling replied.

A female. Someone's daughter.

"I'll make you an agreement," Baraq said.

"An agreement?"

"A deal."

The whelpling came closer to the slot.

"All right," she said. "What kind of agreement?"

"I will promise to eat my food if you will stay and listen to my stories."

"What kind of stories?"

"Very important stories," Baraq said. "Full of secrets."

"What kind of secrets?"

"The best kind, of course. The kind that have to be kept."

The small gap of the slot flashed with the sight of the whelpling's eyes. It made him wish he could see her fully, but he was too weak now to do such moving.

He could feel interest rising through Pella's silence, though.

"All right," she said. "Eat, then I'll listen to a story."

"No," Baraq said. "First you get the story, then I eat."

"What if I listen, then you don't eat?"

"Then don't listen next heat."

In better times, the sound of the whelpling's exasperated sigh would have made him smile.

"Same time," she said. "You tell me the story while you're eating."

"You are a good negotiator," he said. "I like that. It means there is hope for the future."

"Is it an agreement?"

"Yes," he said. "We have an agreement."

He reached the tray down, enjoying the tone Pella had used to form the word *agreement*. That was a grown-up word to her, and her tone said she was proud to be using it. The food was heavy enough he needed both hands to keep the tray steady. The smell of the food was now overpowering.

He sipped the water. It filled his entire body.

As he chewed bread, the sound of Pella's rustling told Baraq that the whelpling was settling down.

"Go ahead," she said. "I'm ready."

Baraq swallowed.

He put his head back against the wall and began.

"Once upon a time, there was a very brave young whelp named Brada who lived in the middle of one of the most powerful Families on all of the Esgarat. One day, he decided that he didn't like things he was seeing. So he decided to make a change…"

CHAPTER 37

Torrance stood at the base of the engine, literally too stunned to move.

It was a small system, perhaps three meters tall and no more than one in diameter.

He touched the flared cone of the exhaust section. The design was primitive—it had almost no fueling coil, and an overly simple chamber to handle combustion. It wouldn't last a minute before it ate itself up. And that was just the beginning of problems he saw with just a simple glance.

He looked around the room for an idea of the size of the final rocket.

A rounded section leaned against a nearby wall. Its curvature said it was probably only far enough around to contain just the one engine.

Like the wormhole pod.

He smiled.

The problems weren't the quadars' fault, of course. Human beings had developed their fundamental approach to rocketry over a period of fifty years or so. At best, this species had only thirty, and that was if they had started the minute the wormhole pod had landed. Beyond that, they were starting everything with a cliff event of what was almost certainly new technology for them—they were dealing with an insertion of new product rather learning concepts through an organic process of trial and error.

He looked at the engine as it hung in the air like a totem to the future.

What fuel were they using? What kind of thrust were they getting? Where did they test? How were they mixing their materials to handle the higher exhaust temperatures?

He sat on a bench, unable to take his eyes off the engine despite his fatigue.

Louratna sat beside him, also staring. Her lips curled into an expression he understood was a smile. The heat of her body felt good beside him. She said something to a worker who had come around the corner, and from a far corner the worker retrieved a box that was almost too big to carry.

He sat it on the floor in front of Torrance.

Torrance looked at her, then opened the box.

Inside was a rounded piece of equipment. He recognized it immediately.

The MCU, Multidimensional Compressor Unit—the guts of the wormhole trigger. It was a piece of the equipment he had sent here.

He took a deep breath and tried to control his emotions.

She focused all three eyes on him.

"Torranze *kasada*," she said, pointing at the engine.

Suddenly, he knew why she had been working with him so diligently.

Suddenly, he understood it all.

"Yes," he replied. "I'll work on it."

A SHELL ACROSS THE SKY

Eden: Esgarat Mountains
Local Date: Eldoro Leading, Year of First *Piela,* Cycle 57

CHAPTER 38

That night, Torrance sat with Louratna over dinner.

She brought him to a chamber that seemed to be an office or a war room of some sort, a roughly round gap dug from the mountain. At its back a shaft fell into darkness. To one side, a passage led a short distance to another open-air view that was even more spectacular than the one Torrance had been to before. Bits of hardware were scattered about, as were rolls of parchment of some type, each filled with markings and diagrams of their own. Slates were scattered about here, also, covered with more jotted notes in the quadars' language. One held a sketch of a full rocket.

The room had battery-powered lighting, but Louratna brought candles this time, which he was fairly sure she did because she thought it would please him. He didn't have the heart or the patience to tell her otherwise. Language expressing nuance of desires was difficult to share. He was tired now, and it was easier to just leave it be.

They ate at a table carved from raw rock. Its surface looked perfectly flat, perfectly smooth as it reflected the flickering flames of the candles with warmth that added to the heat of the evening.

Their dinner consisted of *janga* and *havra*, which always made him happy, and a thin tea Louratna had introduced to him earlier. It seemed to be without caffeine but still spiked his attention, which made him wonder what kind of thing he might be getting addicted to. Probably the least of his worries right now.

He was still trying to decide how to react to the rocket lab.

What were they planning to do? Where was the program overall? Obviously they had hardware.

Were they launching anything? Had they succeeded? Across the chamber, bent and charred remnants of a rocket fuselage suggested the opposite of success.

"How many?" he said, then he made a motion like a rocket lifting off.

Louratna clicked twice and made an offhand motion with her shoulder. Her face darkened and she made a rumbling sound, raising both hands up and wiggling her fingers.

"Boom," he said, seeing she was describing an explosion.

She clicked an affirmative, then shoveled food into her mouth and finished it.

"How many?"

"Many," she finally said.

"You're going to need a bigger rocket if you're going to get quadars off the planet," he said, with several minutes of effort.

Once she understood, Louratna gave a smile that was mostly in her eyes, an expression Torrance took as having as edge of derision, or maybe sarcasm. "Rockets," she replied using the word Torrance had taught her. "Not for quadars."

Something in her voice made him curious.

"*Quezata*," he replied. "Say more." It was a standard phrase he had been using to ask her to continue that line of thought.

"Rocket for Eldoro."

"Eldoro?"

"Alpha Cen A," Louratna replied, using Torrance's label. A smile spread across her face.

"Why?" he said in her language.

She seemed to struggle for a moment, then picked up the stone mug that held her tea. "Eldoro," she said, presenting it boldly. Slowly, she tipped the mug to allow a trickle of its liquid to fall to the floor. She brought her other hand in to tip the mug back up, stopping the flow. Then she held the cup upright again. "Eldoro," she said again. "*Mata.*"

Mata, Torrance thought. The same word they had used when Torrance said he was feeling good. *Mata.* As in *better. Mata* as in *healed.*

"I see," Torrance replied. An unbidden sense of embarrassment came over him. "You know our wormhole pod is draining your sun."

Louratna didn't comprehend his string of words, but this time he didn't try to get the idea across.

Torrance took a bite and a drink, not tasting either.

He had diverted the original pod here hoping that intelligence on the planet could learn about propulsion, and gain the concept that space flight was possible. He never really thought they might have the chops to reverse engineer its design concepts fully enough to determine the wormhole's true purpose. The idea that Louratna could do that was astounding, but here she was, explaining that humans were siphoning energy from their star, and here she was, telling him she was trying to save her planet by sending a rocket into that same star to break that connection.

"That's why you need me," he said, stopping himself in midchew.

Louratna waited.

"Of course," he mumbled. "You don't understand how that works."

The truth dropped like a dud in his stomach.

Despite years of listening to the UG's top scientists discuss the high-order math required to develop and produce multidimensional structures that supported wormholes, Torrance knew he didn't have the capacity to understand the specifics. He had no idea how to destroy the links. Beyond that, Torrance couldn't say what the star was connected to now. Was it a black hole or a squadron of Star Drive spacecraft? Either way spelled doom for the quadars, but he suspected that breaking the links to one or the other required different approaches. Neither one of which he had any idea of how to build.

"I'm sorry," Torrance said. "I don't know how."

Louratna's face fell.

From the corner of his eye, he took in the burned fuselage.

He put his hands on the table. The hard surface felt alive, making his fingers feel as if they went all the way to the core of the planet. He knew Esgarat had a metallic core, like Earth, and that somewhere below this rocky surface were rivers of water the planet breathed upward as vapor. He knew quadars "mined" that water for self-preservation and better quality of life.

He reached for his own mug, thinking about where the water that made the tea came from.

As he held the mug up, the sleeve of his robe fell off his arm to expose his weathered freckles. The image of the cancer-beaten quadar came to him.

Torrance looked at Louratna, again.

He couldn't break the wormhole link.

And he was sure the quadars couldn't build a space program that would get the quadars off the planet anytime soon.

But as he stared at his arm, another idea began to form.

CHAPTER 39

araq drank the last of the water Pella had placed next to his basket. He felt better today. To the best of his ability to tell, it had been three heats since Tierra had last come to beat information from him, which had given him time to heal. The gun wound was covering up reasonably well after the medic's help earlier, and the lunches the whelp had brought had been nearly fresh.

The rustling of her shift as she fidgeted was loud in the otherwise still cell chamber.

Despite the rise in his spirits, he was glad she couldn't see him now. He had to look a fright.

"So they killed him?" Pella said from the other side of the wall.

He had just finished the final segment of his story about Brada's murder.

"Yes," Baraq replied.

"That's what I thought would happen." She clicked the essence of certainty.

Baraq clicked in return. "So you've heard the tale before."

"One like it."

"Then why did you let me tell it all?"

"It made me happy to know you were eating," Pella said. "And it helped me remember my da and ma because they always talked about those stories when we would have dinners together."

"Is that so."

"But theirs was always about someone named Lelo."

Baraq coughed at the name.

"I see."

"His stories were always about fighting against the Families, too."

"Yes, I suppose the two have many similarities."

For a moment the only sound was the scurrying of a rock lizard somewhere in the depths of the nearby cave system. It made Baraq think of when he was a boy and would get himself "lost" exploring those caves. There were hundreds of places to go in them—thousands. He closed his eyes and recalled scaling sheer surfaces far down in ancient shafts that no one went to anymore. He hadn't been supposed to spend time there. The mines were long dead. The passages had no access to water. His mother had made it known just how much trouble he would get if he were to be caught inside them.

So he made sure he was never caught.

"My ma and da went to hear stories about Lelo," Pella said. "And brought them back to our home. They talked about him all the time. But the Families killed him."

"They have a tendency to do that."

"They killed my ma and da, too. So now I don't hear those stories anymore."

Baraq cleared his throat.

"Did your parents like Lelo?"

The hesitation was short, but noticeable. "They believed in him."

"Maybe that's even better."

"I don't know. I like it better when people like me. It's good to have friends."

"Yes, it's very good to have friends."

"I'm your friend," Pella said. "Are you mine?"

"Be careful asking me that, Pella. I'm not sure I make a very good friend."

"I like your stories."

"Would you like to bring Lelo back to life?"

"You can't bring a quadar who's dead back to life."

"You can when that quadar is an idea."

"What?"

"Lelo might be dead," Baraq said. "But the ideas he stood for continue on as long as there's someone alive to carry them even just a little bit further. As long as those ideas are alive, Lelo will roll right on."

Pella paused. Baraq felt her appraise his words.

"I don't understand," she said. "How can I bring Lelo back?"

"Next time you come in here, bring me a copy of the key, and I promise you that Lelo will return."

"I will get skinned if I leave you the key."

"Not *the* key," Baraq said. "A copy of it."

"How do I get that?"

Baraq smiled to himself. "As you leave, steal the key for just long enough to take it to a person I know…when he's done, return the original to the ledge it's on so no one is the wiser. Then, tomorrow bring the copy with you and slide it in to the cell along with the basket. You do this, and I promise that Lelo will return."

"I see," she said, thinking.

"There is a guard who comes to inspect the area after you leave. I hear him pass the corridor. If you are nimble, though, there is time."

Baraq thought he could hear Pella's thoughts as they jumbled.

"Will you do that?"

"It is something my da and ma would have done," she said. "So, yes. I'll do that."

He slid the basket and his empty water bowl back through the slot.

In another moment, Pella was gone, the door shut behind her.

CHAPTER 40

It took Torrance three full days to describe the project.

"We don't need to get a rocket to Eldoro," he finally got across. "Instead, we just need to get to the upper atmosphere."

Then he had to describe the function of aerosols as a controller—the use of scattered particles in the upper atmosphere to reflect more of their dual suns' light from the planet to artificially cool it, which would then, if he was right, serve two purposes. First, it would slow the rate of atmospheric dispersal—cooler molecules moved more slowly and served to protect the planet's atmosphere by keeping it in the gravity well. Second, denser air and the resulting increase in cloud cover would cut the intensity of the UV light, which would reduce the rate quadars might be getting the cancers they were suffering.

Neither was perfect, of course. Neither would solve the problem completely. But it was a process that had worked to save the Earth from its own problems a hundred fifty years ago. Given that the planet was ripe with sulfur he hoped it would serve a reasonable facsimile of the result here. Together, these two things could serve to extend the life of the planet for long enough that, if Kitchell or someone else actually managed to wrangle support for a rescue mission, and assuming UG's spaceships were still attached to the star, humanity might get here and start to work on the problem—a time period that, given the time it would take radio signals of his earlier transmissions to travel, Torrance figured could be a decade or longer when you add in the bureaucratic nonsense that would go into scheduling.

If nothing else, this might give him enough time to work on a new transmitter, but, again, one step at a time.

The whole thing was all a long shot, but it was better than nothing.

Regardless, once they got here, Interstellar Command and the United Government could fix this.

There were ways, after all.

They could move the quadars, or run a link to funnel fusing material from another star into Alpha Centauri A, dumping it in at double the rate it was being used. They could set new links and break these. He was sure better scientists could come up with better solutions.

Once he had properly conveyed the entirety of the mission to her, Louratna took it on as fully as if it was her own.

"Build a shell across the sky," she called it.

"I like that," he said.

After she understood, they realized they had two separate problems—the rocket itself and the aerosol delivery mechanism.

"You stay on rocket," Louratna said. "I can work on shell."

It was a proposal that made sense. Louratna already knew the math and production techniques she needed to devise an aerosol distribution system, but she was still flying blind in the arena of rocketry.

"Deal," Torrance said.

The biggest problem was communication.

Torrance had picked up enough of the quadars' language to be able to handle the basics of subsistence, but developing a rocket required him to build an entirely new vocabulary. Learning it was a painstakingly slow process.

The second hurdle was the fact that very few quadars were as adept at even basic mathematics as Louratna was. To make it worse, many didn't seem to care to learn. Instead, they fell back on trial and error, a process that drove Torrance completely bonkers. Without a common approach, Torrance had difficulty catching errors until it was too late. This meant they left rocket carcasses scattered all over the desert floor.

The third problem was the state of the quadars' manufacturing capability.

They had basic metallurgy, and rudimentary finishing capability, but their machining processes were mostly hand-operated, meaning they lacked precision and weren't reliably repeatable. Their electronics were simple components—resistors, capacitors, filters, and other basic circuitry that they strung together like a kid using building blocks.

Their fuel was a dirty form of kerosene mixed with a weak nitric acid they distilled out of ore from deep inside the mountain. They would be better off with liquid oxygen and hydrogen, but without a refrigerant, he had no way of developing a manufacturing facility for those fuels, and as he remembered hearing Kitchell say "you work with the chips you brought." So kerosene and nitric acid was the only ticket in town for now.

What he wouldn't give for some of the equipment from that Signal Processing Lab, though.

The quadars had electronics, but no counterpart to the quantum chip or optical processor. Hell, they hadn't even figured out the silicon chip, and silicon was a material they had plenty of.

Regardless, high-end computers were out of the question.

Torrance wouldn't let that stop them, though.

None of the first human spacecraft—neither Russian nor American—had computers to guide them. So instead of advanced systems, he decided to focus on inertial mechanics and basic ballistics, technology that fit the mission's real need just as well, anyway.

All he needed to do now was to get the rocket up into the outer reaches of the atmosphere.

Finally, however, there was the issue of the boundaries of Torrance's own knowledge.

He was a systems engineer, which meant he was at home exploring the interfaces between subsystems rather than necessarily understanding the details of each element of rocketry. He quickly became aware that his general understanding of the way things worked was a poor substitute for true expertise. He knew enough about materials, for example, to give broad-brush answers to their questions, but he didn't understand the nuances of what various chemical compositions of fuel did to the combustion process, so he struggled to calculate things like exhaust temperatures and heat transfer rates.

There was more, of course—a thousand other issues over a thousand other details.

The first failure—an explosion while still on the launching pad—was almost expected. Torrance even took some odd joy in watching the thing blow up. It felt like a badge of courage.

He worked around the clock and still there was more to do.

The second failure was aggravating, though.

He missed Kitchell. He missed his design teams. Working with smart people to come up with answers that were better than he could manage himself had an essence of magic to it that gave him energy. He enjoyed the structure of problem-solving that way: Everyone taking a part, each person's expertise not being enough to make it alone but somehow always necessary to achieve the final answer.

All he had now was Louratna, who was as sharp as any engineer he had ever worked with, maybe sharper, but who he still struggled to communicate with.

The third failure made Torrance begin to doubt himself.

Quadars sniped at him. Torrance lost patience. There was more trial and error. More systems that failed. Over and over again they made adjustments and tested. Again and again, again and again until the nearby desert became littered with shards of scrap metal and carcasses of destroyed rockets.

So, it was frustrating in many ways.

But in the end, Torrance realized he felt good.

He was doing important work.

Noble work, perhaps the work of his life.

Esgarat was dying, and if he failed, every quadar on the planet would pay the price.

So despite the daily struggles, despite the explosions on rocket pads that Louratna's crews had built far out over the desert's flat, dry surface, Torrance began to realize that for the first time he could ever really recall, he was truly happy.

CHAPTER 41

The door opened, then swung closed. A moment later, the whelp placed the basket into the slot, and Baraq hobbled the brief steps it took to painfully reach it down.

His ribs burned and his shoulders and arms were bruised. The welt on his cheek still throbbed and radiated pain, but he could see well enough, and as far as he could tell, his nasal passages were clear.

Tierra's assistant had avoided breaking his nose to ensure he could breathe, which made a certain ironic, sadistic sense in the Waganat playbook. They had avoided his gunshot wounds, too.

Probably medic's orders.

He gasped in pain as he took the basket and the bowl of water to his corner. It took both hands to hold them steady.

Later the heat before, after Pella had left, Tierra had brought his assistant to Baraq's cell.

The session was similar to the rest.

It started with questions, *where is the creature?* before leading to painful lashings along his back and legs, screams and whimpers, and blood that dripped to the floor. *Where is Louratna? Where is the creature?* As usual, it ended with Baraq being left to collapse in a pile in the corner.

One thing that was different this time, however, was that Baraq had gritted his teeth with each lash and let each blow draw his focus more tightly to memories of the cave systems. Each kick had given him thoughts of another chute or down-shaft, and when the guard punched his face, Baraq's mind filled with another passage that fleshed out the map he was creating in his head.

He could make it.

If he picked the right time, he could find his way down deep into those caves, and if he made it that far, he would make it out.

"I'm glad you are eating again," his brother had said as the guard locked the cell door behind him. "It makes me happy knowing you'll be around a while longer."

It was the sound of the key in the lock when they entered that made Baraq the happiest.

It meant Pella had been able to return it, assuming, of course, that Pella had lifted it in the first place. Had she stayed firm in her resolution?

He groaned as he squatted down, and he put the basket on his lap. Now that he was eating again, he was glad that the food smelled good. He lifted the cover and found semi-fresh bread and a container of cold root mash that had been laced with *pax* meat.

"Are you all right?" Pella asked.

In a fold of the covering, underneath the root mash, he saw the key. With a quick movement, he slipped it behind him and into his corner, then began to eat.

"Yes, Pella," he said, trying not to sound too grateful on the unlikely chance that a guard may be monitoring them. "I am quite fine now. Thank you very much."

"Will you tell me another story?"

Baraq chewed bread. "I don't know," he replied. "How about you tell me a story this time? Do you know any stories?"

"I don't think so."

"I'll bet you do."

"What do you mean?"

He swallowed the bread and sipped water.

"How about you tell me a story today that your da and ma used to tell you."

"What would you like to hear?"

"Maybe you tell me something you remember about Lelo, eh?"

"About Lelo?"

"Yes," Baraq said, closing all three eyes and thinking about the caves. "I would like that very much."

Pella's young voice filled his mind then. She told a tale of Lelo bringing dinner to friends of her parents. She said he listened and then spoke, said her parents had talked to the hosts and that the hosts had complained about a landslide of stones that had fallen into the pathway, how no motor carts could get in, so working quadars could only travel on foot. A heat later, she said, Lelo and a team of quadars had come and cleared the grounds.

When the story was finished, he sighed.

"Lelo said you can't wait for the council 'cause the council was broken, but that every quadar could do what they need to do, long as they aren't afraid to do it." Pella paused then, and Baraq thought she might be crying. "At least that's what my da said."

"It sounds like your da was a smart quadar."

"I think so."

Baraq thought about the story. He put the basket back in the slot, and finished the water.

"Will you do me another favor?" he asked quietly as she prepared to leave.

"What is it?"

"I need you to get a message to someone. It will help Lelo return."

"What is it?" she said.

"I can only tell you if you promise to give it to the right person. She might be hard to find."

Through the slot, he saw a touch of her, standing tall.

"All right," Pella said. "What is it?"

CHAPTER 42

Louratna stopped at Torrance's chamber each evening. Originally, it had been merely a quiet time where they could share news of progress on their various efforts. Eventually, they had grown into enjoying the time together simply as a way to pass a few moments without the constant stresses of the day intruding.

"Do you think," she said late one evening, "that there is life beyond?"

"I am proof of that, aren't I?" Torrance replied absently. He was very tired, and was struggling over reports from recent efforts to cast alloys that might be better suited to the high-pressure combustion chambers he needed.

"No...."

She went to a slate and marked the shorthand image they used to discuss the concept of time.

He looked into her fading primaries, understanding what she was really asking.

"You mean life after…"

She gave the warm click from the back of her throat. It was a sound he had grown to like. She marked a symbol of a quadar, then crossed it.

"After death," he said. "That's the word in English."

"After death," Louratna replied.

He nodded and gave his own click.

"We call it *indati*."

"*Indati*," he repeated until she clicked the affirmative.

"So, what do you think?" she said again.

He sighed.

The smell of incense in her robe was sharp. Anxiety was a mask over her expression.

He went to sit next to her and put his hand on her thigh. Then he gave his *I don't know* shrug. "It would be hard if this was all," he said, knowing that even after this time together it wouldn't translate well.

She lowered her head to rest on his shoulder.

They sat there like this for a very long time.

"How old are you, Louratna?" He looked at her. "How many years," he said, knowing she understood those words. He put his hand on her shoulder. "Louratna." Then pointed to the symbol for time, hoping she would understand the question.

"One hundred and ninety-two cycles of Esqarat about Alpha Centauri A," she said with something that might have been pride.

Torrance squeezed her knee. "That's a good number."

She shook her head. "Maybe," she said. It was a word they used often when they were projecting if a design would work. They found themselves mixing their languages often, choosing the word or phrasing that was easiest over the more complex.

"Maybe?"

"Before we feared only the council, or the Families. Now…" She shrugged her shoulders and her central went foggy.

Torrance nodded and tried to click to say he understood.

He had picked up some of the quadars' politics through gossip among the manufacturing teams, and from discussions with Crissandr and Louratna. He knew Families were a political structure and that the council made of Families controlled the whole flow. As an ambassador, he understood the complexities of that kind of situation, but he also found that working as an engineer made it so much easier to ignore that aspect of this society for now that he didn't care.

Torrance knew, however, that Crissandr had once been part of a Family.

He knew she had suffered some fate at the hand of that Family.

It also didn't take an Academy valedictorian to know that these quadars living under Louratna's roof considered themselves outcasts of some sort—not trustworthy, not trusted to be *working of the Families,* whatever that meant. At one point, Louratna spent an evening describing how they had kidnapped Torrance from the Families so that he could work on the rocket, and, if what Louratna told him was even close to the truth, he now understood that the quadar species as a whole had just now undergone some kind of horrific war or coup or other conflict over a collection of causes, among them the question of how to deal with the technology he had dropped into their midst.

"I am old, Torrance," she said. "Quadarti expect me to save them from things they don't understand."

Torrance stroked her rough-skinned hand, then reached around to rub the muscles of her neck. Louratna closed her eyes and gave a pleasant moan.

"I think after death is a place where we all live together," Torrance said.

"I thought you said…" She gave his *I don't know* shrug.

"I change my mind about this kind of thing a lot."

"All human beings like this?" she said, using broken English.

He smiled and nodded. "Yeah—we're all very strange. Some of us talk to God often. Others only when they're in trouble."

She didn't follow, but he wasn't sure it mattered.

He also wasn't sure he wanted to get into a conversation about human spiritualism at this point.

Concern creased Louratna's face. The leathery folds under her eyes and the network of wrinkles that crossed her cheekbones made her look suddenly ancient and, at the same time, drew him to her. There was something timeless about this quadar, striving in a hidden mountaintop lab, working in isolation to find a way to save members of her species even if they didn't know about it, or maybe didn't even care.

He rubbed her knee and let her rest her head on his shoulder.

After a time, she reached out her bony hand to take his.

It felt…natural.

"Sometimes a philosopher is hard," she said.

Torrance smiled. "Yes, Louratna, it is hard to be a philosopher."

CHAPTER 43

After the padding of Pella's footsteps faded to nothing, Baraq reached the key, then stretched his hand through the slot as far as it would go. He was barely able to slip the key into the lock, but he made it. It turned with a satisfying click.

Having been sculpted and used by the Family for generations, the caves that fed the primary Waganat complex were generally wide and well maintained. Those that bled into the catacombs, however, were of an entirely different personality. They were harsh places of natural happenstance, tight and dangerous cuts through grimy rock, slants and shelves that shifted, crumbled, and fell in unpredictable ways. They housed insect hordes and cave lizards, and hundreds of species of multiarmed bugs, many of which Baraq ate as he came upon them. Shafts fell in haphazard places, and mineral deposits made climbing surfaces suddenly slick or smooth.

These caves had been a challenge when Baraq was a young quadar, but he was old now. His body was torn and beaten.

Darkness enveloped him, his central suddenly taking the lead, his primaries filling in details as made sense.

The pain of descending the first shaft drove into him.

His hands shook after finding the holds he needed to cross a chasm bridge.

He squeezed through a descending passage, and edged around a ledge that was barely half the width of his feet, leaving behind a trail of blood, skin, and parts of his torn garment. At one point he worried that his trail could be followed, but then thought better. Once Tierra realized where Baraq had gone, he would most likely laugh and decide to let the rock take him.

As he went, though, things got better.

Movement warmed him.

The feel of ancient rock under his outstretched fingers gave Baraq a sense of power that settled over him in some natural way that he couldn't fully describe. His ancestors had crawled from the rock ages before, and there was something ancient to the feel of stone under his fingers that was right and proper. When he pressed close into a tight wedge, he closed his eyes and stayed still for a long time, listening to the stone breathe and feeling the silent pulse below his chest. The idea of staying there and letting the rock take him came in a powerful wave. It would be so very easy to do.

Then the image of Brada came to him.

The memory of his whelp's body jumping with the impact of gunshots, and the image of blood running over his chest to pool under his fallen body.

Baraq opened his eyes, then. He clicked to the rock.

Show me the way, he said.

And then he listened as the rock replied.

Baraq climbed through the network of caves until he came to the crease in the foothills that he knew served as an exit point. Eldoro had set, but Katon was still high, so he rested, listening to the wind and the sounds of creatures scurrying outside until the darkness grew enough to obscure his features if not his presence.

A Family storehouse was nearby, one of fifteen the Waganats used to house product.

It would hold everything he was going to need now.

In the years Baraq ran his shop, he had often visited these storehouses to replenish his stocks. The thought reminded him of those days, each of the products sitting in different sections of his building.

Packing material was in the far back. Paint, required for so many projects, went on a central shelf that was done in a cylindrical fashion to enhance its aesthetic appeal. At least Crissandr said it would work that way, and she seemed to have been right about that. The explosives were held in a containment area out back, available by special request and with a special tax added if you were outside the Terilamat clan. Yards of cord would come already spooled from the factory, and the small timing devices that one of his cousins had devised many cycles back lined the wall behind the counter.

He had sold a lot of those timers, mostly to people who used them for cooking but some to inventors and chemists, others for whatever reasons a quadar might need to mark passage of time.

Though some things would surely have changed, he knew the storehouse layout as well as he remembered his own store's aisles, and he knew its base security systems.

As Baraq waited for darkness, he thought about Brada's views on violence.

Hearing his son talk had often been uncomfortable. It wasn't the idea of violence in general that caused him pain—Baraq understood self-defense—but his discomfort was brought on by his own perception of timing. He didn't like the idea of violence as a first resort, which was how he interpreted Brada's rhetoric.

"We're way past first offenses, Father," Brada told him one time. "The Families have been doing this for years."

But Baraq hadn't seen it like that. Not then, anyway.

It had been his own failing, of course.

Time changes everything, but different quadars move in different frames of time. Baraq lived in his own world—a first event for him could well be an epidemic to anyone else.

When it was finally dark enough, he forced his body to rise through its pain, and pushed his way through the gap to the surface.

Downhill and to his left was the storehouse.

A tent has been erected a short distance away, and a small camp fire was roasting something, downwind. As Baraq emerged, a form rose.

Baraq waited for her to come to him before speaking.

"Ezi," he said. "It's so good to see you."

Ezi pulled the hood off her head. Her face was sharply formed, her expression haggard and drawn. It was clear she hadn't seen much sleep since the day Brada had been killed, but still her eyes danced with a heat that was impossible to ignore.

"It's good to see you, too," she said, examining his bruised face, his bloodied and tattered clothes, and the clearly bent form of his posture. "You're looking well, I see."

The comment caught him off guard.

As he stammered, another form came from the tent to join her, a female whelpling wearing worn pants and a dirty shoulder drape as a protection against Eldoro's now nonexistent heat. As she took a strong stance next to Ezi, her expression told him exactly who it was.

"Pella," he said, glancing at Ezi with an unspoken question.

"After you sent her my way, she wouldn't take no for an answer," Ezi replied, placing her hand on the girl's shoulder. "And since she was the one who risked everything to bring us your message, I couldn't leave her."

He clicked an agreement.

Pella presented him a leg of roasted *jah*. "Will you eat?" she said.

He laughed, and took the food. "Thank you, little one." He ripped a bite off and nearly swooned. "It's much better than what I've been having lately."

"We have more quadars in the hills," Ezi said, handing him a bladder of water and becoming all business in the same way Crissandr had gotten when certain plans had to be followed precisely. "We're ready."

Baraq squinted into the darkening gloom to see heat profiles littered the area.

Quadar shacks were everywhere, as he expected they would be throughout all of Esgarat City.

"*Hedgies?*" he said.

"Some. Or lower Families already pressed outside the ring. But in our case they're mostly Orange Army."

He looked at them.

"What few remain, anyway."

He swallowed hard at that, and took another bite of the *jah*. It was going to be gone before he wanted it to be.

The storeroom loomed like a ghost in the distance.

It was locked, of course, but that wouldn't stop him.

"I can get us in," Baraq said. "But the system will trip, so once we're there, we'll have only a short while to get everything gathered up."

"We already have platforms and assignments," Ezi replied. "If you can break us through the back gates, we can be in and out in half a hand."

Half a hand: the time Eldoro took to move the distance of half an extended hand.

"That will be fast enough. Barely."

"Good," she said.

She made a sharp series of clicks, and motioned with her hand. Movement began to stir around her.

"Eat your *jah*, then, and let's move."

There were two dozen of them—a lucky number, Baraq thought.

They came together at the base of the fence. Baraq entered a combination, which allowed them into the first ring. A set of wire cutters got them quickly into the storehouse compound, but started the countdown. An Orange Army member battered the final door down, and Baraq led them into the storeroom. He split them into three groups, and they went to get their assigned materials while he found the back gate's controllers. He threw the switch, and the bay door rolled up.

Something short of a half a hand later, three platforms came out of the building, wheels squealing in the nighttime chill. Ezi met them behind the steering yoke of a motor cart. She waited while they piled explosives and other material into the back. She ignored what had to be every urge to push off, and instead stayed with them as the Orange Army rolled the now empty carts away.

Only when the entire group had gotten onto the back of the cart did she disengage the brakes and drive the cart away.

Yes, Baraq thought. Brada had been as fortunate with his pair-mate as he had been with his.

CHAPTER 44

"No, goddamn it," Torrance said, waving a quadar away from the casting mold.

The ability to use profanity with impunity had given a certain salt to his language that he hoped he would one day work to fix, but for now made him feel better.

They were in the manufacturing chamber and the facility was working on all cylinders, so noise and heat came from every direction at once. His team had been redesigning the cooling system for the past several weeks, and it was going far too slowly for Torrance's comfort.

"How many times am I going to have to tell you," he yelled over the din. "You've got to straighten it out! The coil can't turn so sharply. Jesus, do I have to do *everything* myself?"

The quadar stepped back and his jaw worked in angry circles for several moments before he bent to his work again without speaking.

Torrance straightened painfully and went to where the engine chassis was being developed.

Torrance glanced at the assembly the team was working on, rage rising.

"No," he screamed.

He didn't care if the culture had a fixation on the number three, the calculations said they needed more than three mounting points. He went to Jatara and held all five fingers up to her face.

"Five, damn it! I said five!"

His three-engine system required a totally different chassis design from the one Louratna had been using previously—his was a cage-like cylinder with five mounting points and reinforcing struts at critical junctions. It was harder to mold, harder to machine, and harder to assemble, but would be better for the mission.

His face grew hot, and it was hard to breathe. All he could see was another disintegrated rocket spread out over the desert floor.

He had to get away from here before he hit someone.

Torrance stomped out of the manufacturing area and down the wide corridor that led to the desert side of the mountain. He passed the fuel processing area, and crossed the central junction that led to several other "offices." Then he left the chamber and followed a path in the direction of a shaft he knew would lead outdoors.

Quadars stared as he went.

They already thought he was crazy, so who the hell cared what they were thinking now? For that matter, who *could even tell* what they were thinking? The entire species was as dumb as the rock they lived in. Totally incompetent.

The air grew hotter as he neared and then arrived at the surface.

Eldoro was in the western sky, Katon at her high point.

He pulled the hood of his robe up over his head, breathed deeply, and tried to relax despite the heat. The two stars were beginning to separate. The season the quadars called Convergence was nearing its end. He could almost stand here without sweating.

The test pad spread over the ground in the distance below.

A group of quadars worked on a launch support platform a short distance away. Another set were preparing the trial aerosol—a sulfur-impregnated solution that Torrance thought would work, and a solution that made sense because sulfur was one thing this planet had an abundance of.

"Torranze," one of them said, raising his hand and stepping toward him. "Question?"

Torrance didn't think he could handle a question right now.

He turned and walked up the slope, leaving the quadar with the word still in his mouth. His robe billowed in the wind, the hood falling back to expose his face to the sun and the wind. He thought about pulling it back up, but left it down instead. Damn the UV.

His hair whipped back and forth in the wind.

The path was familiar by now, twisting up the mountain along his usual walking path.

In a fit of pique, he turned off and went a different way. How lost could he get, after all? It was just a goddamned mountain. Several minutes later Torrance came to a rocky knob that rose from the ground like a steroidal stalagmite. He leaned against its shaded side, feeling tired and totally defeated.

"We're not going to make it," he said to himself.

It was the first time he had voiced the thought. The idea of failure sat inside his belly like raw dough.

He had been dreaming of building a rocket and triumphantly seeing it fly. But that wasn't going to happen. He was too old. Too tired. And the quadars, as fantastic as they were…

He gazed up to take in the formation. It was tall, towering silently over him, shaped almost like a rocket itself.

Shit, he thought at first. Even the planet itself was taunting him now.

But the more he looked at the formation the better he felt.

Wind rasped like music against the rock's surface. He leaned back against it and let the breeze blow. The sound rose and fell in a strange, jazzlike melody that reminded him of the files he had turned into music so many years ago.

He breathed deeply. The chill of sweat evaporating cooled his forehead.

No—this place was not taunting him at all. It was, instead, speaking to him, comforting him with its simple tones, reminding him to look at the big picture.

Looking at the formation closely, Torrance saw ledges he could use for handholds, and a few depressions that would fit his feet.

He grinned, feeling playful.

A moment later he was climbing.

The holds were hard and abrasive. The surface was hot against his cheeks as he clung to the rock. He pulled himself to the top, and then took a seat with his legs crossed, panting, heart pounding, but feeling more powerful and more at peace than he had felt for some time.

He looked out over the landscape.

Esgarat was really a beautiful planet. Savage and brutal, but beautiful in its own way.

The stones were orange and black here rather than brown and dun.

In an odd reversal of tree lines in the more temperate areas on Earth, brush grew in lush clumps at altitudes where the temperature was amenable, then died away in the desert below. A pool of water lay further up, replenished by rain that fell at altitude but would evaporate before hitting the hotter ground below. Odd creatures roamed the area—black-furred rodents, scaled birds with wings that were longer and wider than those at home, almost certainly evolved to survive the thinner air of the planet's hot atmosphere.

He wondered how hot it would get before the birds couldn't fly.

He lifted a hand to shield his view of Eldoro as it beat down, then reached back and raised his hood.

Ugly desperation rose inside him.

Beautiful as it was, Esgarat had no defense against whatever was happening inside this star's core.

He sighed.

Some Wernher von Braun he had turned out to be.

The quadars were here doing what he told them to do, and yet they still couldn't get a rocket off the ground for more than a few seconds.

Sitting here on the top of this formation, Torrance felt a certain truth hitting him.

Part of the problem was that the communication was only going one way. He told them what to do. They did it. Kind of. And as a result of the "kind of," he was coming to the conclusion that the quadars were dumb and klutzy. That was the problem. This was a species that had come so much farther than he ever expected—yes, Louratna was a big part of that, but she couldn't do it on her own. He was the problem here. Him and his need to push the clock on the project.

Part of it was that he was still learning their language.

But honesty forced him to admit that the bigger part of it was that the quadars he was working with were so cowed by his presence that they were afraid to propose their ideas, and that the few times they had tried he had squashed them—often leaning on the excuse of struggling with the language. How often had he said "we don't have time for this—just let me do it myself?"

He thought about other teams he had led.

The best of them always had a lot more to do with people than with technology, and the best people were the ones he had allowed to make mistakes.

Why would leading quadars be any different?

He felt stupid, then.

This was his fault.

Centuries of study and prognosticating from human futurists had preconditioned him to believe that an alien species would be so radically different from his own. But why would that be so? At a fundamental level, why would a quadar be any different than a human being?

He had to change his approach.

He needed to communicate, and he had to bring the team closer together.

Eldoro's heat burned against his robe in a way that made him feel better now.

He had been out long enough.

It took him several minutes to climb down the rock. When he was done, he looked up at the point.

Rocket Rock, he thought as he put his hand on the surface.

What a great name.

CHAPTER 45

Eldoro was nearing highpoint.

In a moment, Baraq would stand and lean on his gnarled walking staff to cross the pathway, then proceed along his Family's complex to enter the public gardens. He would look for the row of the sweet *grisa* trees he knew so well and the thorn-laden hedge of brush that his Family kept trimmed for a multitude of purposes, and he would do his part.

Now, though, he was covered in a light robe that draped over his face, and had the stick resting over his thighs as he feigned sleep against the shop wall across the pathway.

The wall behind him was hot with Eldoro's anger. Its rough clay bit into his tender back plates as he rested his arms over his bent knees. The smell of fresh breads and stewing meats came from the Waganat kitchen. The sound of *kax* and *tal* beasts being driven on the pathways had started early. Motor carts, too, though their presence was dying now in order to preserve their batteries during midheat.

Most of the traffic here was on foot, though.

A few quadars running messages for Family business, and some security bands patrolling to keep order, but mostly the foot traffic was quadars in tattered clothing scrounging for food or asking at the gate for work stipends, their bodies growing toward emaciation; their odors unpleasant, their skin often blotched with black patches that were growing more prevalent as the heats passed.

The device was strapped to his belly and wedged between his legs, covered also by the robe in such a fashion that he would appear to be merely a rotund old quadar. There was a time when he would have thought the device to be foul, but now its boxy form pressed against his stomach with a feeling of purpose, or at least a feeling of correctness, like an equation. Like nature. Like the idea that pushing an object in one direction causes a response in the opposite. Shoot a *neantha* and the rest of the pack will hunt you, a friend of his had once said.

He had seated himself against the wall much earlier that morning.

It wasn't hard for him to put on the pose of age, but pretending to sleep while so many familiar faces walked through the gate and across the lawn had been one of the hardest things he had ever done. At various times he had seen Tierra, Jee, and the "new" guard who had inflicted so much pain on him.

All three, he thought at one time. Another lucky number.

Early in the heat, Baraq watched Pella enter the gate just as she always did, this time carrying another basket that she had volunteered to leave behind in the office of Baraq's brother. A lump formed in his throat when he thought of her. A bigger one formed when she came back out.

He understood the true depth of her passion when she volunteered for the role, but he also knew he would worry about her for as long as he lived.

Baraq himself had wanted to lead the team that was using the caves, but Ezi shut that idea down immediately. "We're on borrowed time and you know it," she said as she laid down the law. "We can't afford the three or four days it would take you to make your way through those caves again."

The fact that she was right was the most annoying part of her argument.

Tierra may be inept, but he was a Waganat, and that meant he had all the Waganat resources at his fingertips. And three carts of stolen explosives would create a sense of urgency. It would not be too long before they were found. Even one day could make a difference.

Highpoint was approaching, though.

It was finally time.

He scratched at his neck, then pulled back the neck of his robe. The timer cord was still wrapped around the device. He had sweated through the strips of rootcloth that held its box to his belly, but they were still tight enough around his back to hold it close as long as he bent over to give it a little support.

He used the stick to help him stand, stabilizing for a moment and letting his tired legs burn as blood returned to them.

"Currency?" a thin voice called from behind.

It was a whelpling, a female no older than Pella. She had come from around the nearby corner.

Keeping his hood drawn, he looked over his shoulder and growled. "I have nothing for the likes of you."

"You'll be kind to my sister, old man," an older whelp said from the opposite direction of the pathway.

The boy was tall and thin in the way of whelps of that age. His golden primaries held a confrontational set, his central was shut tight. The girl was slight, all three of her eyes wide as saucers, her central radiating crimson fear. He had seen similar teams working his customers back in the day—slick pairs who had their plays down and could leave with a few coins or a purse without anyone being the wiser. It was a thing he stayed on the lookout for. He had stopped a hundred such petty burglaries on his premises. These two were new to this, though. Amateurs. He saw it in their hesitation.

"So this is a shakedown," he said.

"Why do you say that?"

"I've seen them before," Baraq said. Eldoro's heat was harsh on his robe, and his legs and back were beginning to hurt with the extra weight of the device.

"I'm sure you have."

"I suggest you be careful who you target in the future."

"I suggest you give us what you have," the whelp said, motioning the drawstring pouch Baraq had tied to a belt that was straining to keep the robe closed.

Baraq smiled. "It's got nothing but a crust of *havra* bread in it, but you're welcome to it if you care."

"We care."

Baraq used one hand to remove the pouch, then gave it to the girl.

She took it and clutched it to her chest and moved to her brother's side.

He looked at the two of them. "You'll want to be moving away from here," he said.

"Is that a threat?" the boy said.

Baraq smiled again, feeling age. "It's a hope for your future," he said as he began to shuffle across the pathway and toward the compound.

He didn't look back, but the two didn't follow him.

For a moment, he wondered how the rest of Ezi's compatriots were coming.

Had they been spotted?

Would they finish their own parts?

Walking with the staggered limp he affected to get the part right made him think he was going to fall over due to the extra weight of the box, but he kept it together and assumed that the combination of his staff and the natural lurch caused by his imbalance was more authentic than anything he could have made up. The device was heavy now, and the band holding it down was stretched too much for his liking. He used one hand to adjust it while he walked the perimeter of the wall that served as the barrier between the Waganat compound and the public.

A few steps later, he came to a forged gate.

It opened with a dry screech that drew attention from the two nearby guards.

Baraq fought every urge to raise the hood enough to glance at them. Instead he used a slow, methodical gait to follow the cleared path that looped through the garden in a way that suggested he was visiting, stopping frequently to bend himself backward and take in a tree or a statue that had been placed just so by the Family's gardeners.

It was the first time he had paid such attention to the Waganat garden in a very long time.

The area felt empty to him now.

Its plants were brittle and barren, having been raided in the first few days of the Family reign for what little bud or fruit it could yield. What was left was mostly stripped brush and the hardiest of trees. A few volunteer roots grew from cracks in the ground.

He crossed to a monument he had seen so often that it hadn't really registered anymore—a piece of art commissioned to honor his father's father, a tall and thick rectangular block of polished mountain ore that ran with dark deposits. In the old days, the Waganats had kept it clean, but now it was covered in dust and dirt, and scarred with rivulets where the burning rain had run over it.

After taking it in, Baraq moved on.

The block would give him cover when he needed it. That was all that mattered for now, though the fact that a monument honoring his father's father would play a role in what was to come made Baraq happy as he made his way to the row of *grisa* trees and hedges that ran along the tall wall that was the true beginning of the inner sanctum of the Waganat complex. The wall ran the entire span of the garden, and rose up to become one side of the business center that housed the Family offices.

Baraq neared the row of trees that still smelled sweet as they baked in Eldoro's heat.

The brush looked sharp and uninviting.

His gaze took in the three locations he was to use.

His mind reviewed the lay of the guard station and the Waganat monument. Its size would block their view of him, so he would have some time. How much was the question.

With one more step he was there.

He bent to lay the staff on the ground, then lifted his robes to disengage the device.

It came apart in three separate packages, each connected by timing cord.

Baraq tossed the cloth band under the hedgerow, and cradled the three components. Then he raced to plant the middle package behind the central *grisa* tree. Playing line out behind him, he bent and crawled the second package along the wall and behind the hedge, hoping the vegetation covered his movement well enough. When the cord ran out, he stopped, set the timer, and crawled back.

A few moments later he had repeated the exercise in the other direction.

Returning to the central box, he set its timer and its flinting mechanism, then scrambled back to where he had laid the staff.

He straightened to flex his muscles. The robe was now marked with dirt and blood in places where rough patches had scraped his knees and hands. Nothing to do for it, though. He bent and took a slow, lurching step, hoping his posture would also hide the fact that he no longer carried the device.

He needn't have worried.

The Waganat guards barely looked at him as he made his way out of the garden, taking extra time to close the gate properly, his hearts pounding. As he walked down the pathway that led away from his Family's compound, he straightened and, remembering Brada's sense of self-confidence, began walking purposefully, no longer limping and no longer using the walking staff.

The aroma of the city rose around him as he strode down the pathway.

The sense of warm metal and baked rock.

The pounding of *tal* beast hooves.

Each step he took seemed to give him energy.

Each moment gave him power.

Finally, an explosion rocked the ground behind him. A fraction of a second later came another.

Then another.

Panicked voices began to ring out as, behind him, the entire Waganat compound erupted in shrapnel and debris. Finally, from the caves deep below, another massive string of explosives ignited with a sound that was deep and muffled, a rumble that was like thunder, only deeper and firmer and somehow more satisfying than any sound Baraq had ever heard.

His stride got stronger and his back straighter.

As he looked ahead, he reached up with the long fingers of both hands, and pulled the hood of his robes back, letting the heat of Eldoro fall over his exposed face.

He reached into a pocket in the robe, and extracted a *Shensi*, a plain mask with a three-point harness. As he stepped off the central pathway and into the alleys that would lead him out of the city, he pulled the mask over his face.

CHAPTER 46

Torrance bowed to the quadars' worship of the number three when it came to test sets for the fuel system and aerosol development pad. Each set now had bays for three separate experiments of three separate compound mixtures, all scaled to smaller sizes.

The team had worked all morning to get the fuel system rig set up.

He inspected the stands—fuel cells each topped off, ignition systems ready to be tripped, thrust meters prepared and linked to their simple pressure readouts. The three systems would each be tripped at the same moment to provide a better comparison of burn rates. A quadar sat at each remote station to monitor levels over the burn.

Test ignition would start as soon as Torrance was ready.

"*Mata,*" he said. "This is good work. Let's begin."

Edart Kel, one of the quadars Torrance considered to be quicker than most, tried not to grin, but Torrance could see the young engineer was pleased. The test devices had been her idea. They had been working together for some time, and she had quite easily picked up the hybrid qualish language that Torrance and Louratna had developed. It was a language he was making up with his main contacts almost daily. The meanings of words and phrases were not yet precise, but it was slowly working its way out.

Now that Torrance was focused on using the quadars for their strengths and keeping them away from things that were…well, not their strengths…he was finding more strengths than he had anticipated.

He and Edart walked together to stand behind a reinforced wall.

Edart waited for Torrance to trigger the ignition system. He motioned that she should do the honors instead.

She turned the switch.

Fuel dumped into three combustion chambers. Ignition systems flared. Fire came, and smoke and sand billowed amid the sound of three rocket engines ramping to full roar.

Torrance smiled and put his hands over his ears.

Edart returned the smile and did the same.

Neither anticipated the leak in one of the fuel lines. Neither knew that at that very moment, a single finger of flame crawled up the line to tank number two.

The explosion was deafening.

Despite their protective wall, the shock wave knocked them over as the test set tore itself into a million pieces. Shrapnel flew from fuel tanks and combustion chambers. A ball of red and black flame rolled over the area, leaving behind a smear of oily kerosene smoke.

When it was done, Torrance rose and dusted himself off.

Edart rose, too, an expression of horror etching her face. Footsteps from rushing teammates came toward them.

"What happened?" she said in her language.

Torrance looked at her.

"We got something terribly wrong—that's what happened."

Edart didn't understand him, so he laughed as well as he could muster.

"It's not a problem," he said, knowing she had heard that phrase in the context he wanted her to hear it. "*Adiago nar, mata*," he said. *It will be better next time.*

She grinned and her eyes got wide. "Boom!" she said, laughing with him now.

"Yes, very big boom!"

• • •

They went over the launch sequence the next morning.

They reviewed the design, and tried to analyze the remains.

Scorch marks on the test pad indicated that the explosion started with the middle segment. The charred remains of two fuel tanks were found spread across the desert, but the third was essentially disintegrated.

"It had to be a leak in the fuel delivery system," Edart Kel said to him.

"Why do you think that?"

"Look at the pattern," she said, running her fingertips along the latest scorch marks. "They burn hottest here. Something must have leaked."

Torrance didn't think that was right, but stopped himself from pushing her.

"What do you suggest?"

"Build another, with focus there."

He pursed his lips. "All right," he said. "Let's give it a go."

The next test actually got off the launching pad before it blew.

Not far—five meters, maybe ten—but it was farther than any other shot so far.

Standing on the launch pad observation zone, Torrance shaded his eyes and looked at the smoldering remains of the apparatus.

Edart Kel appeared to be both tired and hot.

Like the rest of the team, both of them had been up most of the night, finishing details and checking the lists that Torrance was so much a stickler about. He was pretty sure Edart hadn't eaten for nearly a day, and that she was nearly dead on her feet.

Mostly, though, she was pissed off.

"The breaking point is not fuel or controller," the quadar said in the bits of Torrance and Louratna's qualish she had been picking up and adding to so rapidly. "And it's not the pipes—at least not their forms."

Torrance nodded. "You're probably right. What do you think it is?"

"Cooling. The fuel gets too hot, too fast, then...boom."

"That's what I think, too."

"What do we do?"

Torrance shrugged. "Do you have any ideas?"

Edart was clearly let down.

"The good news," Torrance said as he looked over the launching pad, "is that three engines stayed together, and we were in control until they went boom."

"It *was* stable from start to end."

"Short though it was."

They shared a grin.

Suddenly, Edart couldn't help but laugh.

"Come on," Torrance said. "Let's go help the team sort through the wreckage."

Edart groaned.

"I know you're tired, but it'll be worth it. Just make sure to talk to them while you're working. Spread the word about what we learned, listen to their ideas. It's worth it."

"I understand," Edart said.

"You start. I'll go get you something to eat, then join you."

The quadar smiled.

CHAPTER 47

Louratna came to Torrance's chamber later that evening.

He was bent over a painting he had been working on—a view of the desolate landscape that included Rocket Rock. The paints were thick and a little hard to work with, but he enjoyed having something to take his mind off the rocket itself. He had started it outside, and still returned to the scene for moments of reflection, but he found if he tried to finish a piece while at the scene, his personal form of perfectionism kicked in, and he would bog down trying to get every detail right rather than merely capture the essence of the piece.

Louratna sat down in the heavy way she had.

Her breathing came in labored gasps, and her skin seemed to settle around her in gray folds. Quadarti incense clung to her clothes. She was getting to be old, too, he thought.

Torrance put his brush down and wiped his hands on a cloth. "Hello."

"Hello," Louratna replied. "I am sorry to interrupt your quiet time. I know you get so little of it," she continued in her language, looking at his painting. "That's nice."

"Thank you. And don't worry. I get no more time off than you."

Louratna was quiet while he finished cleaning up, then came to sit beside her.

"The canisters are working," she said.

By canisters, she meant that she had perfected a system that could fly with the rocket and dispense a long stream of sulfuric particles in the upper atmosphere.

"That's excellent news. Now all we have to do is get a rocket into the air."

She closed her eyes. In the dim light of his compartment, the lines on her face were dark streaks.

He rubbed the small of her back as he had been doing on occasion. She gave a contented groan and leaned forward to give him better access.

"Are you all right?" he asked.

"What will they do?" Louratna said.

"Who?"

When she raised up, her primaries were filled with deep questioning, and suddenly he understood what Louratna was asking.

"Humans, you mean?"

"They will come to get you?"

Torrance shrugged. "Maybe so. I hope they will, anyway. But I have to be honest and say I don't know."

"I thought you would bring us the answer," she said with a wistful sigh. "And in so many ways you did."

"Shitty answers, though."

"The truth is always a good answer."

He pursed his lips, not knowing what else to say. "Can I get you *aska*?" It was juice that came from a flower that was only in bloom for a few weeks of the year. Torrance considered it nectar of the gods. He had a decanter on the nightstand next to his bed.

"That would be nice."

The sound of his pouring filled the chamber. He handed Louratna a glass. They drank silently together, then she stood up, grimacing as she rose.

"I appreciate your truth, Torranze."

"You're not giving up, eh?"

"No," she said with a twinkling smile. "I will never give up."

She left the room and suddenly Torrance felt lonely.

He glanced at the painting.

Louratna's question was a good one. Assuming the UG actually came to get him, what would happen to the quadars?

Is there any way a man can come into contact with something and not change it?

He thought about the wormhole pod and about Alpha Centauri A, then picked up his brush, and went back to work.

CHAPTER 48

The next day Torrance and Edart Kel walked through the design of the cooling system.

They stood on the massive floor of the assembly chamber, before a table upon which a large drawing was held down by chunks of metal slag at each corner.

"I bring fuel from the tanks through a pair of pipes," Torrance said, running his fingers along the fuel system inlet. "You see the coils wrap there to provide cooling."

"It doesn't work, though," Edart replied.

"No, it doesn't."

"The fuel isn't far enough from the combustion chamber to transfer enough heat."

Torrance sat quietly, waiting.

"What if we had a system that would constantly run water over the chamber?" Edart said.

"The weight of the coolant would be massive," Torrance replied.

"I see."

"What if we skip the coils completely?"

"What do you mean?"

The quadar knelt and drew on the paper. "What if the outside shell is hollow?"

Torrance got one of those sensations that made him smile. "You mean, run the fuel inside the casing to keep it away from the heat?"

Edart clicked a soft series that meant yes.

Torrance nodded. "Yeah," he said, clicking back. "I wish I had thought of that. It'll be hard to cast."

"Only the first time."

The tone of his collaborator's voice made him chuckle. "Sure," Torrance said. "Take a chance, right?"

Edart's expression lit up.

As they left the assembly area the next evening, Torrance felt truly optimistic for the first time in a long while. The casting could be done. And if it was done right, it could work. He didn't know if he was happier that the thing actually had a chance, or that Edart was the one who developed the idea. Just seeing her working the past two days had been great fun.

It made him think of Kitchell.

Which made him wonder what the "kid" was doing.

The grin that crossed his face felt good.

Nothing would be better than walking into Louratna's offices and telling her he was ready to pair her aerosol distribution system with a rocket delivery platform.

He was hungry, but he wanted to be alone.

For just a bit, he thought. Just long enough to get his thoughts together.

Ever since he started working on the rocket, it seemed like he never really had time to think.

Rocket Rock would be perfect.

So, engrossed in his thoughts, Torrance took the familiar path.

Eldoro had set long ago, but the time of year was changing to something the quadars called Katon Following, a period where the gap between Alpha Centauri A and Alpha Centauri B was widening. This meant Katon's light would be enough to see by for several more hours. It was windier than yesterday, and a wispy set of orange and brown clouds raced across the sky. This far up the mountain, the air was heavy with moisture and Torrance was fairly certain that a rare storm was brewing.

Following the path upward, he pulled a cape over his shoulders, shivering as the suddenly cool wind blew against his sunburnt skin. He was trying to keep himself covered most of the time he was on the surface, but he would have to do better.

In the distance a pair of *jah* whirled in the cooling currents, hunting.

Edart had told him there had been a time when she was a little girl that the sky was full of mated *jah*, hunting together, fighting over *pax* or *piela* lizards. Perhaps he should feel sadness at this lonely pairing, but all he thought of when he saw them gliding above was that he would pay a year off his life just to see one of his rockets get that far off the ground.

Rocket Rock came into sight, looking particularly bold as it rose in the darkness.

Torrance didn't notice the quadar who sat at the base of the rock until it moved.

He stopped before it appeared to notice him.

It was a male, sitting with his knees pulled up, arms cantilevered out over them. He was thin and wiry, nearly as heavily wrinkled as Louratna. His body moved sluggishly as he peered intently out over the launch area, though.

The quadar seemed familiar to Torrance, but his angle was bad and he couldn't get enough of a view to place the face.

Intrigued, Torrance stood still and watched.

There was something attractive about this quadar, though. Something magnetic about the way he stared out over the landscape with that lonely kind of sensibility that surrounds a person who's wrapped up in a world bigger than themselves.

The quadar stood, bushed dust from his pants, and started to walk away.

"Hey!" Torrance called.

The visitor turned to him with dismay, then raced into the

darkness.

Torrance gave chase, but it became obvious he wouldn't catch up.

"Damn it," he said, then went back to the rock.

Torrance sighed as he took a seat on the rock where just a moment ago the quadar had been. The other's body heat was still in the stone. He sat there and looked out on the same scene as the quadar who had just left.

It felt oddly perfect.

For the first time, Torrance looked around himself and realized this was his home.

Wherever it was, and wherever he had been, this was where he belonged.

A thick drop of rain hit his forehead. He didn't really want to go in, but it was obvious he had to.

He walked as quickly as he could. The wind whipped against him, and the rain began to fall harder, then harder still. He covered his head with his cape, but pretty soon the rain fell with such force that it seemed to burn his skin when it struck. He walked faster, breaking into a shuffling run.

The rain came even harder.

When he made the caves, he shook water from his back.

His skin was red, and still burning.

By the time he got back to his chamber, Torrance was beginning to get worried. His hands were blistering, and the skin around his neck and shoulders was uncomfortable. The spot on his forehead where the first drop hit felt oddly numb.

Louratna, who had taken to working in Torrance's room through the day, looked up when he entered. She had been working on ballistic theory, but rose the moment he entered, then came directly to him.

"Agggg," he groaned in pain, and saw concern in her gaze. "What's happening?"

"Hold still," she said, taking his hands. Her brows knit together. She picked at the corner of his sleeve, gently rubbing the fabric between her fingers, then sniffing it.

Her eyes grew wide. "Come," she said.

With the same breath, she yelled for attendants. She spoke in a stream of quadar too fast for him to follow. The attendants ran.

"Come," she said again, motioning him to follow. "You have the burning rain."

He trusted her better than to argue, but he went over her comment as he followed her to baths where attendants were hastily pouring water into pools.

You have the burning rain, he thought.

Without asking, she started to pull his robe off him.

"Wait just a minute."

Then the robe was gone.

He covered himself self-consciously and noted his arms were red— as were his shoulders. They seemed to be on fire.

"In," Louratna said, not paying attention to his modesty.

He stepped into the water. It helped. She dunked his head, and it helped more.

The attendants immediately began filling another pool. When that was done, she pointed to the second pool.

"In," she said.

The second pool was cooler, and felt better, the third still better. Louratna let him soak in this one, even going so far as to drop white powder into it that soothed the burning sensation.

Jesus, he thought, as Louratna finally sat down beside the third pool, staring at the back of his blistering hands and flashing on this evening's orange and yellow clouds.

"Acid rain," he said out loud. "Your entire planet revolves around a sulfur cycle." He looked at Louratna, more truth dawning. As the planet cooled, it would rain more, and as it rained, more of the sulfides in the air would merge with water to become sulfuric acid.

Torrance grimaced. He had been so stupid.

Their actions would extend the life of the quadars' atmosphere, but it would likely cause other problems.

He touched his skin, looking at its burnt areas. "Shit," he said again.

"Shit," Louratna repeated, nodding soberly.

CHAPTER 49

Normally Baraq would have gone straight to Louratna's offices. That would have been the proper step to take. But that was not why he was here, so now he stepped through the cave hallway that led to the community kitchen where he knew Crissandr would be.

It annoyed him that the image of the creature continued to cling to his mind, though. He hadn't expected to see it in the wild. To be honest, he hadn't even considered the idea that the thing would still be alive. But the tone of its voice across the mountainside reminded him of the last time he had heard it yelling in its odd language as Baraq left the medical center. He would remember that moment for as long as he lived—the moment he learned Brada had been kidnapped. It was also the moment he should have understood exactly what Brada had gotten himself into. If he were a smarter quadar, his son might be alive today.

Baraq shook those thoughts away as he stepped through the passage.

That wasn't why he was here.

Despite anxiety that draped him, he felt oddly powerful as he strode ahead. He was a champion, now, wasn't he? He had been victorious. Now he was returning from the battle to claim his *kalla*. That's how the Orange Army would see it, and it was the story he was telling himself, though under its bravado he understood the truth of this moment was immensely larger.

He didn't know how Crissandr was. He didn't know how she would feel.

All he knew for sure was that he needed her. That he wanted her.

And that he had left her here to grieve alone.

The scents of *havra* and stewing *tal* grew thick from the direction he walked. The aroma of familiar spices made his stomachs growl.

The temperature rose as he drew closer.

The kitchen was organized into three aisles of meal preparation stations in which quadars worked, chopping, stirring, and cleaning pans and utensils. A fire pit was set into a depression in the far wall, a natural flue drawing smoke up into the mountain to disperse it into the outside air.

Crissandr was washing bowls across the room. Her back was to him.

As he stepped through the area, the room grew quiet until only the sound of meat sizzling on the open fire could be heard.

Baraq felt the pressure of stares. He ignored them and strode forward, gaze focused on the quadar he hoped he could still call his *kalla* as she rubbed down a stone plate.

She did not stop when he arrived at her side, but she knew he was there.

She was older now. She moved with deliberate slowness.

"I'm sorry I left you," Baraq said, choosing his words carefully. "I was wrong, but I was angry."

Crissandr put down the plate, and turned to look at him.

Pain was etched into her face, pain, fear, and loneliness, all wrapped into a single expression. *This is your fault*, that expression said. *You did this.*

"I needed you, Baraq. You weren't there."

"I did what I had to do."

"You think you are the only one who hurt?"

"No," he said. "Please come back with me. Fight with me. I need you."

He waited in the resulting silence, hands knit before him.

"The Waganat Family is no more," he finally said. "We have no family but ourselves and the quadarti we choose to surround ourselves with. You are my *kalla*. The only family I have ever chosen. The only family I will ever choose."

There it was. His heart, open and exposed for her.

"Please," he said.

Someone pulled meat off the griddle.

Crissandr clicked and stared at him with her expression stoic.

She picked up her plates.

"I know what you've done," she said. Then she turned away and walked slowly into the storeroom.

The kitchen crew seemed to let out a collective breath.

All around him, sounds of activity began to creep into his consciousness again.

CHAPTER 50

"Torranze! Torranze! Donzae! Donzae!" Wake up! Wake up!

Torrance had been dreaming about piloting a nuke-drive pod through an asteroid belt at breakneck speeds, something his buddies at the Academy had done one night but that Torrance had been too afraid to join in with. Each of the guys had been suspended for a semester, but their reputation around campus grew to legendary status, and most of all, they had put the experience under their belt. In retrospect, Torrance had been jealous for years.

As he came to consciousness, he remembered jinking left, then using a retro trim to stabilize the roll he had created. He had to dip down to avoid a chunk of space rock, an action he took as he gave a cowboy's whoop. At least, that's what he thought he remembered.

It was some hellacious flying, and he knew it.

"Torranze! Torranze! Donzae! Donzae!" Wake up! Wake up!

Torrance suddenly jumped to full alert, his eyes wide and his heart beating like a pulsar.

It was one of the attendants who often monitored his needs, his golden eyes blazing in the dim light of Torrance's sleeping chambers.

"What is it, Pash?" he said.

"Louratna requests you come."

Torrance rolled off his bedding and made his preparations. A couple minutes later he was on his way.

————

The chill of the deep passage helped Torrance come fully awake as he approached the meeting room, which was a small chamber at the bottom of a tall shaft. The area was brightly lit, yet the upper reaches of the shaft still disappeared into the darkness above. A milky white formation of mica ringed half the sheer walls. It was cool here, and quiet—private given that the only access was from a small passage that twisted and turned for maybe half a kilometer off the primary public passages.

Louratna stood beside a block of stone in the middle of the shaft's floor. The rock had been cut flat and was serving as a table. She wore a white *jook*, an outfit that was half dress, half pantsuit. Torrance couldn't help but think she appeared tired.

Another quadar was bent over the table and moving his hand across a map spread across the surface.

Plates of root and bread held the map down at two corners, chunks of rock at the other two.

"What is it?" Torrance said as he entered.

The new quadar rose to his full height. It was the male he had seen at Rocket Rock. He was as weathered as any quadar he had ever seen, and standing tall, even though Torrance could see the quadar was in some form of pain. Up close, though, Torrance understood exactly why the quadar had seemed so familiar.

"You're the one who showed me the picture," he said in his own mixture of qualish.

The quadar looked confused at Torrance's comment, and was obviously surprised he was here.

"This is Baraq Waganat," Louratna said. "I thought you should meet him before he leaves again." She motioned to the quadar. "Baraq, this is Torranze Black."

Baraq clicked three gentle tones that Torrance understood were a de facto form of welcome.

Torrance cocked his head and turned his palm out in a classic quadar's greeting.

Baraq spoke a rapid burst to Louratna.

She translated for him.

"Baraq says it is an honor to meet you and he's sorry he interrupted your travels yesterday."

"It's not a problem," Torrance said in his best form of the quadar's language.

Louratna continued before Baraq could reply.

"Baraq was the quadar who managed the earliest investigations on your wormhole pod," she said. "He got me involved. Perhaps more important to you, he is the one who sent the messages that brought you here."

Louratna had told him of Baraq Waganat's work, but the connection hadn't immediately formed. As the true meaning of her words settled over him, however, Torrance's gaze locked onto Baraq's.

Torrance stepped closer.

Baraq stood firm, his posture and expression radiating a confusing mix of longing and a strong vein of single-minded purpose that made Torrance's spine tingle. There was something going on in him that Torrance didn't understand.

"I feel like I know you," Torrance finally said as he reached a hand to touch Baraq's shoulder.

The quadar didn't move. Louratna translated.

"Can he help us?" Baraq said to Louratna. Torrance caught the gist of the question, and realized it has been phrased as if he wasn't even in the room.

"He understands the rocket."

Baraq responded.

"What did he say?" Torrance asked.

"He wants to know if your rocket will be able to kill the Families."

The bluntness of her translation set him back.

"I see," he said.

He took in the map on the table, recognizing the layout of the mountains where Louratna's caves were arranged, and, a distance away, seeing the indications of the city where he had almost certainly been kidnapped from before. The diagram had been marked on with dark, sweeping lines, mostly around the city, some elsewhere. It looked like a plan of some kind, or, given this comment, like a war game.

How very human of them, he thought.

"I think it's time someone really explained the Families to me," he said. "Why should we want to kill them?"

"It is a very complicated story," Louratna replied.

Torrance crossed his arms and absentmindedly scratched his elbows. "Well," he said. "I think I've got nothing but time."

It was another long conversation, but, unfortunately not as long it would have been if Torrance was not so well versed in the politics of human nature.

The quadarti social structure was a strange mix of power systems, with genetically segmented Families running an almost feudalistic, commerce-born structure that felt like a cross between a caste system and a hierarchy of the organized crime rings that had influenced Earth politics at various times throughout human history. A shadow council of the Families operated as a legitimizing function, or at least it had until recently when a militant grassroots group led by Baraq's son had disrupted things, then Baraq had apparently finished the job. If Torrance squinted hard enough, he could see that the council wasn't really that different from the UG. Until now, the quadarti class system had been maintained by a combination of economic strata, social stigma, and brute force that kept independent quadars locked into their places.

Given the conversation and the markups of the map, the situation had now changed such that brute force was the prevalent controller of the day. Given the aura around Baraq, it was clear he intended to use as much brute force as he needed to bring about change.

As Louratna promised, it was a complex structure.

The politics internal to the Waganat Family alone was enough to make the ambassadorial side of his brain twirl.

"That's why you're hiding here," he said to Louratna, who had taken a seat sometime earlier and was now chewing on a spiced root. "That's why this whole community is in the caves. You're avoiding the Families and council." It took a moment to find the words *hiding* and *avoiding*.

"The Families clamp down. University cannot teach. Philosophers cannot study. Being here makes things easier."

"That's why you stole me?"

Louratna's primaries danced and her face took on a jovial smile.

"What if they find you?" he said.

"We work hard to avoid that," Louratna said.

"All right," Torrance said. He ran his hand over the map's markups in the zone Baraq said belonged to his Family. "So, what is that?"

"Plans," Baraq responded after Louratna translated. "My brother killed my son, so the Orange Army and I destroyed them all. Now the time is right to move harder."

Torrance's gaze bounced between the map and Baraq.

He understood it all now.

Baraq wasn't here to make a report or even to talk about the wormhole pod. Whatever had been in Baraq Waganat's past was in his past, his future pointed in only one direction.

"I'm going to change things," Baraq said, using words that added up to a sentence Torrance completely understood. "Your rocket would help."

Torrance said nothing, but glanced at Louratna. The expression on her face was enough to say she understood his question.

Are we working on a bomb?

In the end, he stayed silent and watched Louratna deal with the request in her way.

He held his tongue as he dealt with the idea of working on a weapon rather than a science pod. He kept quiet while he dealt with the acid that came to his stomach when he looked at the dark swathes of marker that lined the map.

Her expression said she was struggling as heavily with the news Baraq brought her as she was with the idea that she might be building a weapon. That quadars had separated from the rest of their society and followed her out here showed how much they revered her. But one look at the map and another at Baraq said that world was crumbling now. She was working to save a planet that was being overrun by factions that didn't understand what was really happening to them, and wouldn't accept the full extent of it even if they did. At the rate things were going there may not be a world to save.

Above it all, Louratna was dealing with this alone.

He realized then that this was why she had called him here. Certainly, she had wanted him and Baraq to meet, but the truth was clear—Louratna wanted Torrance to see this. She wanted him to understand. He was a human, an outsider, but in that moment he understood that Louratna wanted him with her, that in some fashion he was important to her.

"Here is the problem, Baraq," she finally said, looking up at the visitor. "Even if I thought it was the right thing to do, I can't give you the rocket for the simple reason that we still cannot get it to fly."

"Even if you thought it was the right thing to do?"

Baraq stepped close enough to loom over Louratna, his fists balled, and Torrance took a step closer.

Louratna ignored Torrance, though. She looked up at Baraq, and swallowed.

"Do you remember when you first brought me the Taranth Stone?"

"That was a long time ago."

"Yes, it was."

"Things have changed."

Louratna sighed, then put her other hand on Baraq's opposite arm. Baraq waited.

"Some things have changed, Baraq, but not the ones that matter."

"What is that supposed to mean?"

"You didn't come here for this, Baraq. Not really."

"I came to make a difference."

"You didn't even know rockets existed until you got here."

Baraq was silent.

Louratna stood and put her hand on Baraq's elbow. "Give her time, Baraq. Crissandr will return to you."

Baraq froze then. His expression grew first pointed, then wide and almost resigned.

Torrance frowned at first, but certain things started to line up.

Crissandr. His tour guide. She was Baraq's pair-mate, or had some kind of relationship with him. Torrance remembered the long silences he had sat through with Crissandr, recalled the soft sounds of her breathing as they sat together looking out on the desolation of the desert.

He hadn't seen Crissandr for some time, but hadn't really wondered why, merely assumed she was off working somewhere else.

"Time is not something I have much of," Baraq finally said.

"Some things happen on their own schedule."

Baraq stepped back and went to the table, scanning the map again. "With no rockets, the Orange Army can't win. You know that, right?"

"Remember who you are, Baraq. There has to be another way."

He glared at her, but she held steadfast.

"What do you think Crissandr wants you to do? What kind of quadar do you think she wants to be with?"

Baraq closed his lips tight, paused for a breath, then gave a single very deep click from the back of his throat. It seemed like a weight fell over his entire body, and years of disappointment seemed to seep from his pores.

"I've failed in everything I've come for," Baraq said. "I need to get back and help the Orange Army recuperate."

He looked at Torrance.

"Thank you for your time," he said.

Then he left the shaft.

Louratna spread both hands on the table and let her head droop.

Not knowing what else to do, Torrance went to her side and put his arm around her shoulder. She stiffened at first, then relaxed. He massaged the muscles of her neck, letting his fingers dig down to spaces between the bones. Louratna sighed and leaned her shoulder against him as he continued to rub her neck.

"He wasn't always like that," Louratna said.

"Quadars change."

"Yes. But Baraq was...different."

"How?"

She just shook her head and said nothing.

"Are we going to be okay?" he asked.

"I hope so."

He didn't say anything else, just kept rubbing her back in gentle circles.

CHAPTER 51

orrance, Louratna, and Edart stood with many other team members in a small clearing on the side of the mountain. As fate would have it, the sky was overcast. Eldoro's lingering heat was a smudge that glazed the western horizon with a golden color that Torrance couldn't remember ever having seen in a sky over Earth. It wasn't likely to rain, but Torrance had learned a long time ago that the world has an ironic sense of humor.

The rocket stood on the launching pad like a needle pointing to the sky.

He stood under the platform and looked up.

The exhaust cowlings were like three dark eyes.

"Think it will fly?"

Louratna walked with her painful shuffle to stand beside him.

"Yes," she said. "I think it will fly."

There was a moment where everything was silent.

Then a light flared under the rocket. Flames and white smoke rolled from the ground up. A cloud of desert dust billowed. The noise rose in a throaty rumble that made their chests vibrate.

The rocket moved upward, slowly at first.

The cloud of dust nearly enveloped it, but its needlelike shape rose above it until the golden flames from its engine were an orange streak behind it. Mass entered the combustion chamber, burned, and was thrown out the back end. Newton's laws worked their magic. The craft rose, and continued to rise, leaving a streak of white smoke in the air like a slash from giant pen.

They craned their necks to watch for several minutes as the rocket continued to rise.

Then it was gone.

An amazing sense of being grew inside Torrance's chest, finally emerging as a halting laugh that he couldn't stop.

The rocket was gone. Escape velocity achieved.

Where once there was metal and fire there was now only a trace of smoke.

The quadars trilled and clapped, the team literally jumping all over each other.

Then Edart Kel was smiling and screaming with her face so close to Torrance's that it filled his whole view.

"Torranze! Torranze!" she called, clapping him on the back with fervor that should have hurt but that now merely said he was alive.

A grin seemed to paste itself on his face.

He stepped away from Edart, and put his arms instead around Louratna, hugging her tightly.

She buried her face in the folds of his robe and wrapped her arms around him, too, her hands pressing against his shoulder blades, the six long fingers of each making distinct impressions against his back.

When she finally pulled back she was crying.

CHAPTER 52

A day after the successful flight, Torrance, Edart, and the rest of their team were in the rocket lab working to install Louratna's aerosol distribution system into the next rocket.

Her scheme was a fascinating arrangement that depended on internal pneumatics and the pressure gradient created by the rocket's climb into upper atmosphere to regulate the dispersal of particles. Like most of her thinking, the approach was both elegant and efficient.

The huge cavern felt somehow smaller today. More intense.

Though it was impossible to tell in the enclosed chamber, it was early in the day. The sound of components being machined combined with the sound of quadars operating the smelting systems to make a steady grind in the background. The sense of anticipation ran high.

The first true flight would happen in two more days.

The next steps would be to develop all the orbital ballistics solutions they would need to ensure full coverage and get the production process to be fast enough to make enough product to maintain Louratna's "shell across the world."

"Once we're operational," Torrance had said to Louratna when they were working on broader plans, "we'll probably need a rocket a day."

All in all, it was an exciting time.

A sharp noise came from the main passageway into the chamber.

Torrance stood tall and gave a prairie dog stare at the source, as did all the quadars in the workshop.

"Was that gunfire?"

A moment later, a quadar with a blocky rifle stepped into the assembly area. Another followed behind. They came down the rackety stair system, firing blasts into the workers below. Another shooter appeared at the opening, then another.

Torrance ducked behind a rock as another quadar began shooting.

High-pitched squeals of terror rose over the sound of machinery. Bullets ricocheted off rock as more quadars fell.

A fuel processor exploded with a deafening roar, killing one of the shooters and leaving a litter of flaming debris across the assembly area floor. The concussion knocked Torrance backward, and a cloud of dense black smoke began to fill the chamber. Torrance picked himself up, seeing dead and wounded quadars as they lay bleeding and moaning.

The sight made no sense.

Quadars, shot and burning, quadars who a moment ago were working on this magnificent technology, now dead.

The smell of burning fuel was oppressive.

"No!" Torrance screamed, then scrambled to his feet.

"Torranze!" Edart raced toward him, flushed and sweating, emerging from behind the wall she had used for cover to hold him back from exposing himself to fire. Her central glowed with fear. "You are all right?"

"What's happening?"

"The Families," she said as if this explained the origin of the universe. "Come on."

She grabbed Torrance by the arm, but he shook her off.

The floor rumbled with a distant explosion.

His thought patterns caught up with her comment. The Families. Yes.

Cause and effect.

The Families would be after Baraq—and they likely wanted

Louratna, too. Baraq had come here. If Torrance understood anything about politics, it was the politics of revenge. The Families could have tracked Baraq.

Alternately, it could be Baraq and the Orange Army, too, coming back to take what he wanted. Torrance took in the burning debris and the dead workers. No, Baraq would have protected the weapon system rather than destroy it.

Whoever it was, though, they were working their way downward.

Gunfire came from several passages.

"Where's Louratna?"

"I don't know, but we've got to get away." She pulled at Torrance's elbow again.

"Not until I find her."

Two of the attackers had recovered from the blast. Bullets were flying again.

The floor shook.

"You've got to go, Torranze!" She grabbed him around the waist and pushed him toward a side passage. "No other way!"

Torrance glanced at the quadars and their guns, then agreed with Edart.

Once he was outside he could double back to help Louratna, but here they were all just sitting ducks.

He used a stone wall as cover while he raced to a side hallway, which was really just a thin vent that was lit most of the way by natural moss. He had used it before, so knew it eventually led outside.

He wasn't used to moving so quickly, though, and the passageway lighting was thin. Shadows lay everywhere. He had to shimmy sideways through one segment, and he scraped his knee on another. Edart kept pushing him, though, and suddenly the bright light of the open surface nearly blinded them both.

Eldoro was still rising, Katon not visible, but they were low down in the foothills, and the heat was already oppressive.

"Come," Edart said.

Torrance saw she was limping, then. Blood ran along her leg.

"You're shot?"

He couldn't tell if she fully understood, but she waved his concern away and led him upward, away from the crease. He stumbled along, glancing over the hill.

Other quadars were running.

Plumes of dust and smoke rose from various openings in the mountain.

After a few minutes' hard exertion, Torrance thought his heart was going to give out. Sometime later he thought for sure it had. His robes were suited for the cool caves, but it was oppressive here. Breathing hurt his lungs, and he had a sudden flashback to the heat of his first days on the planet. The feeling of his tight spacesuit flashed through his mind.

They pressed on, climbing further.

Sweat rolled off his brow and into his blinking eyes.

He started using dried brush and rootstalk as handholds before he realized they were cutting him.

Finally, they came to a protected outcrop of rock.

Edart stopped here, falling into the cooler shade and grimacing with pain as she edged herself over to sit against the rock itself. Her leg was bleeding thick and red, no different from a human's as far as he could tell. Her skin was pale, and her central seemed to be unable to focus. Her breathing came in panting breaths.

Torrance knelt in front of her, gulping for breath.

"Let me see that," he managed.

Edart turned to let him in.

He ripped the cloth of her pants away from where the bullet had entered, and saw the wound was clean. An exit wound showed at the backside of her leg.

She was lucky.

All he had to do was to stop the bleeding.

No tourniquet, he thought. He was no doctor, but the bleed-out didn't seem to need that—instead, he had to close the wounds and get pressure on it. Now.

"Hold here," he said, pressing one of Edart's hands to one side of the wound, "and here," he said, putting her opposite hand at the other end—then he pressed them together. "Got it?"

Edart clicked affirmative between a groan.

He shrugged off his robe, then ripped an arm off it. Folding it over, he reached it around her leg, keeping the broadest part of the bandage on the side where the bullet's path was closest to the skin. Pushing Edart's hands away, he tied it down.

Then he was done.

The bulk of the bleeding was staunched.

"Thank you," Edart said in her own tongue.

They sat together for several moments, collecting themselves in silence. They were on the highest levels of the foothills. The toothy peaks of the range towered over them.

Torrance paused, then closed his eyes and listened to the sound of the wind and the rustling of the brushy plants that grew in cracks of the planet.

He opened his eyes and stared at Edart.

"Do you hear?" he said.

"Hear what?"

"Nothing," Torrance said.

Tired, he stood and peered carefully around the ridge of rock they were using as a shelter.

There were no gunshots.

No rumbling of bombs or other explosives.

The attack was over.

They were on the far ring of the valley that comprised the primary entrance to Louratna's network of caves. Across the way, Torrance saw a large gathering of quadars with mechanical jeeps and *tal* beasts. A column of the attackers emerged from the main opening, two of them leading Louratna, bound and gagged between them, pushing her ahead with tight grips on her arms.

Torrance swallowed hard, watching as they brought her before a quadar who was obviously in some form of command.

They forced her to her knees before him.

He strode around her, perhaps talking, perhaps questioning.

Yes, questioning.

Louratna made a response, and the commander slapped her.

He towered over her, speaking again. Other workers were being filed out—prisoners of some sort, probably to be put to work some-how, Torrance thought.

The commander hit Louratna again, then motioned to the line of prisoners.

One was brought to him, and he removed a pistol from his belt and put it to the prisoner's head. The quadar crumpled. Torrance saw a puff of smoke from the handgun, and a moment later heard the crack of the weapon's firing.

The image stopped his heart.

He had seen dead people, and even been in the area when Karl Malloy had shot Thomas Kitchell. But he had never seen a pure execution. The sight of the body froze him in place.

The commander then walked around Louratna.

She was on all fours now, crumpled on knees and elbows.

The commander seemed to be speaking to her.

He stopped and pointed the weapon at the back of her head.

Torrance closed his eyes and pulled himself back from the view. His heart pounded.

A second later there was another crack of the gun.

When Torrance turned back to see what had happened, there were two bodies on the ground.

CHAPTER 53

orrance, Edart, and a handful of other quadars climbed through the passages that led back to the main halls. The rock was quiet like death is quiet, the passageways empty except for the bodies the Families had left to rot or be scavenged.

"They gave them to the mountain," Edart said.

That sounded too damned poetic for his taste, but if it was true, the Families had left gifts everywhere.

He went to the assembly area first.

The lighting was dim, now, consisting only of the green and aqua moss that clung to large patches of the wall.

The team was scattered—Ket Alto had been left sprawled over the fuel system he had been in the process of revising, Mako facedown in the central area. He had probably run from gunmen who arrived on the desert side of the hall. Several quadars were burned beyond recognition. The smelting operation was destroyed, the fueling center charred and burnt to a crisp.

Jesus, he thought. *What kind of people do this?*

Then he flashed on images of *Everguard,* and recalled the strike the United Government had made on Atropos City. He thought about Miranda Station and the hops Universe Three made into the asteroid belt. He thought about how Eldoro, Alpha Centauri A, was still being drained one way or the other. There was a time, he thought then, that it might matter if that drain was due to a black hole set by Deidra Francis and her physicists or due to Star Drive engines run by Interstellar Command and theirs, but here on Esgarat that differentiation was meaningless.

The Families had their reasons, he supposed.

No different from his own species.

Ironically, in a far corner, Torrance found the center stage of the first wormhole pod he had sent to the planet, still intact.

Edart came to Torrance's side as he was kneeling to examine the assembly.

"How will we ever rebuild?" she said.

He stood upright and scanned the rubble of what remained of their rocket program.

"We don't," he replied.

Gritting his teeth, he walked away.

Torrance sat at a stone platform carved in the middle of the onyx passage that Louratna had sometimes used to receive visitors. Feeling drained and too hollow to cry, he didn't know what he was going to do. Didn't know what there was to do.

Anger coiled up in his gut.

Footsteps came from behind him.

"Torranze?" a soft voice said.

A stone bowl was placed on the table beside him, the quadar's six fingers receding, then appearing again with one of the nearly flat spoons they used.

The quadar sat beside him. Its body was warm.

He turned to look.

"Crissandr," he said, surprised.

"You've got to eat."

"How…?"

"The mountain hides," she said.

He nodded as if he understood, then looked at the bowl.

It was root mash with *piela*. She had brought water from below also.

"I am sorry there's no bread," Crissandr said.

Torrance eyed her, then spoke in the quadar language. "No cause to apologize."

It was a phrase Louratna had taught him early in their conversations.

He took a spoonful, and chewed slowly. If he could have tasted anything, it probably would have been good.

"The Families will pay for this," he said.

"How?" she replied.

He looked into the darkness of the cavern around him. It felt close to him now. Oddly, it had been the darkness that had first caused him to focus on the precise place that he was at all times while he was inside the cave. At first that darkness obscured, but in living here he had come to see how it all came together—the map of the place was scored in his head. He knew exactly where he was now, for example, and could probably close his eyes and make it to the assembly area and the common kitchen.

He remembered Louratna.

The way she looked at things. Her sense of humor. Her ability to make him feel like everything he did was good. Her single-minded focus on saving her species even as they were working to destroy themselves.

"When I came here," he said, "I was alone."

He twirled the spoon absently, then glanced at Crissandr from the corner of his eye. She was staring at him intently.

"I thought I would die then—I should have died then. Out in the desert."

"But you didn't."

"No, I didn't. Some quadar I never met raked me out of a hole and saved me."

He sighed.

When had he changed his focus from contacting the Solar System to saving this planet? When had he become so certain that Interstellar Command and his United Government wouldn't come? More important, when had he stopped caring if they did?

In so many ways, this place had become his home.

When had that happened?

"Louratna always made people into things they never thought they were," Crissandr finally said.

"Yes, she did."

She reached up and held his shoulder. He craned his neck and wrapped his arm around her to take her in.

"You made her what she wished she could be, Torranze," she said. "I want you to know that. The quadars here, we called you pair-mates, because we all saw what you were to her."

He swallowed hard. Yes, that was fair. In so many ways Louratna had been his pair-mate. Now the Families had taken that all away.

"Thank you," he said.

He sighed, and let the mountain filter into him.

"I don't know how I'm going to make the Families pay, Crissandr," he finally said. "But I'm going to find a way."

The quadar nodded and got a resolute expression on her gaze. "We all do what we need to do," she said.

Then Crissandr jogged his arm.

"But first you have to eat."

EPILOGUE

Karshi Fael had just decided to find shelter when she heard the thudding explosions from under the mountain.

It was early in the heat and she was on a ridge of the foothills, a place she was frequenting recently because it had a plentiful patch of *katja* and because it was the time of year that the *jah* paired themselves and soared on the high winds, a sight that always made her feel something she considered sacred. Here in the vents of the mountains, the air became cool at times, and the aroma of that same cool air made her happy, too. This mountain was as much a part of her as her central plate or the six fingers on each of her hands. Like most free-rangers, Karshi was most comfortable on the rock and in the wind.

The sound came from under Louratna's camp, which alone was not surprising.

Karshi had been watching the quadars in the philosopher's network making noises for many years, though she was oddly intrigued to see how things changed when the strange creature had joined them.

She wondered how it had come to be here.

It seemed healthy, and it seemed to be helping them.

The problem with this thundering sound, though, was that it came from so deep in the mountain, and that it wasn't alone.

Karshi had been gathering root in these areas since she was a whelp.

She understood its passages.

After the first rumbles, she climbed to the higher lines where the air got cooler, then scampered along the flat ridge of rock that blinded her progress from the valley below.

The sky above was a bloody orange, almost red with Eldoro's early heat.

When she got to a central observation point, Karshi sat still.

She recognized the symbols that adorned the flags of the quadars who were gathered at the mouth of Louratna's caves. They were Family blazons riding on the motor carts with their battery powers and their cracked wheels of ribbed rock. Her practiced gaze picked out sentries, dead in their positions. Her practiced fingers pressed against the heated rock and felt the vibrations of more explosions.

Fearful voices called.

Smoke rose from vents where smoke should not be rising.

Many of Louratna's quadars emerged from the protection of the mountain, and as Karshi stood up to get a better look, a group of quadars from the Family brought Louratna out to their leader.

She knew what was going to happen before it happened.

She understood it, too. At least she understood as well as anyone really could.

These quadars were fighting each other like there was some kind of game going on, trying to win in some way that no free-ranger could ever truly understand.

She didn't turn away as the leader shot a quadar down beside Louratna.

Nor did she flinch when that same quadar killed Louratna herself.

Instead, when it was over, Karshi Fael merely stood up and walked away, using the sharp ridge of toothy rock as cover for her retreat and looking up at the sky where a set of pair-mated *jah* soared on a draft of air, heads bent to the desert floor, looking for an oblivious *pax* rodent or *piela* lizard to forage.

There is no game, she thought, as she retreated from the scene.
There is nothing to win, and nothing to lose.
There is only your life, and what you choose to do with it.

THANK YOU!

THIS IS THE END OF STARCRASH

If you enjoyed this story, please consider stopping by your favorite
online booksellers' websites to leave a review.

Word of mouth is the most powerful force in the universe when it
comes to the livelihood of your favorite authors. Even a few words can
help!

THE STORY CONTINUES!
INTERGALACTIC WAR IS CHAOS

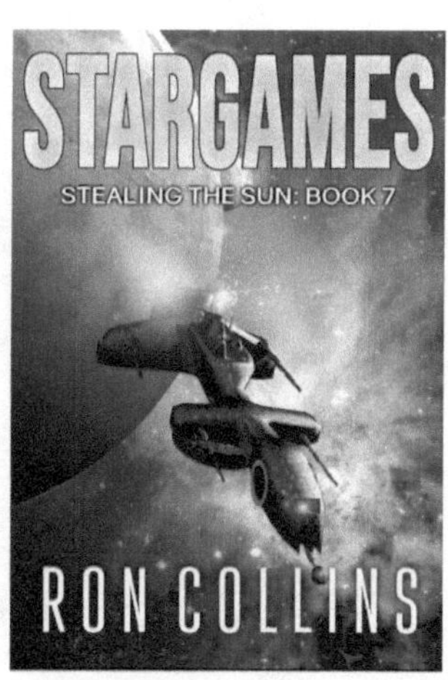

- Deidra Francis: Director of the Universe Three rebels.
- Allie Feder: Brilliant wormhole physicist
- Zina Nichols: Ambitious United Government intelligence agent
- Thomas Kitchell: Esteemed scientist, hero of the *Everguard* mission, friend of Torrance Black

New forces gather. The United Government search for Universe Three's home system narrows, leaving the rebels with slim options. How far is Deidra Francis willing to go to give her people a chance to live free?

The answer: As far as it takes—or farther.

Nothing less than the survival of the human race lies in the balance.

STARGAMES, the seventh book of *Stealing the Sun*, a space based Science Fiction series from bestselling science fiction and dark fantasy author Ron Collins.

———

Or, save a little and get the next three!

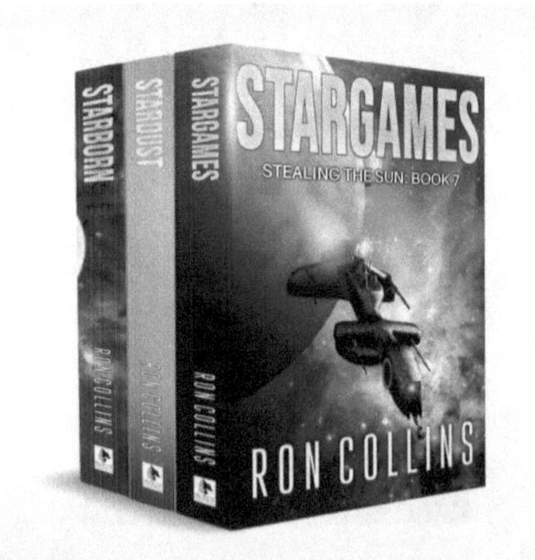

READER LIST SIGN-UP

Get copies of STARCRUISE (a stand-alone short story in the STEALING THE SUN SERIES), and Glamour of the God-Touched, volume 1 of Saga of the God-Touched Mage for Free!

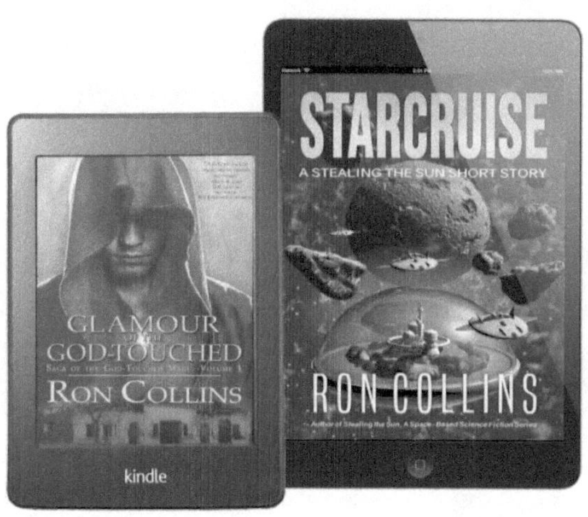

Sign-up at: https://www.typosphere.com/newsletter

ALSO BY RON COLLINS

Novels

Stealing the Sun (9 books)

Saga of the God-Touched Mage (8 books)

The PEBA Diaries (2 books)

The Knight Deception

Wakers

Poetry

Five Seven Five

(Science fictional examinations of the elusive haiku)

Collections

Collins Creek (Three Volumes)

Tomorrow in All the Worlds

Picasso's Cat & Other Stories

Five Magics

Seven Days in May (with John C. Bodin)

Nonfiction

On Writing (And Reading!) Short

(A Science Fiction Writer's Quest for Stories that Matter)

ABOUT RON COLLINS

Ron Collins is a best-selling Science Fiction and Dark Fantasy author who writes across the spectrum of speculative fiction.

His short fiction has received a Writers of the Future prize and a CompuServe HOMer Award. His short story "The White Game" was nominated for the Short Mystery Fiction Society's Derringer Award. With his daughter, Brigid Collins, he edited the anthology *Face the Strange.*

He has contributed a couple hundred or so short stories to professional publications such as *Analog, Asimov's,* and several other magazines and anthologies (including several editions of the Fiction River Anthology Series). His latest science fiction series, *Stealing the Sun,* and his fantasy series *Saga of the God-Touched Mage* are available from Skyfox publishing.

He holds a degree in Mechanical Engineering, and has worked to develop avionics systems, electronics, and information technology before chucking it all to write full-time.

facebook.com/roncollinssfwriter

twitter.com/roncollins13

instagram.com/roncollinssfwriter

bookbub.com/authors/ron-collins

goodreads.com/Ron_Collins

amazon.com/Ron-Collins/e/B00AP2IYEW

ACKNOWLEDGMENTS

As always, I need to thank my early readers, John Bodin and Sharon Bass, both of whom nagged me appropriately when I was running late, and then gave me their normal outstanding points of view. Thank you, so, so much. Thanks as always to Lisa Collins, my wife and my copy-editor, for her normal outstanding job and putting up with me being grumpy on the days it wasn't working so well. And I also want to thank all of the readers of this series—especially those who reached out to ask where book six was. Nothing motivates me more than knowing someone likes what I'm doing.

You all are the best.